Best Wishes,

Tim Bowling

the paperboy's winter

Tim Bowling

PENGUIN
CANADA

PENGUIN CANADA

Published by the Penguin Group

Penguin Books, a division of Pearson Canada, 10 Alcorn Avenue, Toronto, Ontario,
    Canada M4V 3B2
Penguin Books Ltd, 80 Strand, London WC2R 0RL, England
Penguin Putnam Inc., 375 Hudson Street, New York, New York 10014, U.S.A.
Penguin Books Australia Ltd, 250 Camberwell Road, Camberwell, Victoria 3124, Australia
Penguin Books India (P) Ltd, 11, Community Centre, Panchsheel Park,
    New Delhi – 110 017, India
Penguin Books (NZ) Ltd, cnr Rosedale and Airborne Roads, Albany, Auckland 1310,
    New Zealand
Penguin Books (South Africa) (Pty) Ltd, 24 Sturdee Avenue, Rosebank 2196, South Africa

Penguin Books Ltd, Registered Offices: 80 Strand, London WC2R 0RL, England

First published 2003

10 9 8 7 6 5 4 3 2 1

Manufactured in Canada.

NATIONAL LIBRARY OF CANADA CATALOGUING IN PUBLICATION DATA

Bowling, Tim, 1964–
    The paperboy's winter / Tim Bowling.

ISBN 0-14-301228-2

I. Title.

PS8553.09044P36 2003   C813'.54   C2002-904372-7
PR9199.3.B6358P36   2003

Visit Penguin Books' website at **www.penguin.ca**

For my children
Levi, Sadie, and Dashiell
and for the friends of childhood

It is people at the edge who say
things at the edge: winter is toward knowing.
—*William Stafford, "Sayings from the Northern Ice"*

the paperboy's winter

prologue

BY THE TIME I WAS FIFTEEN, I had begun to share my father's night-owl ways. We would stay up until the wee hours, as my mother resignedly called them, watching old movies on TV—everything from Buster Keaton to Bergman and Fellini to truly forgettable movie-of-the-week fare. During commercials we would talk casually about fishing or sports or the daily news, and sometimes, when the movie ended, the conversation would grow more serious and we would stay up till daybreak, especially if what we'd watched had been interesting.

One movie in particular always stayed with us, not so much because of the story itself, though we were moved by it (my father, no doubt, in a more complicated way) but because the title song became a private joke between us, something we relied on whenever faced with a perplexing or mildly unhappy situation, or even just to fill a long silence. Out on the river, for example, when my father had just set his net and all I could see was the burning end of his cigarette in the stern, a red star among all the pale ones low on the western horizon, he might suddenly say, in a voice rich with memory and comfortable amusement, "What's it all about, Alfie?"

And even though I knew he couldn't see my face up on the deck behind the drum, I would adopt a puzzled, sorrowful expression, just like Michael Caine's in the last black-and-white frames of that movie. But since I lacked that character's long history of woman-izing, and in fact had little romantic history at all to that point, I could never get the expression right. My father, despite having been happily married to my mother for years, always managed it better. I put the difference down to age and experience, and assumed that someday I would master the expression naturally, just as I would someday fish my own boat and get married and live in my own house.

Fifteen years later, none of that had happened, and my father was dead. Without his quiet, affectionate interest in my life, I had begun to drift, to find it difficult to rally to any serious engage-ment with the world. I was like an actor who suddenly found himself performing before an empty theatre, without even any other actors to spur him on to greater achievement. And somehow the gentleness of my father seemed to have faded from my country as well; all was faster, harsher, colder. As if shocked into sight, I woke to a place and a time from which I was, at heart, dislocated.

But fortunately there were responsibilities and affections to keep me moving forward, and it was to these I now strictly attended.

I had come home again to the West Coast, to Chilukthan, to visit my mother who, after three years of widowhood, still seemed as lost as she had on the day of the funeral. There was little I, or anyone, could do to help her, but since that little was so impor-tant, I made every effort to provide it.

But the physical effort of being home was uncomfortable for me. The shadowy, gently haunted place of my boyhood—a town of swaybacked barns and crumpled wharves, rusted, abandoned train tracks vanishing into the salt flats and sunken fishboats turning skeletal along the muddy riverbanks, of wild blackberry bushes deep and dark as pirates' grottoes and condemned, century-old houses standing like tall tombs in grass up to their broken verandas—had almost vanished, replaced by strip malls, fast food franchises, and gated condominium developments named "Heron Shores" and "River Point." I was finding it harder and harder, each visit home, to feel my father's presence in the landscape. In the winter, there were fewer gillnetters pulled up on the dyke, brine-hulled boats out of whose cabins I could hear his faint whistling of "Santa Lucia." In the fall, the rich musk of dog salmon no longer hung in the streets and conjured his gumbooted shadow out of every corner streetlamp's drizzle. In the spring, where had the storms of wild cherry and apple blossoms gone, those delicate notes of change that once, along with the salmon scales, thickly layered his palms? And in the summer, where were the salmon? Their annual return seemed always diminishing, as if they were no more than the wake of my father's unwilling departure. Season by season, year by year, the past was becoming a sequence of images glimpsed out of the corners of my eyes.

But one summer afternoon, as I waited on Chilukthan's new main street for the bus into Vancouver, as I squinted into the sun-glare off the plastic of the town's developed core and, half-comically, half-desperately, whispered "What's it all about, Alfie?" to the few circling seagulls who might have shared my salt longing for what couldn't be recovered, I did not expect the past to appear so visibly, in such a way that I could not simply dally in its vague images, but had to coalesce and concentrate them.

The day was sweltering. It hadn't rained in weeks, and people were taking full advantage of the sunshine: motorcycles and convertibles swarmed in the streets, girls in bikinis rollerbladed past, shirtless boys on skateboards darted everywhere, and those who were older, many pulled along by gasping dogs, wore mostly shorts and thin shirts. Yet it was a weekday, and when I stepped onto the crowded bus and negotiated my way to a seat, I noted many commuters dressed conservatively, as if for business, and looking none too happy because of it. The bus was like a small travelling section of a rainy November Monday that people begrudgingly boarded, realizing that work had no real place in the paradisal ideal of a coastal summer.

Already uncomfortable from the extra heat of so many unsmiling bodies crammed together, I stared disconsolately out the window as the bus jerked to each stop outside Chilukthan's two main shopping malls. I had recognized no one as I found my seat, nor did I see a familiar face amongst the dozens climbing in and out of cars in the malls' packed parking lots. Now, as the bus jerked forward again, and those who had just boarded searched for seats, I stared dozily toward the front, wondering if my expression came even close to Michael Caine's when the singer plaintively asked him what it was all about.

Musing thus about my father, missing him more with each trip home, I was suddenly, shockingly, wrenched back a quarter century.

At the front of the bus, beside the driver, stood a figure so immediately familiar to me, yet so unremembered, that I had to blink the sweat out of my eyes to make sure he wasn't a mirage. But the quickening of all my senses told me I wasn't mistaken. How could I be?

His beard was as full as always, but less smooth and now flecked with grey. He wore no skullcap and his greasy hair, only about jaw-bone length, was combed over in one direction, like a small boy's.

His clothes were simple and familiar: blue jeans held up with a thick black belt, a flannel plaid workshirt unbuttoned over a dingy white T-shirt, and scuffed work boots. The boots struck me most, since I could not recall ever seeing him in anything but gumboots.

But then I looked closer at his face. It was not nearly as dark as I remembered, was almost pale in fact, with no colour in the lips. Yet the eyes—did I only imagine that they burned as blackly as before, giving off the smell of creosote and coal oil? I could not see them clearly, for he had not looked my way. He held out a card for the driver, a card he then gripped tight in his hand, as he had once gripped the small creatures of the marsh.

I was seated halfway down the bus with many people obscuring my view of the front. But I saw him squeeze into one of the side-facing seats just behind the driver. A chubby teenaged girl wearing a Walkman and eating fries out of a McDonald's bag sat on his right, and a thin, middle-aged man holding a briefcase sat on his left.

I could not look away. I had not seen Ezra Hemsworth in years. My mother or father had mentioned in passing the complaints that had been made against him by residents of the townhomes and condominiums along the river, complaints about his not respecting private property, about his cursing, spitting, and urinating off the stern of his boat in broad daylight. But that was years ago. Back then, he still fed the rabbits and songbirds in the marsh, and, though he no longer brought a bucket of oolichans or a Christmas tree to our front door, he had occasionally worked with my father on the potatoes out on Pheasant Island. On rare fall mornings he had stopped at the house to get a ride out to the fields, and even waited in the living room a few times until my father was ready.

These "visits" had been extremely awkward, as Ezra hardly spoke at all, just sat dully rubbing his woollen socks together as if they were kindling to start a fire. "And the smell," my mother had said. "Worse than ever. I don't think he bathes any more. And there's always a grease stain on the back of the chair where his head has been. It's so sad, Callum. Such a kind soul as that."

Now, looking at him, it seemed impossible that he had ever been striding rapidly through the streets of town. He sat stiffly on the increasingly crowded bus, an absent grin on his face, his hands palm-down on his lap. His profile was sharp as ever, hard-edged as an anvil. Every few seconds he turned to stare at someone, a stare that respected no conventions and caused the recipient to look away in embarrassment. At one point he shifted slightly to study the chubby girl beside him. She was so discomfited by the attention that she got up and pushed her way through the standing passengers to the back of the bus. Ezra followed her with his eyes, his grin unchanged, and did not turn back when she had reached her destination.

With a start, I realized he was staring at me through the same gap between heads and shoulders that I had been using to stare at him. Fighting the urge to look away, I grinned and raised my hand in greeting. But he did not change expression or wave back. He did not seem to notice me at all. Yet he was looking right at me. Was I so changed that he did not recognize me? Or was the change solely in him?

We were on the highway now, speeding past the few potato and cornfields left between Chilukthan and the Deas Island Tunnel. Ezra had not looked away. I became aware of the sweat on my brow and under my arms. It was like being stared at by a sentient moon, a force so present and focused that a whole world could take it for granted. I had dropped my eyes, but now forced them up again. The bus sped down the gradual decline into the tunnel. Ezra's face began to fade into the dimly lit darkness, his features to bleed at the tight margins. Soon we were under the river, and the whole bus hushed, became a torn row of pews. The black, the river, the reverent silence, and that free-floating, uneasy expression just at the edge of the flickering light brought another summer back, so forcibly that I was soon lost in it, thrown under the retrieved life, as if I were a piece of driftwood prey to the purposes of the above-rushing tide.

"Jesus," a voice said, and my eyes that were open, opened again.

The chill of pre-dawn, as much as the hushed, awe-stricken voice, woke me. Shivering, I blinked the sleep away and soon remembered where I was, my eyes adjusting to the darkness just lifting off the river. I stared over the skullcapped men gathered in the sterns of the gillnetters to the high, ink-black outlines of the mountains beyond Vancouver. It must have been about four or five o'clock. I took a deep breath of the mud-clogged air, enriched with the smells of briny water and the slime of fresh-caught salmon. Close by, hardly audible above the gusting wind, an engine idled, missing every few seconds. Another voice, my father's, said with amazement over the sound, "You can't get it on board."

I stirred uncomfortably, not eager to rise from my seated position on the deck. The dull warmth of the manifold pressed through my layered shirts and sweaters, but I was still freezing. Though it was mid-August, and the night had been mild, the break of day was always damp and bone-numbingly cold. I stretched my legs out on the dew-wet boards of the main hatch and stared at the mingling beams of pickup lights off the sterns of three gillnetters forming a loose triangle on the tide. My breath dissolved before it could obscure my vision of the other breath clouds and rising cigarette smoke. Below the drifting white I noticed that our net was on the drum, the web dripping as if it had just been rolled in. Every thirty seconds there came a heavy thump on the planks underneath, made by a large salmon in its death throes. Our boat and another drifted alongside a third boat that still had some of its net in the river, which accounted for the idling sound. Off to my right, partly across the narrow channel toward a silt island of bullrushes forming its eastern bank, a candlelike night light marking the end of the net bobbed drunkenly on the current, blinking on and off in an erratic pulse. Yet we were hardly drifting at all. Then I heard the flags rippling high on the masts of the boats, and understood that the wind was up, furrowing the calm channel into a small chop.

My father and two other men, one in each stern, kept bending far over the sides of their boats then straightening up again. I watched with slight interest, still drowsy and unwilling to leave the faint warmth of the manifold. As I was only six, I knew I wasn't expected to help my father much and could rest when I wanted. And yet the charged atmosphere made me fight off sleep until I could find out what was happening.

After another minute of rapid, excited exchanges that I didn't catch, punctuated by the eerie flapping of the flags, the wind-driven chop of the river, and the misses of the engine, I heard my father call to me.

"Callum," he said, his voice still hushed. "Callum, wake up."

"I'm awake," I responded, rising even before he told me to do so.

"You've got to see this," he continued in the same odd tone, odd because my father was generally even-mannered. "Come on, hurry up."

I forgot the cold and clambered alongside the drum and into the stern. It was slippery with blood and flecked with scales reflecting palely in the faded yellow light. I squeezed in beside my father at the side of the boat closest to the drifting net, not even looking at the other men. On the triangular black surface of river between the boats, only a few white corks rose and fell with the chop; several others had vanished, held so far under water that their vague shapes weren't even visible. But this was not so strange. Any large deadhead would pull a long section of the corkline under. I was about to turn to my father for an explanation when the man in the third boat suddenly increased the gas to his engine and stepped on his drum pedal.

"Wake-him-up-a-bit-wake-him-up," he said rapidly, the words blending into one word above the sound of the engine and the straining drum.

I kept looking down, frightened and excited. The part of the net hanging from the rollers to the river tightened briefly, the green nylon meshes filmed with water, and then the man cut the gas and the net loosened. The ensuing quiet was even more strangely pregnant than it had been. I waited, my mouth slightly open, my heart beating fast. Staring at the roiling black, I felt a powerful desire to break it somehow, even if I had to throw myself into it. More seconds passed. I hung farther over the side of the boat and felt my father's hand settle lightly on the base of my neck. The river rose and fell, rose and fell, as if it were breathing.

Very slowly, a dingy whiteness, broad as the moon path and slightly phosphorescent, floated up from the depths. My father's hand tightened on my neck.

"Watch now," he cautioned, and I straightened up a little, my attention fixed on the shape, the glowing whiteness spreading like a film over my eyes.

"Jesus!" the man in the second boat breathed into the air.

The shape kept rising at the same slow pace for what seemed an hour but was only seconds. Then, suddenly, it broke the surface, the head seeming to hang independently above the black chop for a few seconds until the body emerged from below. I jerked back, my father's hand sliding away. Then, as suddenly as it had risen, the white glow dropped back into the black depths with a surprising absence of sound, as if it really was the moon path going under.

I knew almost immediately what the shape had been, but I could not name it. Somehow the familiar word didn't seem to fit.

The man in the third boat cackled delightedly, breaking the brief trance I had fallen into.

"Sturgeon," my father whispered, as if he knew that I was having trouble accepting the truth of what I had seen.

"Sturgeon?" the man in the second boat remarked incredulously. "Whale's more like it."

I was still staring at the river. Had I really seen the whiteness? All was black again, except for the few dirty-white corks. Was that massive, anvil-flat head really down there, resting in the veil of meshes it had lifted? Had I dreamed it, and was only now waking to rise from the warmth of the manifold and the cold dew of the deck?

"Looks like you'll have to cut your net," my father said.

At the sound of the man's gleeful, chuckling response, I looked up at him.

Weather-beaten, mud-stained, he was as black as the great sturgeon had been white. Only a sliver of pale skin showed between his thick plush of beard and his eyes, which were ringed in darknesses, like a raccoon's. He wore an oily black skullcap over his stringy, unwashed hair, and a thick black woollen sweater, so snagged and torn that it looked like a patch of broken earth. Standing to one side of his cramped stern, just on the fringes of the mingled yellow light, he looked rapidly back and forth from the net to our faces in turn, as though unsure of how the different parts of the scene were connected. But he was grinning too, though in a manner that didn't appear exactly pleasurable; there was another quality in it, incomprehensible, unsettling. He gave the impression of being completely alone even as he responded to my father's comment.

"Can't-cut-the-net," he said rapidly, the words again merging into a single word, the way Ezra Hemsworth always spoke.

Just then, the stern of his boat began to move upriver slightly, against the flow. The corks on the surface plunged soundlessly under and the length of net hanging from the rollers yanked tight.

"Jesus H. Murphy," the man in the second boat almost sighed. I finally recognized the gaunt, stubbled face of Johnny Toukalos; he was one of the regulars, along with Ezra, on this drift of the river.

The loose, black triangle widened as the great fish pushed against the current and pulled Ezra's boat away from ours.

Ezra cackled long and loud, as if in triumph. Yet he still seemed almost solemn. Confused by his behaviour, I looked at my father, but he was gazing intently at the river, the smoke from the cigarette held loosely between his lips wreathing his head.

Meanwhile, two other boats had idled alongside from downriver. The added motion, sound, and light made the scene even more mysterious, darker and darker, emphasizing our complete separation from the world below the corkline. I began to sense that only the boat physically connected to the fish had any intimate involvement in its struggle.

The newcomers cut their engines and soon appeared under the pickup lights of their sterns. The sickly-sweet smell of gas soaked through the smell of mud and fish slime, but soon wafted away on the wind. I recognized Mr. Mawson, another regular on the drift. The younger man was less familiar, though I knew him to be one of the Brunovs, a family that lived on Pheasant Island, a few miles downriver.

"Six, seven hundred pounds, judging by the head . . . ," my father explained, returning his own gaze to the river. His words trailed off into another freighted silence.

"It'll be a hundred years old at least," Mr. Mawson added quietly.

I tried to imagine a fish over twice my father's age, but the young Brunov shattered my reflections. "Shit, seven hundred pounds. That's what? Four hundred bucks?"

Quickly calculating, I realized we'd have to catch three hundred sockeye to make that much. No wonder Ezra didn't want to cut his net.

None of the other men seemed to react to this information. My father did not even lift his eyes from the river.

Ezra, meanwhile, had begun muttering to himself and fiddling with ropes in his stern.

"Why can't you?" my father suddenly asked him, as if nothing had been said since Ezra's last remark.

His head still down, Ezra mumbled just loud enough to be heard, "Can't-live-in-the-net."

At first, I didn't know what he meant. But then I realized that he was concerned about the fish.

"Doesn't he want it?" I whispered to my father.

Before he could respond, the young Brunov said, "Shoot the fucker. Can't do nothin' else."

Ezra muttered even more rapidly now and bent so far over in the stern that I almost lost sight of him. My father, Mr. Mawson, and Johnny Toukalos remained silent.

The flags rippled, the current slopped, and Ezra's engine puttered brokenly. After a while, my father said, "You can't pick it."

Ezra did not look at him.

"He's too big. You won't be able to cut him free."

"You'd have to wait him out," Mr. Mawson added. "He'd likely snap through when he felt like it."

Again, Ezra paid no attention.

"Four hundred bucks," the young Brunov said bitterly. "What the fuck would you let it go for?"

Ezra looked up now, his expression cold, matter-of-fact. "Can't shoot it," he said to my father calmly. Then, more excited, he added, "Can't-shoot-a-fish-goddamnit-goddamnit."

My father nodded and blew another smoke ring into the cool, damp air. It was no real surprise that Ezra wanted to keep the sturgeon. I already knew enough about fishing to understand that fishermen had little sentimentality where killing was concerned. Ezra just didn't want to lose the sturgeon if it wasn't going to survive. By this same logic, my father always cursed more when a large spring salmon, already dead, fell out of his net before he could gaff it. But still, I couldn't understand why Ezra wouldn't shoot the sturgeon. If he couldn't pick it out of his net, and he didn't want to cut a chunk of net free with the sturgeon in it, then what difference would it make how the fish died? And, even more interesting to me, how was he going to kill it?

All this speculation hung in the charged air and held us in place. The black triangle between the sterns was broken only by the chop.

Ezra's mood seemed to have changed. He was grinning strangely again, and wore the fisherman's common expression of excitement in the way he moved, decisively and instinctively.

"Lucky bastard!" the young Brunov snapped out, returning to his cabin. Then his boat roared to life and, churning up the water beneath the stern, sped upriver.

My father announced that the tide was starting to move. What he really meant was, "We've got to make another set. We can't wait around all night." But I could also tell that he had been hesitating, not only out of curiosity, but for Ezra's sake. No matter what happened now, Ezra was going to lose valuable fishing time. And yet, if he caught the sturgeon, a four-hundred-dollar fish, what difference would the lost sockeye make?

We all waited for him to speak, but he seemed to have forgotten our presence. He just picked at the bottom of his beard with one long-fingered hand and stared at the western horizon still black with stars clustered vividly as the scales on the boat planks. Slowly, to the northeast, the sky was brightening. A faint pink hue showed above the mountains and spread as gradually as seeping blood, higher and higher. At eye level, along the riverbanks, the vague shapes of trees and bushes crouched in the last, lifting motes of darkness. Soon daybreak would dissolve the yellow light in which we were standing and change the black of the river to a murky brown.

The boats drifted a little faster, the current pulling them toward the bottom of the channel to where it branched westward, oceanward, down an even narrower side-slough. And still Ezra stared through us, his eyes shifting rapidly but not seeming to take anything in. The wind, increasing with the tide, flayed the flag high above him just as it flayed the surface of the river into the same black motion.

Finally, Ezra began to mutter to himself again, rapidly, incoherently. Then the flowing of his voice disappeared under the sudden roar of his engine and drum as he stepped on the drum pedal to bring in his net.

My father, Mr. Mawson, and Johnny Toukalos exchanged resigned glances and shrugs.

"Best leave him to it!" my father yelled above the straining of the engine and drum. Fishing closed in a few hours and we had to make as many sets as possible in the hope of increasing our week's catch of sockeye. But something in my father's look and tone, and in the expressions of the two other men, suggested that Ezra had plans of his own and they were nobody else's business.

I remained in the stern while my father started the engine to take us upriver to the top of the drift. Ezra did not look up from leaning far over his rollers as the three surrounding boats and their lights moved away. I watched him strain at the leadline gripped in his hands, not with frustration or fatigue, but calmly, as though he was prepared to repeat the procedure for hours. As the darkness closed around Ezra and his faint circle of dull light, he picked up a long aluminum pike-pole from alongside his drum and swung it high over his rollers, as if divining for something.

An hour later, long after Ezra had drifted out of sight down the side-slough toward Pheasant Island and the gulf, my father and I were at the top of the drift again, preparing to make another set. The blackness in the air and on the river had gone, replaced by a smoky grey. A low mist snaked whitely through the sloughs and channels of the delta, as if the river were breathing just as we were. The wind had calmed. Bird-chatter had begun to rise out of the reed-thick marshes, but this sound seemed to be part of the same silence to which the wind and current belonged. I stood at the deck wheel, awaiting my father's command of "upriver" or "downriver" depending on how he wanted to lay the net across the channel.

Slowly, from the bottom of the drift, the roar of an engine overwhelmed the bird-chatter. We waited and watched, having recognized the engine. Before long, Ezra's boat appeared along the near bank and slowly approached. I could tell by my father's hesitation that he shared my curiosity (few things could make him delay a set). What had Ezra done with the sturgeon?

"He's hardly moving," my father said.

Given the roar of the engine, the boat should have been speed-ing up the bank. Instead, it moved forward at a plowing tractor's pace.

Our own boat was drifting downriver and would soon be too far down for us to start the set. Quickly, my father put the boat in gear and increased the gas. "Up," he commanded gently, as I had let the bow swing toward the centre of the channel. Over my shoulder, I watched the black shape of Ezra's boat climb the muddy bank, so close that it was almost among the graveyard of deadheads that had been towed there off the drift. Why was he moving so slowly?

We began to set, angling across the channel, turning up and downriver to loop the net so the meshes would hang loosely, making it harder for the salmon to break through them. The tide was running so fast that we were halfway down the drift before we had finished setting the net. My father told me to shut off the engine. When I emerged from the cabin into the sudden absence of close noise, I could tell by my father's fixed stance that he was still puzzling out Ezra's strange progress.

"What's he doing?" I asked, stepping alongside the drum. I could just see, several feet back of Ezra's stern, a pale froth churned out of the grey river.

Without turning, my father shook his head slightly. "He's towing the sturgeon, by the look of it."

I waited until my curiosity became too much. "But why, Dad?"

"I don't know, Callum," he finally said. But his words hung heavy with a possible answer, and I tried to figure out what it was. Fifty or sixty fathoms out from our stern a salmon hit with a small, white splash like the uncorking of a champagne bottle, but there was no accompanying sound above the dull roar of Ezra's engine.

I watched the fish kick and struggle for a while, and considered the possibilities. The thick smell of blood and slime rose out of the stern to merge with the mud-heavy air. A shower of skinny green-yellow leaves gusted off a poplar tree on the bank of the silt island we were drifting past and speckled the dull surface of the river just above our boat. My father's cigarette smoke climbed higher and dissolved into the grey dome of overcast that the break of day had revealed. It would probably rain soon. I watched our scotchman, vivid as a clown's nose, pass against the darkness of Ezra's boat and then re-emerge on the other side. In a few minutes we'd be drifting into the side-slough. I thought harder.

"He's drowning it!" I suddenly announced, surprising myself.

My father nodded.

Then he turned to me quickly and commanded "Start her up!" We had almost reached the slough mouth, past the point where we normally began to pick up. I hurried into the cabin, started the engine, then hurried back to the stern to help my father as he rolled the net in. A minute later we had slipped into the slough, our scotchman just pulling inside the far point as always. Ezra's boat had vanished from our sight.

one

WITH MY PARENTS and two younger siblings, I lived in a small bungalow on a street of cracked pavement and ancient plum orchards that ended abruptly at the bank of the Fraser River. Potato trucks and salmon boats were our traffic, and laughing dogs the colour of ripe pears and blackberries were our constant companions. At Hallowe'en, we scurried through the rain-slick streets, gathering candy in the same pillowcases we entrusted our dreams to; at Christmas, we tramped through the bog to find a perfect tree, knowing that the lowest branches would be cut off to make room for our presents; and in the long-shadowed, long-grassed summers, we roamed the mucky low tides in search of beer and pop bottles to trade in for the money to buy comic books.

But on that winter afternoon of 1975, it was my more lucrative source of income that really mattered. I had recently begun delivering the daily newspaper, and that was how Ezra Hemsworth suddenly entered my life as something more than a strange background figure in that mysterious world my mother always referred to as "the waterfront."

In those days, the *Vancouver Sun* was an evening paper delivered mainly by eleven- and twelve-year-old boys on Mustang bicycles, and the paper shack was a common suburban cave of obscenity, laughter, violence, emotional torture, and camaraderie. Just as in a playground at recess, you could find all the secret manipulations and open loyalties of life in those banged-together plywood shacks where the big-city trucks from the Pacific Press Building on Granville Street would drop off the day's wired bundles of print for the shack manager, usually an older teenager, to cut and distribute to his younger menials. Our shack sat at the edge of a vacant lot just below the high gravel dyke of the harbour. The shoulder of what was known as the "river road" simply dissolved into the tramped-down grass that circled the ugly, dark-green, tin-roofed building stained with seagull droppings and the time's popular graffiti—"Kilroy was here," "Jesus saves, Esposito scores on the rebound," as well as the more colourful and personal comments on select girls and teachers.

By three-thirty in the afternoon, Monday through Saturday, anywhere from a dozen to three dozen bikes, depending on how many friends each paperboy had brought along, leaned neatly against the shack or lay splayed on the grass like huge birds that had crashed out of the sky. First come, first served, was the official policy of our shack manager, a sharp-nosed fifteen-year-old named Clive Withers, notable for his terrible, purple acne, hair the colour and sheen of oil drained from an engine, and a violent temper. But since official policy was entirely at Clive's whim, arriving first did not necessarily guarantee that you'd get your papers first; it all depended on your current position in the manager's favour. At ten, and new to the job, I was one of the younger boys, and tried hard to be inconspicuous, arriving not too early and definitely not late, hoping to avoid the daily torments that Clive heaped on those who happened to ignite his bullying.

But on this particular afternoon I had lingered too long in the Haunted Bookshop. Run by a genial, pot-bellied man named Mr. Bradlee—whose ill-fitting, never-quite-clean T-shirts and work pants and a full beard snarled as an old bird's nest gave him the appearance of a rather seedy Santa Claus—the bookshop was a cramped, magical place smelling of must, mildew, stale tobacco, and a hundred different scents of bubblegum. It was split almost perfectly in half, one side packed with ten-foot-high bookshelves into which adults would vanish without a word, only occasionally coughing from behind some well-thumbed mystery, romance, thriller, or other mainstream title, and the other side entirely devoted to Mr. Bradlee's real passion, collectible comics and the amateur fanzines produced by fellow devotees of comic book culture. A wooden counter extended all the way from the front door to within five feet of the back of the shop—a distance of perhaps forty feet—where it then turned abruptly toward the wall, away from the paperback shelves. Behind this counter, standing heavily but easily against a wall plastered with colourful posters of superheroes—Spiderman, the Fantastic Four, Captain America, Silver Surfer—rare issues of comic books encased in protective plastic sleeves, and some local fanzines sporting surreal, pen-and-ink images that hinted at the drug culture but not so obviously as to attract notice from our town's arbiters of morality, Mr. Bradlee smiled indulgently out at his enthusiastic, noisy, sometimes intensely studious young customers.

We spent hours doodling on the huge white sheets of paper taped to the countertop, copying the illustrations from the comics or inventing our own, and writing everything from limericks about our peers to epic, ongoing narratives inspired by our more fantastical, mythical readings in such comics as *Conan the Barbarian* and *Red Sonja*. And when we weren't busy creating, we took refuge in the corner of the shop opposite the paperback shelves and read all the crumpled and ripped dime comics, the *Archies* and *Uncle Scrooge* reprints that had little collectors' value. Often we would burst into giddy laughter so disruptive to the concentration of the adult browsers that Mr. Bradlee would be forced to reprimand us, quietly but firmly. He well knew that the small profit his business brought in—only enough to supplement his regular income as a garbageman in the city—came from the paperback trade. But it was also clear that, in a way that we could sense but not really appreciate, he respected us more than his other patrons.

In any case, we were in school most of the time the shop was open, when his wife, a thin, nervous woman with protruding eyeballs that made her resemble something that had hopped out from one of the more sodden cracks in the walls, stood behind the counter. And during summer vacations, the weather was too nice for us to spend all our time indoors. So Mr. Bradlee was able to indulge our antics fairly comfortably in the late afternoons and on Saturdays throughout the rest of the year.

Of all his young customers who descended on the shop to wile away the drizzly hours of autumn and winter, only Eric Turnbull and I achieved the special status of avid collectors and amateur scribes and artists. Many others came to buy comics—especially noticeable were the sullen, bespectacled teenagers for whom we invented scornful nicknames based on their joylessness and astonishing mistreatment of the expensive comics they purchased (*The Warper, The Grim Ripper,* etc.). But only Eric and I (and to some extent a quiet teenager named Jamie) regarded the place as a combination arcade and sanctuary, and so haunted it that our faces became almost as familiar as the owner's.

But this one Saturday I was alone in the almost-empty shop, huddled in the corner, reading and avoiding going out into the blustery, rainy afternoon.

Perhaps it was the sudden deepening of the silence, the absence of the last shuffling, throat-clearing adult in the shelves opposite, or the faint, echoing ring of the old cash register that brought me back from the little coloured squares on the page to the grey light seeping in through the rain-spattered window. Whatever the reason, I looked up with a start, blinking myself back into the familiar world and hour, the shivering twilight settling down like soot, wetted and darkened even further by the ceaseless drizzle. Mr. Bradlee slouched on one elbow behind the counter, grinning over an opened comic. Beyond him, through the front window, I could just see the lace-like fronds of the huge weeping willow rise and fall slightly on the breeze, as though I were peering into an aquarium at the fins of some ancient, slow-moving fish.

"I've got to go," I almost shouted, terror-stricken at the image of Clive Withers waiting, arms crossed and scowling, in the open doorway of the paper shack.

"See you Monday." Mr. Bradlee smiled up from his book, turning slightly toward me over a huge ketchup stain on his dingy white T-shirt.

I grabbed my bike from the trunk of the willow, nervously aware that the overhanging streetlamp was poised to ping on, and pedalled furiously down the street past the dim fluorescent gas pumps of Onnoways' garage and the stern, granite facade of the lawyers' office, straight for the concrete loading platform of the Foamboard Building that marked the end of the main street. I almost spun out turning the corner onto the river road. In the near distance a shiny strip of yellow light fell out of the paper shack's doorway. To my dismay, no shadows flitted across it.

"Oh please, oh please," I whispered, throwing my bike heavily onto the beaten ground, "don't let me be the last."

But it was no good. Before I even reached the doorway, Clive poked his pinched, purple-mapped face into the light and snarled, "Where the fuck have you been!"

I swallowed hard and scurried past him without responding. Nothing I said could make any difference, and since silence had always been my refuge in that place of dangerous, shifting politics, I hoped that it would serve me well again. I was wrong.

"It's about time!" he roared, and grabbed me by the shoulder, spinning me around. His long hair seemed to drip off his forehead; I could almost feel it sizzle against my cheeks. "I've been waiting for you for half an hour!"

"I'm sorry," I began weakly. "I was reading and . . ."

"What!" He looked around as if desperate for witnesses to back up what he had just heard. "You were what?"

A sickening feeling overwhelmed me as I realized my mistake. "Nothing," I muttered, hurriedly shoving the thick Saturday papers into my canvas sack. "I forgot, I'm sorry, I'll be here really early tomorrow, I'll . . ."

He whapped me on the back of the head with his open hand. "There's no paper tomorrow, stupid." Then he spat down at my running shoe and emitted the scornful, barking laugh he always used when something struck him as particularly pathetic. "Reading, he says. He was reading." His already high-pitched voice became mincing. "I'm sorry I was late, but Lassie was in trouble and I just couldn't tear myself away. Oh Jesus," he shook his head, his voice back to normal, "I always knew you were some kind of sissy. Reading!"

I was on the verge of tears because I knew from careful obser-vation what happened when he got his hooks into something meaty; the torture could last for weeks, and would likely be enjoyed by everyone else in the shack. Only one thing could make it worse, and I was just savvy enough to avoid the trap. No matter what happened, you could never plead for a break, never compound your fault with an obvious show of weakness. And I was aware that, since I was younger than the others, Clive expected me to break down in tears.

I didn't. I suffered his abuse in silence, moving quickly when he swung his hand or spat again, and then lugged my loaded sack back into the blustery gloom.

The darkness closed around me like wet burlap. A chill wind blew off the dyke and sent shivering gusts of rain through the dull amber glow of a streetlamp on the river road. Suddenly, I realized that not only had I been late getting my papers, but I would be late delivering them (which might cause complaints), and my mother would worry when I didn't show up on time for supper. And all this because I had been reading! Maybe Clive was right to make fun of me, I thought, struggling to fit my bulging canvas sack into the wire carrier attached to the front of my bike.

It wasn't easy. On Saturdays, I had nearly fifty papers to deliver, fifteen more than usual because some people only wanted the weekend edition. I wasn't small for my age, but I was still only ten years old and often had difficulty handling the weight of the extra papers, as well as the comics, flyers, and other supplements stuffed in to pad each copy.

Eventually, I clambered onto my bike and wobbled precariously up the loose shoulder onto the river road. It was a half-mile to my first delivery, a houseless stretch along the dyke not pleasant to travel in miserable, dark conditions. My route began in the most wind-flayed and desolate part of town, among the sagging shacks of poor bachelor fishermen who had only mongrels for company. Here, few lights shone, and the cluttered yards, often shrouded in hanging fishnet and crammed with broken skiffs, seemed to belong more to the nearby salt marsh than to the firm ground. In the daylight, I enjoyed this area—its maritime sloppiness appealed to my sense of adventure, and I was familiar with torn nets and old boats. But darkness turned my enthusiasm to cold terror. I had read enough comic books to know that anything could be living in the marsh.

The best thing to do was to build up speed along the river road, enter the glow of the last dim streetlamp like a comet, and burst forward to the first shack. Satisfied with this plan, I rose up off my seat and pressed down hard on the pedals again and again until I was almost out of the darkness and into the faint glimmer of light where I'd have to leave the pavement and climb the gravel dyke into the marsh. The rain pelted my cheeks and forehead so that I had to keep my head lowered, which is probably why it happened.

My front wheel hit a rock, shifting the weight in my carrier and twisting the handlebars out of my grip like live snakes. I careened sideways, unable to recover my balance, and toppled more than plunged to the slick pavement. On the way down I somehow jammed one leg into the frame so that, when I landed, my leg was twisted awkwardly under the bike.

When I realized what had happened, I tried to keep the papers that had scattered onto the road from blowing away, but I could not pull my leg from the frame. I began to cry in sudden, frustrated gasps. The wind picked up as if it had been waiting for an opportunity to carry all my papers off, and I couldn't hear any other sounds except that low, victorious moaning and my own broken sobs. I forgot about my papers when my leg began to throb and I noticed a tear in my jeans through which I felt the stickiness of blood. All I wanted now was to get home, have a steaming bowl of soup or a mug of hot chocolate, and put the paperboy part of my life out of my mind. But first, I had to *get* home.

Lying back on my elbow, sniffling, and occasionally trying to move my leg, I didn't notice I had company until a nasally, rapid-fire voice pierced the wind-deepened silence just over my head.

"Ass over teakettle, eh? Goddamnit-goddamnit, get wet as a duck's ass if you just sit there."

I looked up into the face of a man, neither young nor old, whose few inches of exposed skin—above his full, black beard and below a woolknit, black skullcap pulled down over his eyebrows—shone shockingly white around his dark, searching gaze. He was bent forward at the waist, close enough to me that I could smell the strong odour of gasoline and river mud coming off his grubby canvas jacket. His mouth had the thick-lipped half-pout of a rock cod's. The lips were ruddy, and he licked them rapidly, at thirty-second intervals, with the tip of his tongue. That motion, plus the length of his bony nose, the tip of which overhung his top lip, made his tiny, bloodshot eyes seem so far away that it was as though his face were divided into two faces, the upper one coming suddenly to life when his voice and tongue stopped moving.

He grinned slightly as he stared down, but the effect wasn't cruel or mocking. It just seemed to be an expression of gratitude for the wind and rain and darkness. Besides, I knew just enough of the man from being around the wharf with my father not to fear him. Yet I was not easy in his presence, which he seemed to understand. Straightening up to his full height—about five foot six—and pushing his skullcap back off his eyebrows, he cackled gleefully, "Mackie's boy aint ya? How's the old bugger doin, goddamnhim, up-to-no-good-the-old-bugger-eh?"

I nodded, feeling better for the company but more aware also of the throbbing of my leg. "He's okay, I guess."

Ezra's grin broadened briefly, then he looked at my bike and scowled. "I seen you go down Jesus Christ I was up on the dyke there and there ya went just-like-that, pretty damned hard too, hurt any?"

"A little," I answered. "My leg's stuck."

He squatted by the front wheel, and had just reached forward to the frame when a car pulled up, its headlights painfully brightening the streetlamp's shimmer. I squinted and flung one arm over my eyes. Ezra muttered something I couldn't make out.

"What's going on here!" a deep, authoritative voice boomed. Then a car door slammed, and I opened my eyes to see a tall man looming in the headlights. I did not recognize him, but his commanding presence immediately comforted me.

"I fell," I explained. "And he was going to help me get my leg out of . . ." But when I turned toward Ezra, he was gone.

The rest of that night passed predictably enough, except for one small event. The man managed to extricate me from my bike, loaded it and my canvas sack into his trunk, and then drove me home. Once I had washed my cut, changed into dry clothes, and generally recovered from the shock, I realized I still had to deliver my papers. Unloading my sack, I counted only thirty-nine papers—eleven had been scattered on the river road to become nothing but pulp for the wind. That meant I'd have to buy eleven papers and pay for them out of my own pocket, money that would normally go to improving my comic book collection. And by this time of night, there was no guarantee that I would even be able to find eleven copies still left in the stores.

Depressed, I had to be prodded out the door by my mother's offer to contribute a dollar toward the reduction of my sudden debt. I was so busy calculating the numbers—how much the papers would cost, how much that would lower my weekly earnings, how many days I'd be working for nothing (about two, I figured)—that I almost fell over the plastic bag perched at the top of the porch steps. When I opened it, I was stunned to find it contained a dozen neat, bone-dry copies of that day's *Vancouver Sun*.

"Now who on earth put those there?" my mother asked, her pale face ballooning over me where I knelt on the linoleum floor, handling the papers as if they were rare back-issues of *The Amazing Spiderman* or *Daredevil*.

"It must have been Ezra," she smiled, remembering what I had told her of my fall. "A heart as big as all outdoors, that man. Give you the shirt off his back."

My father, listening from the living room, added in an amused voice, "Not that you'd want it."

"Very nice," my mother winked at me, "coming from a man whose shirts would be just as dirty if he didn't have his own personal cleaning service."

But I wasn't in the mood for their banter. Somewhere, below my immediate elation and relief, I felt uneasy. The dark face that had leaned down to me out of the rain; why did it suddenly seem a part of my world yet separate from it too, compelling and disquieting as the moon or stars?

two

IT MUST HAVE BEEN early December, after the last dog-salmon opening, because I had helped my father take his fall net off the boat and store it in the net shed. Now, with the fishing season shut down until the springs and early sockeye returned in March, our household would be calmer as the stresses of my father's job briefly disappeared. Or at least this is what we thought, huddled inside our drenched and shuddering bungalow as the heavy winds and rain of the past few days continued to rattle the blackened living-room window. It was such a miserable night that I was astonished to see a hunched figure suddenly emerge at the top of the dyke, just where the orange fluorescent lights of the cannery glimmered. Then the figure vanished, only to reappear a moment later in the streetlamp glow in front of our house. A few seconds later, we heard the pounding.

I reached the kitchen door just as my mother pulled it open and a gust of briny riversmell blew in, rich with the mulch of dead fish and rotted bark. Outside, in a pelting rain so thick that he seemed to be trapped in a woodcut print, Ezra raised his dripping, water-spangled beard into the porchlight and shouted, "Better-tell-Mackie-to-get-down-to-the-float-she's-almost-under-now-for-chrissakes!"

My father had already pulled his gumboots on and was reaching for his floater jacket. "Tell him okay, I'll be right there," he said wearily to my mother, then muttered something to himself about corking.

"What's going on! What's going on!" my pyjama-clad brother and sister chimed in unison, jumping around my father until he told them to settle down. As calmly as possible, I dressed and took a flashlight out of the nearby drawer. I hoped to give the impression of indispensability so that there would be no question of my staying home, even though it was a school night and close to my bedtime.

The plan worked, but only because my parents were too preoccupied even to notice me before I had followed my father into the streaming dark.

We lived about a half-mile west of town and the harbour, close to the river road, which meant we had to struggle along the high dyke in almost total darkness for twenty minutes, only the wavering beam of the flashlight brightening the gravel in front of our boots, before we reached the slick, roughly planked gangway leading down to the wharf. At the far end of a linked series of mossy floats, the *Nautilus,* my father's twenty-four-foot, flat-bottomed, wooden gillnetter, sagged in its mooring, its short mast looking dangerously shorter than normal.

As we approached, carefully negotiating the plywood boards joining the floats together, we heard the screek-screek-screek of the old metal hand-pump hard at work, sounding like the cries of a weakened gull. I trained the flashlight beam on the sound, and there stood Ezra on the deck just outside the open cabin door, yanking the steel-rod pump handle back and forth. His skullcap had fallen off, and the rain had matted his long, black hair to his cheeks.

"Callum," my father said firmly, "shine that light someplace else."

My father stepped on board, then hollered over the whooshing of the wind and the gush of rainwater out of the pump, "Okay, Ezra, I'll take it from here!"

But the screeking noise continued without pause, and even grew louder and faster.

"Ezra!" my father hollered again with a kind of nervous insistence.

The pump kept going. I forgot my father's order and shone the beam back onto the deck. Ezra's right arm pounded up and down like a piston, his head lowered almost into his chest. The edge of the light reflected my father's orange jacket, the only bright colour in the scene. Beyond the figures of the two men the river flowed black and steady, in rhythm to the motion of that one black arm, driving through the slash of rain. We just stood there, watching. The echo of my father's edgy words rolled on for what seemed an eternity.

Finally, hesitantly, he reached out a hand. "Ezra!" he tried once more, and lightly touched the rising left shoulder.

The blow fell rapidly. I wasn't even sure I had seen it, except my father lay sprawled back against the netless drum, its proximity to the deck all that saved him from landing hard in the stern.

A strange quiet descended. Ezra's breath and my father's drifted slowly together in the air over the deck, in tiny clouds of shagged white. Ezra stood among them, bull-heavy, his chest heaving, his eyes blinking furiously at nothing in the dimness. Then, very slowly, he turned toward my father as if he had just noticed his presence.

My father, meanwhile, had not moved. His gumboots were propped against the edge of the main hatch, and his right arm, draped over one side of the drum, kept him from lying prostrate over the centrepiece. I watched the flow of his breath as it rose to meet the opposing flow, almost scared for it in the coming collision. For the first time in my life my father appeared vulnerable to me, stilled in the presence of something more powerful than even the river or the wind. I shifted the light back to Ezra's face, the strands of soaked hair clutching his cheeks.

"Callum," my father said calmly, "shine that over here so I can see what I'm doing."

I did as I was told, and my father soon righted himself. He stood between the drum and deck, his head at the height of Ezra's boot tops. For one terrible second, I saw him as a coloured spike Ezra would start pounding into the wood of the stern. But I soon sensed what my father already knew: Ezra had come back to himself from wherever it was he had been.

"Give me a hand, Ezra, would you?" my father said, reaching up.

Ezra did, and, seeming not to feel the weight, almost flung my father onto the deck. "Had-to-start-on-her-couldn't-wait-for-you," he launched in, as if nothing unusual had happened. "Jesusjesus-wouldn't-have-turned-her-over-in-a-few-minutes." He paused, then thrust his face into the rain that continued to pelt down. "Pissin'-like-this-you-better-get-the-automatic-going-Mackie-for-chrissakes-be-down-here-all-night."

My father nodded, then bent over and picked up the top end of the pump lying in the doorway of the cabin, its bottom end still immersed in the rain-swollen current rising around the open engine. "Supposed to be working now," he said. "Better check the battery once I get rid of this." He gestured toward the darkened cabin.

Screek-screek-screek, the pump started up once more. I kept the flashlight off my father's face, the beam illuminating his midsection, but eventually I angled it toward Ezra. I was still amazed that neither he nor my father had referred to the sudden violence of a few moments before. Had I imagined it?

After a while the rain stopped and my father lifted the hand-pump from the sodden bottom of the cabin. He asked me for the flashlight and shone it on the engine, a black, greasy Oldsmobile, bulky and squat as a huge typewriter.

"Must-have-wet-the-plugs-this-time," Ezra cackled. "Come on, Mackie, goddamnya-goddamnya, turn-her-over."

My father disappeared into the cabin. Then the engine coughed and sputtered, once, twice, before it finally caught and roared into life.

"Jesus-Jesus!" Ezra howled, shaking his head rapidly from side to side, which shook the wet strands from his cheeks. He seemed to have escaped fully now, and with the rain stopped and the wind dying down, a sense of normalcy flooded back.

My father, emerging triumphantly from the cabin, obviously felt the same. "Can't beat this old girl," he grinned. "She's got the life's blood in her, all right."

He let the engine run awhile to charge the battery, which he then hooked up to the automatic pump, saying "That ought to hold till morning even if the rain starts up again." Then he and Ezra joined me on the float and we all moved toward the gangway.

About halfway there, Ezra stopped abruptly and clapped my father on the back. "Come-on-in-for-a-drink-Mackie-you-old-bugger."

My father hesitated, shook his head slightly, opened his mouth to speak, and then closed it again. Finally, with a shrug, he said, "No harm in a drink, eh Callum? Just a quick one?"

I nodded, in no hurry to get home, then followed Ezra and my father across the slippery decks of two gillnetters moored side by side.

The third boat out was Ezra's. A few feet wider and longer than the *Nautilus,* it was like other Fraser River gillnetters, masted, cabined, drummed, licensed. Yet it stood out in one remarkable way: there was nothing warm or homey about it. No sentiment had been showered on this tar-black, green-slimed hulk of wood, dangling its stained scotchmen (not pumpkin-fat and bright, but dingy and deflated into the shape of oily teardrops) and flying a tattered, faded piece of the Greek flag no larger than a dishcloth, the lone sentimental reminder of the previous owner. Even the former name, *Aegean Princess,* was barely legible along the bow, and no new letters ever took its place. Fishermen who would refer to each other by boat name, as in "Who's that at the top of the drift? Oh, it's the *Nautilus,*" could not refer similarly to Ezra's boat, but could only remark, "There goes Ezra."

I had often seen Ezra's boat at the wharf and out fishing, but I had never been on deck, let alone inside the cabin, so I followed my father excitedly as Ezra preceded us through the skinny doorway into the wasp-coloured light of a single hanging bulb.

The interior was spacious enough—my father didn't have to adjust his six-foot frame much as he passed to the right of the wheel and dash and stepped into the cabin proper—yet it had the cramped, claustrophobic atmosphere of a cave. Apart from the almost-darkness, there was the strong smell of stale sweat, unwashed clothes, and fishblood that would have been unbearable if not diluted with the heavy, almost smoky odour of stove oil. But even more noticeable than the absence of light and the smell was the clutter. In the sink and on the attached counter sat empty cans of soup with the jagged lids sticking up, similar tins of evaporated milk, old teabags shrivelled as dead mice, crumpled potato-chip bags, a butter knife with a congealed blob of butter at its tip, some bloodstained plastic wrap (perhaps off a piece of hamburger or cut of steak), a chipped ceramic coffee mug, a plastic milk carton squished into an accordion, a rusted combination can opener–corkscrew–jackknife, an unopened package of mending twine, some loose radio batteries, and some dirty plates, bowls, and cutlery.

Opposite the sink and counter, a padded, leather-upholstered bench semicircled a small enamel-topped table on which lay some tools—a monkey wrench, pliers, and a Phillips screwdriver—more chip bags, a fishbook with the dried blood imprints of fingertips on its cover, and an engine part that might have been a carburetor. The leather bench was torn in places, buckled in others, and bits of white stuffing had burst through. Above the table, a grimy porthole the size of the tiniest winter moon stared across at its equally grimy twin above the sink; neither looked to have been opened for years. Where it wasn't buried under engine batteries and brown-paper shopping bags block-lettered with "Shop-Easy" and "Super-Value," a greasy beige shag carpet, now worn flat as moss, visibly covered the floor. And finally, in the bow, a small opening narrowed to the bunk, a just-visible heap of sleeping bags, mack jackets, thick woollen socks, sweaters, and other clothes.

Ezra was hunched down beside this opening, firing up a small kerosene stove, his back to us. He made no attempt to clear a place for us to sit. In fact, he seemed to have forgotten that we were there.

My father nudged me toward the table, then slid in beside me on the leather bench. We didn't move anything, just waited silently for Ezra to turn around. I could hear the current trickling underneath us and the wind clanking a loose chain on a nearby boat.

Eventually, Ezra faced us, with no expression of hospitality. Mumbling, he pulled off his wet jacket, crossed to the galley, then returned to the table holding a bottle, the chipped coffee mug, and a plastic cup. He slid onto the bench opposite us, poured some of the contents of the bottle into the mug, pushed it over in front of my father, then sloshed a little into the cup and inched it in my direction, without comment or change of expression. Finally, he lifted the bottle and took a long swig from it.

"None for the boy, Ezra," my father said gently, pushing the cup back.

"Warm him up some, Mackie," he grinned, but left the cup where it was.

We stayed for perhaps twenty minutes, during which little give-and-take conversation occurred, just a few exchanges initiated by my father. At one point, he thanked Ezra for coming to tell him about the boat being flooded, to which Ezra merely grunted, "Better get her corked again if you want to keep her floating till spring." Mostly, my father talked, not lightly but not forcedly either, reminiscing about fellow fishermen, stories that Ezra grinned broadly at, and nodded to, seeming content just to listen, as though he were a child hearing bedtime stories that he knew by heart.

"Remember that one fall opening?" my father would begin. "When Rod set his net in the fog, about midnight, then crawled into his cabin and fell asleep?" He chuckled and took a brief swallow from the mug. "He woke up at daybreak and could hear bells. It was like he was back in England, he said, them ruddy bells." Here, my father laughed at his own poor attempt to mimic an English accent. He was even more animated now. "So old Rod, he says, what in blue blazes, and drags himself up on deck, rubbing the sleep out of his eyes. And what do you think he sees?"

Ezra had leaned forward slightly, and now his tongue darted out, rapidly wet his lips, and disappeared again.

"Cows!" my father laughed. "A whole herd of them, gathered around the boat, munching away, looking at him like he was the biggest jackass going!"

"Drifted into Swenson's field," Ezra grinned. "Got stuck there too."

"Had to wait for the next tide," my father added, elbowing me lightly in the ribs. "Now you know why I never go to sleep when I'm fishing."

"Too goddamned hungry," Ezra grinned again. "Eh Mackie? Can't miss that one smiley swimming by goddamnya-goddamnya."

My father shrugged happily. "Can't sleep anyway, even if I tried. Scared of those bells, I guess."

Ezra guffawed, throaty and loud. Then the silence resumed.

The oil began to bother me, and I coughed twice to let my father know. Also, I was uncomfortable in my wet clothes and a little disappointed in Ezra's virtual muteness and in the lack of telling personal details to be found in his home (for he had no other, I soon discovered).

My father, responding perhaps to my coughs, suddenly scowled. "Jesus H. Murphy, Ezra, you're going to kill yourself one of these days if you don't watch out with that stove."

Ezra only blinked indifferently.

"Can hardly breathe in here now," my father continued, sliding out from behind the table. "Anyway, we've got to get back. Thanks for looking out for the old girl. And for the drink."

"All right, then," Ezra nodded, polite but subdued. When my father and I turned to leave, he did not follow.

It was a relief to be back on deck. The stars had come out in frozen clusters, across which some black clouds, pushed by the wind, scudded in shredded pieces. I breathed in great gulps of the rain-sweetened air, so refreshing that I did not even notice how chilled I was until we had climbed the gangway and were hurrying along the dyke for home.

Once we had passed the last empty streets and warmly lit houses at the edge of town and plunged into the darkness, my father stopped and, cupping his hand around a struck match, lit a cigarette. I took the opportunity to ask, tentatively, about what had happened on the *Nautilus*.

He waved his hand dismissively, and a little trail of smoke followed the motion. "Oh, that was nothing. I ought to know better than to startle a fellow when he's concentrating so hard. Especially Ezra. He's more coiled up than most."

"How come?"

"I don't know, Callum. That's just the way he is, always has been."

We started walking again, high above the river's low, rushing tide, past a sagging net shed with a canvas-covered boat up on blocks beside it, dry-docked for the winter. After a while I said, as more of a question than a statement, "He never said he was sorry."

"No," my father responded between drags. "I doubt he even knew what he'd done." As if recognizing the mysteriousness of this comment, he quickly added, in a sober tone that told me he had no more to say on the subject, "Ezra's a bit off, Callum. A good fellow, really, but not like most people."

We had reached the huge metal sign of the Home Oil gas station, the point where we always left the dyke to take the shortcut through the ancient orchard of gnarled plum trees to our street. This sign, round and white as a full moon, shone its tall red and blue neon letters into the darkness, and marked the one small industrial area on the dyke before it curved off blackly toward the potato fields of Pheasant Island and the salt marshes of Canoe

Pass. Forty feet out from the base of the dyke, opposite the sign, two fifty-foot-tall cylindrical steel tanks glimmered dully in a cemented rectangle of ground closed in by a barbed wire fence. Outside a gate in this fence, a gravel driveway for oil trucks meandered through a field of short grass to the river road. The tanks themselves were always a surprise, Chilukthan's version of a large city's "refinery row." They were taller than anything else around (including the dyke), and reverberated with an eerie hollowness whenever we were daring enough to chunk stones at them. All sorts of dials and knobs and spigots stuck out from them, and steel ladders were welded to their sides so that workers could climb to more valves and dials higher up. A complicated tangle of pipes with square metal boxes attached snaked all around the cemented base of the tanks. I had often wanted to get beyond the fence and climb the ladders to the tops of the tanks, but I had never found the courage (my parents, too, had repeatedly warned me away from them).

Equally compelling, but in a different way, the sign on the dyke nightly unveiled its letters upriver toward the sleeping town. For years, from the top of a concrete pole shut off behind a chainlink fence, the dull neon had read HOME OIL. But several months back, the IL had burned out, leaving HOME O, which was a source of much humorous comment, both on the waterfront and in the paper shack. "Going to meet the big homo?" someone might snicker as you headed off along the dyke. "Give him a kiss for me." But since time wears the edges off every joke eventually, the sign went mostly unremarked now, to the point where, if you referred to the HOME O sign, only the lamest comedians attached any ribaldry to it.

I paused under the sign now and looked out on the river. The station's fuel barge, a long wooden pier with two pumps where fishermen regularly stopped to gas up, extended thirty feet into the channel. Occasionally, I would walk with my father along this pier to the company's small, square office building on the dyke, a place shelved with marine supplies and a counter and cash register where we would pay for our fuel. But since my father usually carried his own jerry cans of gas down to the wharf from Onnoways' station close to the harbour, we rarely stopped at the Home Oil pier.

For this reason, the whole place—the pier, office, sign, but especially the tanks—fascinated me. Standing there again, under the blue-red light sifting wetly down onto my face and hands, I felt a half-terrifying, half-pleasurable shudder pass through my body. And I realized, with a sudden chill, that I felt exactly the same way around Ezra Hemsworth. There was something different about him, as if he needed to keep the core of himself secret from the world. That strange, coiled darkness—it seemed to be building all the time, waiting for release. And the weird thing was, that darkness was familiar to me; I knew it from somewhere. But where?

As the wind gusted the briny mud smell over the dyke, the answer soon reached me. Of course! Ezra possessed all the mysterious qualities of my favourite comic book characters.

I shuddered again, deliciously, and the whole black night crackled away like a swirling cape beneath the stars.

three

MY FATHER'S BAD COLD did not reveal itself until a few days after we had first pumped the boat. More rain fell in the interim, great driving tempests of it that flooded the potato fields and swelled the ditches to road level. If the weather had been warmer, we might have referred to this unending storm as a monsoon, but since the temperatures were only a few degrees above freezing we had to resort to other descriptions. "Right royal nuisance" was my father's choice, as he trudged back and forth from the house to the boat, trying to save Ezra from making the trip to tell him or from doing the actual pumping. I agreed with my father's opinion, since delivering newspapers in the driving rain was sloppy, uncomfortable work. My back tire sent a skunk-stripe of mud up my back and I had no end of trouble keeping my papers dry. On top of that, I had to withstand the teasing nicknames Clive Withers had bestowed on me. "Egghead" and "Bookworm" were not so bad; I was almost confident enough to take pride in them in a quiet, shrugging way. But "Lassie," with its connotation of girlishness, was very upsetting, and Clive, with a torturer's instinct for weakness, soon added "Nancy Drew" and "Trixie Belden" to the list. It took every ounce of will I had to leave the cozy, musty sanctuary of the Haunted Bookshop for the unpredictable torments of the rain-rattled paper shack.

Yet there were compensations. Poor weather made some of my customers more generous (especially the older people), and I occasionally received invitations to stop for a cup of cocoa and some cookies. Since it was December, I could now anticipate the largesse of Christmas tips, which could only be larger than usual if the rain continued to make my customers feel sorry for me. Also, the rain deepened the pleasurable solitude of reading. It added an under-rhythm of words to the page, so that even the most exotic story retained a comforting homeliness: the terrible thirst in *Lawrence of Arabia,* for example, was not quite so terrible with the drainpipes gurgling just outside. The stories were oddly more real, as if the rain had put the stamp of dampness on them, and said, "You can gallop off into the sun, but you'll never chip that moss off your horse's hooves."

Meanwhile, I had begun to enjoy delivering newspapers. There was something magnificent and empowering about the job, perhaps because it left me to a great extent on my own to determine my schedule and even my income. If I wanted to ride like the wind and finish my route in half an hour, I could; or if I preferred to lollygag around the shack and then coast through the streets, getting home in the dark, I could do that too, as long as none of my customers complained. Even better, each paperboy was responsible for increasing the size of his route by going door to door and signing up new subscribers. The incentive to do so was entirely in keeping with the capitalist ethos of the newspapers themselves: the more customers I had, the more money I made—also, each month, the boy who signed up the most new subscribers had his name entered into an annual draw for a new bike or an all-expenses-paid trip for him and his family to Sea World in Florida. Only the most naive, unseasoned boys, of which I was certainly one that year, aspired to winning prizes; the others scoffed at the whole business. "What would I want to go to Sea World for?" ran the general opinion. "I can see all the fish I want to down at the wharf."

What really rankled some of the older boys, however, was the fact that we had no choice but to sign up at least a few subscribers; failure to meet a minimum monthly quota would result in having your route taken away. As a result, toward the end of each month, a complex series of bargains and/or extortions occurred, in which the less enthusiastic boys would attempt to buy or trade someone else's subscriptions. On rare occasions, when the pressure reached a fever pitch, threats of violence would also be used, but these were risky, since bullying for subscriptions was greatly frowned upon and would also result in the loss of your route—a few of the more cynical thirteen-year-olds used to complain that if it was okay for the *Sun* to bully them into signing up new subscribers, how come they couldn't do a little bullying in return? But these boys were slackers, and, as Clive said, "didn't know dick about business."

Their refusal to participate enthusiastically in the subscription drive infuriated Clive because he felt pressured by the district manager to inspire us on to greater and greater deeds of entrepreneurial achievement. And December, being the season of fiscal frivolity for most people, as well as of goodwill, was deemed the prime time for us to do everything in our power to swell the circulation numbers of the *Vancouver Sun*.

As a result, the atmosphere around the shack was particularly poisonous and tense, and the endless rain didn't help matters much. One afternoon, just before the cold snap hit, I pedalled over from the bookshop, not early and not late, to discover a green Oldsmobile Cutlass parked beside the shack, looking odd among all the scattered bikes, as if the driver had deliberately run down every paperboy in his path. Inside, standing against the far wall with his arms crossed, was a short man with huge, dark hollows under his eyes and a bristly blond crewcut. I had never seen him before, but I could tell from the ominous silence and subdued faces of my peers that he had to be Mr. Vreen, our district manager. He was almost a mythical creature, known to us mostly by name, as when Clive would snarl, "I'll tell Vreen," or "You just wait till Vreen hears about this!"

Certainly, his physical presence in the shack was a surprise. I sidled in, disappointed that, as mythical creatures go, he was decidedly ordinary in appearance. Slight, dressed in black slacks, a black, thigh-length raincoat, and a scuffed grey fedora, he looked as harmless as someone's ancient grandfather, no taller and no more imposing than Clive, with whom he was conversing, one thumb pushing absently at his bottom lip. For his part, Clive resembled a whipped dog. He kept his head bowed so long that I was sure his hair would finally drip right off and leave him bald. And when he did look up, his expression was a startling mixture of obsequiousness and fear.

About a dozen of us stood evenly spaced around the wooden paper-stuffing shelf that ran along the four walls of the shack and extended about two feet outwards. In the dim light sifting in through the chinks up below the tin roof, I could just make out that a few of the older boys were smirking. The rest, however, looked unmistakably curious, as puzzled as I was by the unusual visit.

After a couple more minutes, Mr. Vreen turned to face us. As soon as he spoke, I understood Clive's palpable trembling. The man's voice was harsh as gravel spun under a tire, and when he used it, his thin top lip curled back to reveal a front tooth so sharp that it might have been a fang. And he had a way of rubbing his hands together that suggested he was well used to grinding boys into dust, and even took great pleasure in the process. I cringed even as the few smirks around me vanished.

"Well, boys," he began, "Mr. Withers here tells me that some of you aren't interested in new bikes or trips to Florida. Is that so?" He glared at the nearest boy, who instinctively recoiled, shaking his head at the same time.

"No? Well, now, that's funny. I would have thought that boys interested in new bikes and sunny vacations would be out there eagerly signing up new subscribers. But from what I can tell, that's just not happening." As he spoke this last sentence, he began to circle the shack like a sergeant checking out his recruits. I held my breath along with everyone else. Only the rain sounded, rattling down on the roof.

Finally, Mr. Vreen stopped in front of Donald Bints, one of the older boys and a slacker by any definition. Bints—we were all called by our last names—did the least amount of work possible. In the year that he'd had his route, it had dropped from thirty-five papers to twenty-seven, yet he somehow managed, just barely, to meet his quota every month. "They don't say nothing about losing subscribers," Bints would laugh, as another of his customers, tired of his poor service and bad attitude, cancelled a subscription. It was a mystery to all of us how he had hung on to his route so long. Clive certainly hated him; the two were always at each other.

Now it was clear that Clive had sicced Mr. Vreen on poor old Bints. I felt sorry about this, because there was something inspiring as well as irritating and depressing about him. Bints was an undernourished type, bony in the face and shoulders, with a haircut so short that it was almost a red stubble. His thick-lensed, thick-framed glasses, dark as circles of soot, were attached tightly to his skull with a thick black band, a precaution against those who were always hitting him and knocking his glasses off. When you threw in his large front teeth and the fly-swarm of freckles on each side of his skinny nose, Bints added up to the shack's resident clown, a status confirmed by his most striking characteristic, a strange kinetic energy that contrasted dramatically with his laziness. Bints was as near to a skittish colt as it was possible for any human to be. I often thought that his whinnying laugh must have been an affectation he'd developed to perfect the image.

Of course, almost everyone made fun of him. And yet—this was the inspiring part—he never seemed bothered. In fact, insults and physical abuse brought out his most antic qualities. And how much he was abused! Despite it all, though, he was a survivor, and I admired his daring and his resiliency because I was less confident, albeit more "normal."

So, to see Bints face to face with Mr. Vreen made us all tremble with anticipation. Clive in particular looked as if he was about to cry out gleefully, "Crush him, Vreen! Crush him!"

If Bints was scared, though, he didn't show it. He jittered back and forth from one foot to the other, a half-grin on his face. But he wouldn't meet Mr. Vreen's eyes. Perhaps, just perhaps, Bints was going to fail us—and that was how it seemed suddenly, Clive and Mr. Vreen against the paperboys.

"Bints. Route 35," Mr. Vreen said speculatively, his voice rasping like a stone lid being slid off a tomb. "Three subscriptions last month. Four cancellations. And no new subscribers so far this month."

"Yes, sir!" Bints barked out, standing to attention and grinning goofily at us, pleased with his mock-military manner.

Suddenly, Mr. Vreen slapped him on the side of the head, hard enough to shift his glasses off-centre despite the band. "A real clown, eh? Mr. Funny, huh?"

An even more disturbing quiet descended over the shack, even though Bints's snuffling had been added to the rattle of the rain. Somehow, we seemed to have left the outside world behind and were existing in some kind of surreal nightmare. The blow had shocked us all.

"Fucker, you fucker," Bints muttered, between gasps. But Mr. Vreen paid no attention. He had made his point and was already moving on.

"Now, boys," he said, turning. "I'm a fair sort of fellow. I could take away Mr. Bints's route right this minute, but I'm not going to do that. Do you know why? Because I believe in giving people a second chance, that's why. Besides, I had a nice chat with his mother yesterday, and she asked me to have a little chat with her Donald, put him on the right path, so to speak. A very nice woman, Mrs. Bints. She deserves better. Boys ought to help out their mothers, don't you think?"

We nodded in unison. But Bints, true to character, didn't take long to recover. "I'll help the old bag out!" he shouted. "Right out of the house and into the river!"

No one laughed, but I was secretly relieved to see Bints back to his old self.

Mr. Vreen simply ignored the remark. He stepped into the centre of the shack and said, "Which one of you is Taylor?"

I was too terrified to speak up, so Clive, still chuckling about the slap, walked over and pointed at me. "That's Nancy Dr . . . I mean, that's Taylor."

Mr. Vreen stepped closer. I could feel my heart pounding as he leaned in and I caught a whiff of his cloying aftershave.

"Eight new subscriptions already." He smiled with hearty approval. Then, after a pause, he added, "How old are you, son?"

I blurted out my answer.

"Ten?" He raised his eyebrows and turned back toward Bints. But Bints had vanished from the shack. "Well, it seems Mr. Bints has left us for the moment. No doubt he's embarrassed that a boy nearly three years younger is a much better worker."

I knew this was utterly false, the part about Bints being embarrassed. Suddenly I felt awful, like a traitor to some cause I didn't even know I belonged to. Sensing the other boys' disapproval, I understood, for the first time in my life, how an adult's praise could be dangerous. Confused and embarrassed, I realized that it might have been better if Mr. Vreen had slapped me. Instead, he kept smiling down for an interminably long time before saying briskly, "Keep up the good work, Taylor!" Then, turning back to Clive, he snapped, "I'll be watching those numbers." With that, he cinched the belt on his raincoat and strode through the open doorway. A moment later, his engine revved and his car pulled away with a spin of the tires that was like one last harsh command.

Once they were sure he had gone, everyone started talking at once about what had happened.

Meanwhile, Clive had started tossing out the paper bundles, barking "Come on, hurry up, get going!"

As we began stuffing papers into our sacks, wondering if Bints was going to return to do his route, he cantered in, grinning as usual, his glasses back in place. Good old Bints, I thought, remembering his comeback shout more than his tears. After all, it wasn't fair for a man to hit a boy.

After we'd laughed at him for crying, and called him "Mr. Funny," and tried to cuff him on the side of the head, somebody asked where he'd gone.

He unleashed his whinnying laugh, and, bouncing on his toes, said, "Had to find some dogshit, didn't I."

Our bewilderment delighted him.

"The bastard left his briefcase in his car, and the doors were unlocked."

"You didn't?" someone howled, but we all knew that he was telling the truth. Bints didn't need to lie.

"You're in for it now," Clive gloated.

But Bints just shrugged. "I'm not scared of Vreen. What's he going to do, fire me?"

"Yeah," Clive nodded fiercely, angered as always by Bints's attitude. "Yeah, he'll fire you."

"Big hairy deal. See if I care."

Clive purpled with exasperation, because it was so obvious that Bints really didn't care.

Eventually I left the shack, grateful to Bints that his return had made everyone forget Mr. Vreen's damning praise of my work ethic. I still wanted the extra money that new subscriptions brought in (mostly to improve my comic book collection, which I planned to do by attending a big comic book convention in Vancouver in January), and I had hopes for the new bike, but the encounter between Bints and Mr. Vreen had deflated my enthusiasm. Pedalling away in the rain, I saw again that sudden slap: it was as though I had been sleeping and the slap had shocked me awake. Which world did I belong to? Where did my allegiance lie?

I rode on past the fishermen's shacks, off the dyke, and toward the town centre, all the while deepening my conviction that Bints, despite being the target of so much ridicule and abuse, was someone whose smile I'd rather receive than that of Mr. Vreen. Yet I certainly couldn't imagine being Bints's friend. So where did that leave me? I rode on against the hard rain, splashing through puddles, racing the dusk and my own growing confusion.

Only when I reached the shabby, one-level duplex at the end of Finley Street, a run-down structure with flaking grey paint and a tilted veranda at the front and back (which made it seem like two sinking ships instead of one, both decks flooded), did I return fully to the present. I had been watching this house carefully for weeks. The previous residents at the back of the building had been three foul-mouthed and sullen young men. Even their German shepherd, which they always left chained to the broken veranda, had a nasty temperament and would rush to the edge of the walk and snarl and snap at me as I rode by. Normally, I would have tried to sign up anyone along my route who was not already a subscriber, but I could never muster the courage to run the gauntlet of those bared fangs, especially since I imagined the same sort of greeting awaited me behind the cracked screen door.

So I was both relieved and hopeful when the former residents moved out and the back half of the duplex sat empty. Not only was the nasty dog gone, but I suddenly had the prospect of a new subscriber.

To my disappointment, a new resident was slow in coming. Peering through the dirty windows one day, I understood why. The place was tiny, little more than a filthy main room with a hallway almost as narrow as the cabin door on the *Nautilus* leading to the back. The walls were covered in a dull-green wallpaper, torn in spots, and the windows, though south-facing, were low to the faded hardwood floor and skinny, making the room murkily dark even in broad daylight. The massive, rain-shuddering willow shrouding the veranda effectively blocked out whatever sun did emerge from the gloomy skies. My hopes for a new subscriber diminished as I walked away: who could possibly want to live there?

I had almost given up expecting someone to move in as I rode across the plywood plank bridging the swollen ditch at the front of the duplex. But this time I encountered something other than the usual dismal silence. A small, bright orange U-Haul trailer was backed up to the veranda, and a slope-shouldered man with a round, florid face was carrying a mahogany cabinet up the three mossy steps to the screen door, held open by an umbrella stand filled with black umbrellas. Despite my newfound resolve to slow down on the subscription drive, my first thought was mercenary. The fleshy solidity of this man, his slightly greying temples, and his plain business suit suggested he would be a newspaper reader. I slowly pedalled around the beige Plymouth attached to the trailer and rested my bike against the trunk of the willow, sheltered from the still-heavy rain.

The man noticed me as soon as he came back through the screen door. He plodded across the brownish grass toward me, his broad, brown tie flipped up over one shoulder like a hound dog's tongue. The effect was comical, but I couldn't even smile at it. I almost thought the man was going to sink into the wet earth before he had a chance to speak.

"Hello there," he said, bending in under a willow frond and blinking a few raindrops out of his eyes. "I gather you're the paperboy?"

This was encouraging, and I nodded.

"How would you like to make two dollars?"

"Sure," I answered without hesitation. Ever since I'd become a paperboy, the prospect of money had grown addictive.

The man sighed so deeply and at such length that I thought he was blowing up an imaginary balloon. "I have to get back to the office," he explained, "but I could leave the trailer." He paused, and eyed me more intently before continuing. "There's nothing very heavy. Yes, I think it would be all right."

I knew what he wanted, and I thought it would be all right too, except I wondered about locking up when I was done.

He seemed to read my thoughts and, smiling so that his face became even fuller, said, "Okay, but you'll have to come in and meet Mother first."

I followed him into the dark, dreary room, immediately oppressed by the low ceilings and that stale-air smell vacant places always have. The man had not brought much in out of the trailer so far, just an old, horsehair armchair, a coffee table, a few cardboard boxes, and the mahogany cabinet. At first, I didn't notice the woman seated in the armchair, perhaps because she was slight and frail enough to be little more than a shawl someone had dropped, or perhaps because she wore dark sunglasses and her head was swaddled in a magenta scarf, wrapped like a turban. It was easy to lose her against the background. I really only looked closely at her once the man addressed her, tenderly but firmly.

"Mother, this is the paperboy. He's going to finish bringing in your things."

Remembering my manners, I stepped forward, just as her pale, long-fingered hand, spiderwebbed with dark blue veins, lifted to her nose. She held an embroidered handkerchief, and then I realized that she was crying. Her thin body—made thinner by a long, black woollen coat that reached almost down to her leather, white-buttoned shoes—trembled almost imperceptibly.

"Mother," the man repeated, a slight break in his voice. "Please, I have to get back, I . . ."

The handkerchief drifted down slowly as a snowflake to rest in the black lap. Through the rest of our conversation, I fully expected it to melt. But it shone there now as the woman, in a voice stronger than I expected, quivering but sure, said, "All right, Leslie. I'll be here when you want me."

I thought the man was going to burst into tears. "I'm sorry, Mother, I wish . . ."

"It's all right," she consoled him. "I'll be fine. You run along." Then, unwinding her scarf, she smiled up at me. "I'm afraid we've not been properly introduced. My name is Mrs. Reginald Edmundson. But you may call me Vera, if you like."

I stared back at her. Even with her glasses on, she was striking. Her hair wasn't full but very long, grey streaked with black, like a fog with night sky showing through. She had a firm jaw, high cheekbones, a long, proud nose over a tiny mouth, and skin that, while wrinkled, didn't show her age in the way that her hands and voice did.

"And your name, dear?" she asked, her smile mechanical though not without warmth.

"Oh yes," her son, rallying, joined in. "I forgot to ask you."

"Callum," I said in my best speaking-to-old-people voice (many of my older customers had hearing problems).

"Callum," she repeated slowly. "Well, Callum, it's a pleasure to meet you." She extended her hand. My father always said, "When you shake someone's hand, be firm. There's nothing worse than a handshake like a wet dishrag." But I had never been invited to shake an old woman's hand before. Awkwardly, I held it, almost gasping at the coolness. Then, following her lead, I pressed it just slightly.

"Very nice to meet you," I almost shouted.

"Callum," she winced, "you'd be very good in the pulpit, do you know that?"

I must have looked confused because the man touched me lightly on the shoulder and explained, "My mother's not deaf."

"Oh." I felt a flush rise to my cheeks.

"Let the boy alone, Leslie." She fell back against the chair again. "I'm sure we'll get on fine."

The man signalled me toward the door. "I'll be right back after work, Mother. And we can arrange all your things."

"Things," she repeated dully. "Yes, of course, things."

Out on the broken veranda again, the man pulled a clean two-dollar bill from his wallet and handed it to me. "There aren't many things," he said, catching on the last word as if hearing his mother's echo over his shoulder. "Mostly boxes. I shouldn't think it will take you very long. Just put everything in the middle of the room." He frowned out over the brown grass as if it were a choppy sea he had to swim. "I left my jacket in the car," he said absently. "Callum." When he spoke my name, I was surprised that he remembered it. "I'm trusting you to . . . I mean . . . you'll be nice to her, won't you? You won't shout or bang the door or drop things . . ."

"No, sir," I reassured him, not at all used to being in that position with an adult.

"Thank you," he said quietly. And then, as though speaking to himself, he added, "She'll be fine here. It's not so bad, really. At least she'll have her privacy." But the rain and the brown grass and the broken porch defeated him. His jaw muscles twitched and he blinked rapidly. He sighed again and, hunching his shoulders, plowed through the rain to his car.

I watched him unhitch the trailer and drive off before I remembered that I had a job to do.

During my comings and goings, Mrs. Edmundson didn't speak; she just stood motionless by the skinny side window that looked out over the cracked walk and the gravel alley down which her son's car had disappeared.

When I had brought in the last box and placed it gently with the others, I stood as still as she, uncertain what to do next. Should I just leave? Should I say something first? Briefly, I thought I should ask if she wanted to subscribe to the paper, but I decided to wait for another day. For a while I simply stared at her, startled again by her hair, which, released from the scarf, fell to her shoulders in straight lines. Her profile, though, was softer and, even with her strong jaw and nose, almost vanished completely between her hair and the dark window.

When I realized she wasn't going to turn to me, I cleared my throat and softly said that I was finished and was leaving now.

"Thank you, Callum," she finally responded. Still without turning, she added, "I'm afraid I'm not very good company this afternoon." There was a regal gravity in her voice that I had heard before; often, my elderly customers spoke as if each word was precious as bone china, or with a kind of halting discretion that suggested it would be improper for the words to get too close to each other.

"That's okay," I responded, at a loss.

The silence deepened. I felt bad about leaving her, but I wanted even more to get away from that gloomy, musty room. I was already behind schedule, and if I didn't hurry, I wouldn't finish my route before dark.

"Well, see you," I mumbled, and gently closed the screen door behind me. Soon I was pedalling down the gravel alley, unnerved by the sensation that she was watching. But once I had begun my deliveries again, I stopped thinking about her still figure and speculated instead on how I'd spend the two dollars her son had given me.

By the time I reached home, soaked to the skin as I had been for weeks, I had spent at least ten dollars in my imagination and was fully committed once more to signing up new subscribers, no matter what the social costs.

Yet as I lay in bed that night, replaying the hard slap Mr. Vreen had given Donald Bints and picturing Mrs. Edmundson's motionless stance by the dirty window, the two disparate images coalesced until somehow I was seeing Ezra Hemsworth once more, frozen in the seconds after he'd struck my father, his shagged breath swallowing his dark, unknowing face. I was so startled that I almost jumped out of bed and went to the window, half-expecting to see his swift figure come up over the top of the dyke. Instead I closed my eyes and the image passed, blurred back into the distinct worlds of the paper shack and bookshop, the wharf and school and home.

four

AMAZINGLY, THE NEXT MORNING the world had changed. On
waking, the first thing I noticed was the silence, or rather the
absence of what I'd been so used to hearing for weeks—the hushes,
whispers, sighs, and taps of the rain that made the days a permanent
womb from which one was never quite born.

But the rain sound was gone—no gurgle in the drainpipes, no
vague splatters against my bedroom window. A hollow coughing
came from my parents' room, three quick bursts, then a half-
minute pause, then another round of bursts like heavy, hurried
footsteps that never came closer or went any farther away. Something
unusual was happening. It was as if someone had put his boots
on but couldn't make up his mind about leaving.

I got out of bed and went to the window. The bright view made
me squint. Where were the puddles in the muddy yard, their
brown depths marbled with heavy raindrops? What had happened
to the dark and shivering horses' manes of the willows and the
guttered-down candlesticks of the plum trees? And the sky: why

wasn't it low and grey and tilted like an old stone bowl being emptied? All the brown and grey was gone, all the crankcase oil drips off eavestroughs and branches had stopped, all the head-down, chest-forward, boot-slopping human progress had vanished and a new creature with new motion had appeared in the shape of Mr. Ely, our next-door neighbour, who was moving slowly from his back porch to his shed, each bootstep a questioning lunge; he seemed to be wondering whether the ground itself had disappeared.

Snow! And in December too. My pulse quickened as I took in all the astonishing newness of the familiar. Yes, the gnarled, black plum trees were there, but how different they looked, like an army of dwarves lugging leaky sacks of flour to the dyke. And icicles! I stared at a large one depending from our toolshed and felt a sudden urge to run out and snap it off.

But more than all this, I was drawn to the two competing levels of earth and sky, unrecognizable after so much rain and drizzle and overcast. The brilliant, endless vault of blue above the shocking white: how was it possible for one night of stars and sleep and silence to so utterly transform everything? I stared at the dazzle of sunlight on the pure, untravelled distance from our yard, through the orchard, and off to the dyke, and felt the paralysis of abundant choice. I forgot all about school and my job and homework and comic books, all the usual defining circumstances of a weekday morning. I watched Mr. Ely, red-jacketed as a pheasant, come to a dead stop outside his drift-hidden shed door, his knees lost to the white earth, his breath pouring out in a steady spiral as if his mouth were on fire, the daylight sharpening his profile until he was as clarified as a glass figure set out for the seed-searching sparrows to light on.

I dressed and walked down the hall to the half-opened doorway of my parents' room. My mother must have heard me, for she soon emerged from the darkness, white-robed as the yard outside, and, lightly touching my shoulder, turned me toward the kitchen. "Your father's not feeling well," she said, failing to hide the anxiety in her voice. "Do me a favour, Callum, and help your brother and sister get ready for school."

"What's the matter with him?" I asked, troubled by her tone.

She shook her head slightly, and I noticed the dark bags under her eyes and loose strands of black hair dangling over them. "Oh, it's just a cold," she replied with forced optimism. "All that pumping in the rain did it, I suspect."

Reassured, I helped my equally excited siblings dress in winter clothes that had rarely been needed (though my mother was never one to be caught unprepared where her children were concerned). Eventually, I ushered them outside into the cooling nip of the air, where Pepper, our springer spaniel, greeted us with even more enthusiasm than usual, as if he too understood the promise of the day.

"Can we ride our bikes, Callum?" Angie asked, hardly able to get the words out in her eagerness. Steven was already hurling himself into the deep white, re-emerging like a gopher, shaking his head and glancing around in all directions.

"I don't think so," I said, realizing we couldn't even ride our bikes—the changes had already begun and we hadn't even left our yard. "We'll have to walk."

The twins cheered this decision so enthusiastically that I didn't even consider how the snow would make it difficult for me to deliver my papers. Once Jerris had come flying out of his house to join us, his hair as vividly red as his father's jacket, we trudged happily schoolward, chattering so steadily that we drowned out the chickadees huddled in the laurel hedges and shrubs that lined the streets.

And so the morning went, and most of the afternoon, unreal in its charged engagement, even for our teachers and other adults, most of whom seemed different too, kindled by the change and our enthusiasm. The classroom, latterly a warm, brightly lit refuge from the damp greyness, now became a prison that tantalized us with its views of a nearby dreamworld, the likes of which we had encountered only in the pages of C.S. Lewis. All day I kept expecting a faun to tap his cloven hoof on our classroom window and invite me out to tea.

Recess was a chaos of hastily assembled snowmen, fierce snowball fights, face washes, and dared snowball tosses at windows, passing cars, older kids, and teachers—everything a brilliant blur of toques, mitts, jackets, boots, and scarves.

I wasn't at all surprised that Jerris stood at the centre of the storm, hurling, jumping, shouting, his hair unruly, his jacket wide open and eventually discarded. A year younger than I, Jerris had been my best friend for five years, ever since his family had moved in next door, arriving in a full-to-bursting station wagon. The only small children in our neighbourhood (except for Angie and Steven who, at two, were not much good as playmates, and the child Mrs. Ely was then carrying), we immediately became, as my mother put it, "thick as thieves." Mr. Ely skippered a seine boat, so Jerris and I began on a common, comfortable footing that made the wharf and the river priorities for roaming. How fast a summer day can vanish when you're intent on picking every piece of fruit swelled to ripeness by the sun and rain. How slow a lesson in adding and subtracting drags on an autumn Monday when the chucked beer and wine bottles of weekend drunkards settle slowly into the muck of the lowering tide. We were so inseparable that, if you had driven along the Chilukthan river road when school was out, any time between 1972 and

1975, you'd have seen us moving up or down the dyke in a pinwheel of excitement.

Even now, in the last month of 1975, our friendship was solid, but different interests had slowly emerged to loosen our bond. Jerris enjoyed comic books, mostly westerns like *The Rawhide Kid,* and we had wiled away many hours in our salty plywood tree fort high in a Douglas fir or in the back seat of an abandoned car by the river, flipping through the coloured pages. But he was not much interested in books, or even the more serious collectible comics. Reading was too sedentary for him; he preferred to be both the Kid and the Indians and desperados he encountered. Rarely did Jerris appear without a pheasant or seagull feather in his hair and a stone or clump of mud in his hand. And if you weren't careful, that stone or mud would be thrown in your direction, followed by a peal of Indian yipping and then a shadow slipping away with the speed of an eclipse.

During this particular recess, Jerris hurled snowballs wildly in every direction. He pegged a grade seven boy, and then spent several minutes outrunning him, his tiny body better suited to racing over snow. I cheered him on until the bell rang and the chase dissolved and the playground emptied. I waited by the entrance door. Finally, Jerris appeared, mittless, red-faced as his hair, freckles vivid as constellations on both cheeks, and breathing so heavily that he could have been a genie emerging from an uncorked bottle.

"Didn't catch me," he gasped. "Got him a good one too, right in the head." His grin was so broad that I thought his face would crack.

"I know," I said. "I saw."

The hallway behind sounded perilously silent. "Come on," I urged, "the bell's going to go."

Jerris hesitated, weighed down by the choice he faced every school day. Then he swiped another cold handful of snow off a nearby window ledge and declared, "I'm not going back."

I should have warned him he'd get into trouble, but he already knew that. Besides, saying so would have driven the wedge just a little deeper into the gap widening in our friendship. He looked at me for a few seconds, not in a pleading way, just open and hopeful, and I almost went with him as I would have done the year before. But I couldn't do it, not because I was afraid, but because the classroom with its many different relationships held a growing fascination for me.

Jerris understood that, so he didn't exert any pressure. "See you," he said quietly, turning back to the brilliant blue and white day.

Moments later, my teacher's words were stunned into silence by the smack of the snowball on the glass. Only I recognized the act as a gesture of affection, an attempt to fully include me one last time in the world I had begun to walk away from. My other worlds, of newspapers, comic books, and schoolwork, had an increasing hold on my time and attention. Different friends, enemies, and acquaintances now inhabited my social reality.

After the three o'clock bell signalling the end of classes, I stood with Eric Turnbull in the hallway outside the main office. We were grinning down into the large papier-mâché and wooden-figure manger scene that had been set up as part of the school's Christmas celebrations.

"Still there," Eric nudged me, barely restraining his laughter.

"Yep, still there," I agreed, trying not to catch his contagious mirth for fear I would give the game away.

A week before, while out on a hall pass, Eric had covertly reached into the manger, lifted the baby Jesus from his cradle, and taped a tiny school-album photograph of his own face over the Saviour's face. Then he laid the baby back in the cradle so that onlookers could join the three wooden wise men in admiring the cherubic features of the Son of God.

But Eric did not even distantly resemble the infant Jesus. For one thing, Eric's head was huge and covered in black curls. Also, he had a slight overbite, which didn't give him a horsey expression so much as it kept him looking younger than he was. There was so much curious intelligence in his dark gaze that, if he hadn't had such a childish mouth, his manic enthusiasms and practical joking would have been remarkably incongruous. Even so, teachers and most other adults were routinely disappointed with Eric. How could such a bright boy be such a little goof at the same time? We saw this question in their eyes so often that Eric had started to say that an alien intelligence had taken over his "mortal form," but that he, Eric, was trying to win it back. Every time he "capered about," he would grin and say, "It's another small victory for the human race. Take that, alien entities!"

Yet Eric was sometimes very serious, especially when pursuing a new enthusiasm. But even on those occasions, most adults didn't like him. Only a few other than his own parents—most notably Mr. Bradlee at the bookshop—were prepared to recognize the slapstick humour and the serious phases as two sides of the same rare coin.

I greatly admired Eric because I could push neither my goofiness nor my seriousness to such extremes. He was a year older than I, and two grades ahead (having skipped one of the primary grades), so I was content to follow in his wake. We had become friends in the bookshop one afternoon, finding a common preference for Marvel superheroes over their DC competitors, the teenaged, angst-ridden alter ego of Spiderman seeming more

believable and intriguing to us than the stiff, gentlemanly persona
of Batman's uncostumed self. From that day, he had become a sort
of role model, though our relationship was never the unbalanced
one of prophet and disciple. The closest Eric ever came to being a
religious figure for me was that December when, holding in my
laughter outside the main office, I saw him wrapped in swaddling
clothes under the adoring eyes of Mary.

Day after day, as the holidays drew closer, we would check the
manger to see if Jesus had his face back. And we waited with a
certain pleasurable anticipation for the scolding voice to come out
of the public address system to order Eric down to the principal's
office. How long could a practical joke be funny if no one but the
jokers ever noticed?

After a while, we turned away from the baby Eric and plunged
outside into the snow, laughing through the thick-padded streets
to the bookshop.

The town was oddly quiet. A few cars nudged forward like
spawning salmon, and for once we did not have to worry about
being splashed. The whiteness overwhelmed. Everything had an
underwater quality, as if we were on the bottom of the ocean
blinking through great drifts of salt. The granite clock tower by
the museum, a few doors up from the bookshop, seemed poised
to hoot out a lighthouse warning. But where were the shoals?
The moonish clock face showed 9:33, as it had done for
months, but it was easy to believe that the cold air had frozen
the hands. We went under their stilled pointing, past the pool
hall and antique store, then the skinny vacant lot, its knee-high
grass still strewn with the rubble of the house knocked down a
decade before, the barbershop (one chair, a zigzaggy black-and-
white TV, and glossy photos on the walls of men's hairstyles that
had been out of fashion for years), and a dress shop whose

window mannequin looked as if she had been expecting someone to ask her out to the prom since 1950. Finally, we reached the standing plywood sign on the sidewalk; it was in the shape of a pinstripe-suited duck, chomping on a cigar (Howard the Duck, to be exact, a wisecracking comic book character currently popular).

We burst into the shop, and the musty, yellowish scent of old pages greeted us warmly, followed by the even warmer greeting of Mr. Bradlee.

"Hi fellas," he said, grinning between bites of a sloppy submarine sandwich. A large, fresh mustard stain graced his white shirt front. "Good day at school?"

We told him that the baby Eric was still in place, a fact that made him chuckle heartily.

"Nobody's noticed it yet?" he asked incredulously.

Our confirmation delighted him.

"Priceless, that's priceless. I'd sure like to see it sometime." Then, catching himself, he slowly shook his head. "You want to watch out, though. Some people can get pretty touchy about that sort of thing, monkeying around with religion."

But we knew he was only going through the motions, protecting himself from possible criticism. He owned a business in a small town, after all, and a certain amount of goodwill was required.

"Oh, Callum," he suddenly announced, "I almost forgot. Your mother phoned. She wants you to call her back." He lifted the phone onto the counter.

Trust my mother to expect me to go to the bookshop despite the snow's disruption. That was just like her. Though not a big reader, she had a high regard for the activity.

When I dialled our number, I immediately felt guilty because I had forgotten all about my father's cold.

"I don't want your dad going out today," she almost whispered. "So he wants you to go down and check the boat for him. He says you'll know how to use the pump if there's water in the cabin."

I said I would check the boat after I'd finished my route, and that I'd be late because I couldn't use my bike in the snow.

From the moment I put down the receiver, the day progressed even more strangely and slowly. Despite my best intentions, I did not leave the bookshop immediately. By the time I stepped outside again, a few flakes were falling, like a preamble to the million-moted dusk hovering just beyond the deepening blue. I had hours of work ahead of me, even if I hurried. But since when had December ever given us such an unreal seascape to float through?

As I expected, the paper shack was even more chaotic and dangerous than usual. Because the snow had made driving difficult, the *Sun* truck was an hour late, which meant an extra hour of ducking snowballs, avoiding face washes, and hoping that the verbal and physical abuse wouldn't turn toward me. But Bints, as always, took care of that. His whinnying responses rang out with an increasing forlornness through the darkening afternoon.

I hovered on the edges of all the activity, throwing snowballs during the full-scale battles but avoiding the individual tosses that might have drawn too much attention. At one point Clive sneered at my fondness for reading, but his heart wasn't really in it, since my talent for signing up new subscribers kept him out of trouble with Mr. Vreen, who happened to make another surprise visit just after the truck arrived. He strutted into the shack wearing a raccoon-striped fur coat and fur hat with ear flaps, and in that chummy voice adults often use when they want to be friendly toward children, bellowed, "Well, I'll bet that Florida trip is looking pretty good to you boys now!"

He was so wrong that we couldn't even bring ourselves to look at him. Who would want to escape the supercharged world of the snow? Only a few days before, Mr. Vreen had been an ominous, mythical creature. Now he was just an embarrassment, and a cruel one at that. We didn't even expect him to say anything about the dogshit in his briefcase. After conferring briefly with Clive, and offering some hearty encouragement that we ignored, he left as suddenly as he had arrived.

Eventually, I slung my full paper-sack over my shoulder and trudged off to start my route. Darkness fell quickly. Soon every fifth or sixth house shone with Christmas lights, becoming a multi-coloured rectangle glimmering invitingly, a reminder of the warmth I would find at the end of my labours. Once I had reached the duplex on Finley Street, though, the only light guiding my path shivered down from the faint stars. I cautiously made my way around the back to where a sliver of yellow light lay on the snow. Mrs. Edmundson must have settled in. I pressed close to the building and heard the quietest strains of a violin through the wood. But when I peeked around the window frame, I saw no one through the glass. The boxes were gone and the room appeared orderly, but Mrs. Edmundson was not in her armchair. I suddenly pulled my head back. For one terrible second, I feared that she was still at the window and that I was staring right through her, our faces separated only by the thin glass. And yet something about the violin music bespoke an absence, a ghostliness. I shuddered at the sound. The music, the empty room, the light spilling onto the deep snow lightly engraved with bird-tracks: all this made me feel both inside and outside the darkness. It was very strange. If not for the weight of the papers, I might have felt even more detached. The dark alley lay ahead of me, and two dozen more porches, the mile-long walk to the wharf, and the wind-gnawed, black stretch of dyke homeward. I had no time to waste.

Yet something held me outside that window. Perhaps I was simply tired and the faraway violin lulled me into a brief rest. Perhaps I was afraid that Mrs. Edmundson had collapsed or died. Or perhaps I sensed that the chill in the air belonged to more than the air, and that it intensified the longer I stood still and let it sink into my skin.

The newspapers put an ache in my shoulder, and the moment broke. An hour later, the silence and the strangeness had delivered me to the bank of the river.

From high on the dyke, I could not see the tide beneath the dim wharf lights, so it had to be low, its last oily blackness seeping out to the gulf. I knew it was moving because of the trickles and gurgles around the pilings and bows of the moored gillnetters. And since the one familiar harbour deadhead was turned downriver in the dimness, I also knew that the current was running out. Above its restless noises, the wind added its countering oversound, a low and steady keening. The wharf was desolate. Lacking a flashlight, I had to be especially cautious descending the almost vertical gangway. The edges of the wharf were lost under the deep snow. But as I gripped the wooden rail, my eyes briefly lifting to the blur of flakes across the orange lamplight circle at the base of the gangway, my boots found the hollows of other bootprints. Grateful that I didn't need to break a path, I stretched from print to print until I reached the bottom of the gangway and the first float, one of a linked series resting on chained logs and attached to creosoted pilings that extended a hundred yards upriver, dark but for the faint starlight reflecting off the snow.

Only when I had adjusted to my precarious surroundings by taking several deep breaths did I notice something miraculous. At first, I was puzzled by the extension of snow beyond the edges of the wharf, wondering how snow could possibly float on water.

With a start, I realized that a layer of ice had enclosed the boats and pilings. I had never known the river to freeze. The summer fleet, still faintly redolent of salmon-blood and brine, was frozen in its moors. Little heaps of snow had gathered on the swaying links of the mast chains, turning them into long vertebrae, as though the night itself suddenly needed a spine to hold its position over the earth. The gurgling and trickling noises were the current running underneath the ice, and this realization chilled me even more.

I was afraid. How could I be sure I wouldn't walk right off the wharf and crash through the ice? As I started, I found with relief that the bootprints continued. Using them as well as my memory, I progressed cautiously along the frozen summer.

Halfway to my father's boat, a shout exploded directly ahead of me. "Hemsworth! You bastard! Come on out of there!"

It was a man's voice, deep and fractious as if the ice had cracked open. Silence followed. Then I heard an angry muttering, a sound like a lock being rattled, and silence again. Finally, another shout: "You stay the fuck away, you hear me!" This time, the silence lasted longer. Terrified, I realized that the only way back to the dyke was through me. I didn't want to run back the way I had come for fear of slipping, so I had no choice but to move out of the bootprints. Just after I had done so, and carefully lay chest-down in the unmarked snow, a dark figure stomped past, furiously kicking up a white spray, either sure of his direction or not caring where he went. From my position I could see only the dark legs behind the flying powder. Once I was certain that enough time had passed, I stood and looked back toward the gangway, but the figure had already vanished.

The troubling music of the river resumed, and I continued along in the bootprints until they ended at Ezra's mooring. Was he on board? I listened in vain for some indication, then pushed on even more slowly, since the bootprints had ended.

Finally, I reached the *Nautilus,* ghostly in its plush white mantle. There wasn't much water near the engine, but I pumped for a while just to be safe. As I worked, and my breath clouded over my eyes, I sometimes glanced up, convinced that someone was nearby, watching me. But there was nothing there but darkness and swirling flakes. When I had put the pump away and shut the cabin door, I stared out at the black channel, wondering if the ice stretched across the fifty yards to the far bank. I gathered up a snowball off the roof of the cabin and threw it as far as I could. I was a little disappointed when it landed with a splash, but the knowledge did nothing to dispel the ominous atmosphere.

I relaxed only once I had reached the dyke again and could rely on the firmness of the gravel beneath the snow. But even as I scurried along against the nipping wind, I felt eyes burning into my back.

five

MY MOTHER HAD A FAVOURITE expression for describing people whose recurrent intrusion into her days was unwelcome. "Keeps turning up like a bad penny," she'd say of certain politicians or town gossips, but as much out of weariness as irritation. If she had harsher words for her fellow creatures, we were never privy to them. My parents were of a generation who believed that children were neither your friends nor miniature adults, and thus had no business hearing things that didn't concern them and that they could not fathom emotionally.

So I knew it was futile to ask probing questions about my elders, no matter what rank they held on the social scale. Ezra Hemsworth could admittedly be "different" and "a bit off," but since further explanations did not belong to the child's world, they were not forthcoming. Of course, I was not afraid to ask my parents (out of some slim hope that the rules would be forgotten momentarily), and sometimes I did learn a few interesting details. But until I was in my mid-teens and became more of a friend to my father, information had to be gleaned from other sources or not at all.

This was especially the case when I reached home on the night of the snow. My father was still in bed, a rare and therefore upsetting circumstance, so I had no opportunity to ask him anything even if I thought it was worth the effort. And my mother, clearly preoccupied with her nursing responsibilities, suggested by her manner that she'd have little patience for my sticking my nose into matters that didn't concern me.

Yet I could not ignore the unusual reappearances of Ezra Hemsworth in my life. Was he a "bad penny"? He didn't seem to belong with the politicians and gossips, nor did I feel weary or irritated thinking about him. In truth, I felt a growing excitement.

As I lay in bed, really thinking things through, I realized that I knew a few things more about Ezra than what I had discovered recently.

He had two older brothers, both of whom my father described with mild distaste as "go-getters." One worked in real estate, and the other owned a junk shop where Jerris and I sometimes collected the deposits on the beer bottles we had found. As far as I could gather, neither man was much respected. I had once heard Mr. Graveridge say that "those two would sell their souls to the devil if they had any." Mostly, I knew them by their vehicles. They both drove at high speed, the real-estate agent in a beat-up Buick usually half-filled with "For Sale" signs, and the junk-shop owner in a rusted pickup usually carrying an old fridge or stove or other appliance. I often had to watch out for the two vehicles at intersections, for neither driver paid much attention to stop signs.

As for Ezra, he looked enough like his brothers to be related to them, but the family resemblance stopped at the dark eyes and bony nose. Whereas they had little time for anything but work, he was well known for his odd willingness to participate in water fights with teenagers who hung around the river and worked as deckhands, and for his penchant for straightforward and heart-stopping practical jokes. His favourite trick, which he had inflicted on my father, was to hide behind a corner of a building, especially late at night, then jump out and bellow at his approaching and unsuspecting victim. A similar "joke" involved tossing lit seal-bombs near gathered groups of fishermen and laughing maniacally when they jumped around in stricken confusion.

Beyond that, what little I knew of Ezra had simply been confirmed by recent events. I had witnessed his impressive feats of strength before, had seen him toss engine batteries as though they were pebbles and easily trundle loaded net-carts that would have made most other men strain their blood vessels to bursting. His unpredictable behaviour was, in fact, no revelation either. Many times I had heard fishermen warn others that Ezra was "out of sorts today" and to "steer clear of him." Or they mentioned knowingly that he'd been "into the sauce," something he did sporadically but with great abandon. Mostly, however, Ezra's black moods involved little more than a sullen silence or low muttering, though occasionally, as when he'd been pumping my father's boat, he would enter that curious zone where it seemed he had no relation to time or place at all. But certainly moodiness was not an unusual characteristic among salmon fishermen, most of whom behaved oddly by other people's standards, perhaps because of their blood-close association with the moon and the tides, or perhaps because the work itself attracted an unconventional sort of personality.

But this undersocialized condition was not all a matter of darkness. As my mother had put it, Ezra had a heart as big as all outdoors. Even before he had bought me a dozen dry newspapers and had come to tell my father that his boat needed pumping, I was aware of his unusual acts of kindness. He commonly put seed out for songbirds during the winter and befriended the always-growing populations of cats and rabbits (abandoned to the marshes by pet owners who hadn't taken the procreative talents of these species into account). Yet he could kick a dog or fling a cat when in one of his black moods, and he had a fisherman's no-nonsense attitude toward death, where killing and protecting could exist together and not be contradictions.

Whatever Ezra was involved in with the shouting man on the wharf, I sensed that it would lead to further excitement. I was amazed that it had taken me so long to realize what a rich source of adventure Ezra offered. All I had to do now was make sure I was on hand to witness the action.

Satisfied, I lay in bed and felt with a thrill the snowflakes approaching through the darkness, becoming heavier and whiter, and whiter still, until I closed my eyes and the whiteness drifted in and carried me off.

When I woke the next morning and looked out my bedroom window, it was as though the previous twenty-four hours had not happened. Amazingly, even Mr. Ely, vivid as a blood smear on a swan, was advancing slowly again from his back door to his shed. Once more I dressed eagerly so that I could hurry out into the untouched snow.

But the day was different, of course. When I reached the kitchen, I found my mother saying goodbye to our family doctor as he pulled his coat on and buckled shut his black bag.

"Not to worry," he said in his slow, underwater voice. "Mack will be fine. Plenty of bedrest and fluids." A portly, tired-looking man with lizardlike eyes, the doctor had a way of making others feel better just out of gratitude that they didn't have to live his life.

"Thank you so much for coming," my mother repeated. "He had such a bad night and I wanted to be sure that . . ."

"Quite all right," he sighed as his hand drifted toward the doorknob. "Plenty of rest and he'll be himself again soon." He spoke longingly, as though about himself. "A week in bed will do anyone a world of good."

Once he had floated like smoke through the doorway, my mother turned and again asked me to help out with my siblings. "Your father still isn't feeling well," she explained. "It's nothing to worry about, but he mustn't be disturbed. Mrs. Hettle is going to take Angie and Steven after school for a few hours."

I nodded, already thinking ahead to my day. Since the doctor wasn't worried, and my mother believed the doctor, I had no cause for alarm. Before leaving the house, I did peek into my parents' room, hoping to say hello to my father, but he was asleep under his mass of blankets. So I tiptoed back down the hallway and, with a sigh of relief, opened the kitchen door and stepped outside.

It was colder and the air smelled different. What I hadn't noticed with the first shock of change the day before seemed intensified now. Woodsmoke poured out of the Elys' chimney in a great climbing spiral of grey against the pale blue—and I could almost taste it on my tongue when I swallowed. But something was missing too, the heavy, soaked mud smell of the river and marsh that always wafted over the dyke, a clotted blend of decay and brine, dead fish and the last tides pickled in the wash of the ocean and pushed back upriver to rot. Now a sharper, cleaner smell commanded the morning. The smoke burned over it all, as if the world had ended in fire and was emerging anew out of the opposing element.

Was the snow deeper? The plum orchard looked even more squat than usual, the black dwarves losing their battle with the leaky sacks of flour. Beyond, the dyke rose higher against the northern horizon; now it might have been the bottom layer of a low cloud instead. But the sky was cloudless, a river-depth of blue. The wind had given up its usual gusting and moaning for a slow intaking of breath, hardly audible, and the snow had muffled all the wanderings over fields and through streets. When Pepper suddenly barked once, thirty feet off to my left, it sounded like someone splitting wood.

The snow crunched slightly as I walked on it, the thinnest layer of crystal glistening and dazzling on the surface. Only Pepper's head showed above the dazzle, thinly veiled in his own heavy breaths. Somewhere underneath, the chain that held him to the yard lay coiled, still as the spine of a sleeping snake. It was that kind of morning, when snakes could have bones, and barks fell like axe blows, and my own steps crossed over a mirror that broke beautifully and came back together and cast only a reflection of the vivid sunlight. The dog's head steamed beneath my mittened hand, and the smoke reached higher and higher. Suddenly, I could not remember what I was doing or who I was. It was exhilarating and frightening, like lying flat on the grass in the midsummer heat and feeling the spin of the planet.

Nothing brought me back, no cry or shout, but I came back. And I did not know that I had gone, I did not remark the strangeness at all. My mittened hand on Pepper's head broke the veils of his breath, and I turned toward the house to see my brother and sister entering the orchard on their way to school. Jerris emerged behind them, bounding over the snow, and I suddenly remembered to warn him about the grade seven kid who was still seeking revenge.

He grinned his freckles wider apart and said he didn't care, and I knew that was the truth. Jerris lived permanently on the knife-edge of punishment, even at home, and so an impending retribution was second nature to him.

"What did you do yesterday?" I asked, suddenly curious about how all those hours out of school could be filled.

He shrugged. "Not much. Hucked snowballs at people, mostly." Jerris was usually nonchalant about his adventures, unless something particularly interesting had occurred.

"Yeah? Hit anybody?"

He grinned even wider at the recollection. "I pegged this big truck right in the driver's window and it stopped and this guy got out swearing and yelling at me and chased me for a while but he never caught me." Winded, and in the spirit now, he listed a few people he had hit.

At one name, I immediately interrupted. "Ezra? You hit Ezra? Where?"

"Aw, just in the back. I couldn't get close enough . . ."

"No, I mean where was he? On the wharf?"

Jerris squinted with suspicion. "I don't know. Why?"

I told him about my own adventure on the wharf, how I'd had to jump out of the path of the shouting man.

"Oh yeah?" he said excitedly. "Who do you figure it was?"

"I don't know. I couldn't see him. I was hiding and . . ."

He frowned. "Couldn't you have sneaked a look?"

I felt I needed to defend myself against Jerris's disappointment, mostly because I knew that, in my place, he would have done better. "I couldn't even move," I blurted out, "or the guy would have seen me, and who knows what he might have done? He might have chucked me in the river."

Jerris was too interested now to pay any attention to my argument. "What did he say again? Stay away from what?"

"That was it, just stay away. And he called him a bastard, and I think he tried to get into his boat too 'cause I heard the lock rattle."

Jerris's eyes were sparkling and I could tell that he was forming a plan. We traded a few speculations on what Ezra might be up to, but these were completely unsatisfactory since we had no idea how he might anger someone else. Jerris likely knew more about Ezra than I did—Mr. and Mrs. Ely were less discreet than my parents— but he was also less likely to pay attention to adult discussions. He took the river and its people so much more in his stride. What Jerris knew, he knew in the way that a strong wind knows a pile of sawdust.

By this time, we had started for school and were among the plum trees when Jerris stopped suddenly. "Hey," he shouted, grabbing my elbow, "let's follow him today, see where he goes!"

I hesitated. The snow had created a charged, anything-can-happen atmosphere at school, and I hated to miss out on any fun that might be gone completely the next day. And yet, the idea of skipping out to follow Ezra had a powerful appeal. On top of that, I felt the last, lingering loyalty of my first real friendship. As I looked at Jerris, noting the eagerness in his expression, I somehow understood that we would not have many more opportunities to come together like this. Jerris knew this too, and if we had been older, one of us might even have said, "For old times' sake."

I finally burst into a grin and said excitedly, "Okay, let's follow him!"

Jerris let out a Rawhide Indian whoop and we were away, hell-bent for high water or whatever tide the river had in store for us. But even as we rushed for the dyke, jumping and hollering, I thought, "I'll go to school after lunch, I'll say that I had to help out at home this morning because my father was sick."

The dyke rose ahead of us glittering white, and we ran for it as if it were the safe mesa behind which we could take cover from the flying arrows.

Once over the top, we paused to catch our breath—and marvelled at the strangeness of the world we found.

Bank to bank, the harbour channel was covered in snow. The boats were frozen in place, as if they'd been slipped into giant wine bottles, and all the floats and sheds and shacks seemed as though they'd been splashed with bucketfuls of whitewash. The bullrushes, bereft of their seedheads in winter, had suddenly regained them. Little tufts of cool down graced each skinny spire clustered against both banks. Farther across the river, on the small harbour island, the fronds of the marsh willows had become bony fingers pointing to where their flesh had been buried, and the once-black branches of the poplars now curved in to make huge ribcages against the sky. Beyond that, the salt marsh for once was true to its name, and stretched away in a great grainy dune of white toward the main river to the north.

As we stood on the dyke, a great blue heron squawked loudly and flew upriver right in front of us, its ceramic body a kind of burnt blue and its long orange legs dangling thin as pencils. Normally we would not have blinked twice at the ungainly, prehistoric bird, but the bone-pure, stripped world over which it flew had so shocked us that we latched on to the heron as something familiar. Only it wasn't familiar either. I wondered how it could feed if the river was frozen. It squawked again, as if in complaint, and then kept squawking all the way into harbour. Jerris and I were pulled along in its disquieting wake, not speaking until we reached the government wharf.

Jerris started for the gangway and I followed.

"What are we going to do?" I asked suddenly, wanting to stop and think things over.

Jerris didn't even turn back. "Got to see if he's on his boat first."

The wharf looked deserted. A trail of bootprints stretched in front of us, and we stepped into it. It was completely silent. The light breeze couldn't even move the mast and anchor chains, they were so iced over. All I could hear was my own breathing. Finally we stopped on the wharf near Ezra's boat.

"How are we going to tell if he's there?" I asked nervously. "Come on, let's forget about it."

Jerris scowled at me. "We can't follow him if he's on his boat."

I backed away a few steps. "We can wait and see if he comes out," I finally suggested.

Jerris shook his head. "That could take forever. I'll just sneak up closer and see if I can hear anything."

And he was gone. I felt the air swelling with a shout and imagined a dark figure rushing past again. But the silence remained.

A minute later, Jerris returned over the two decks of the near gillnetters. "He's not there," he said conclusively. "I couldn't see or hear nothing."

Relieved, I started back the way we had come. On the dyke again, I asked "Now what?"

"He's got to be somewhere," Jerris said, kicking at the snow. "Maybe he's where that guy didn't want him to be."

School suddenly seemed like the better idea. But looking for Ezra had already proved to be more exciting than I had antici-pated. "That could be anywhere," I responded, then had a sudden bright idea. "Maybe he's at Dirk's, having breakfast."

"I'll bet he is!" Jerris whooped into motion again, speeding down off the dyke onto the river road.

Ten minutes later, standing across the street from Dirk's, trying to be inconspicuous underneath the museum clock and its eternal 9:33, we waited for Ezra to emerge from the café. We could see his dark figure through the large plate-glass window. He was eating so fast it looked as if he were striking himself repeatedly in the face. Even so, we felt we had been waiting for hours when he finally stood, left the table, and emerged outside.

He held a large brown paper bag in his ungloved right hand and swung it slightly, like a coal-oil lantern, as he moved. In his drab-green canvas coat and black skullcap, he was easy to keep in sight against the white-blue backdrop, but he walked so quickly that we had to half-run not to lose him. Bent forward, head raised at sporadic intervals, gumboots hardly touching the ground, Ezra seemed as though he were searching for some precious item he'd lost but only had a limited amount of time to find.

"Look at him go!" Jerris gasped. We increased our pace, careful not to be too obvious in our pursuit. But Ezra never looked back.

By now, we had hurried a half-mile down the main street and had turned east onto Trunk Road, the main east-west dissector linking Chilukthan to the rest of Canada in one direction and to the Gulf of Georgia in the other. The town's business centre, very small and contained, had not shifted much from where it had been in the nineteenth century, centred on the main street. Trunk Road, for a half-mile in either direction from the main street, had a few scattered businesses—a grain and feed store, another gas station, a grocery store—but mostly it was residential and undeveloped, with stately but shabby homes sinking slowly into giant surrounding properties of high cedar hedges and fruit and dogwood trees, or huge vacant lots overgrown with blackberry bushes and morning glory (in one of these, someone even let his horses graze).

We followed Ezra east away from the centre of town, past the field with the grazing, puff-shrouded horses, past the collapsing gentility of verandas and gables and rose-bush trellises, past the weighted-down, flattened grasses, once waist-high and now crushed to the boot tops. Every few minutes a car or truck passed us, and still Ezra did not look up, even when one of the trucks honked at him.

"Where's he going?" Jerris asked, and we both knew without speaking that this had something to do with what I had seen on the wharf the night before. Ezra's haste, the swinging, lightless paper lamp, his direction away from town, seemed ominous. Suddenly he stopped and stood staring on the shoulder of the road. We had been following so quickly and for what seemed hours—though it was no more than fifteen minutes—that we could hardly believe it. At first, we did not realize why Ezra had stopped or what he was staring at. A large field with a hundred-foot-high poplar in the middle of it, boughs caked with snow and shivering flakes down each time the wind gusted slightly, lay behind him. But he was staring across the road at another field, one newly transformed by the season.

"Lums'," Jerris announced, a puzzled look on his face. I followed his stare to the rows of cut Scotch pines and other ever-greens, a maze of sweet-scented boughs and sap-sticky trunks constructed at the edge of the otherwise open field on a floor of sawdust over which big metal floodlamps hung like giant bugs. To one side of the maze entrance sat a grimy trailer, small enough to be pulled by a car. Its hitch and wheels were fixed in place with cedar blocks. A little spiral of steam drifted out of the roof. Propped against the trailer, facing the road, was a large plywood sign that read XMAS TREES $5 SMOKED SALMON $2 A SIDE. To the other side of the entrance, a short Chinese man in dark glasses and a bright orange toque was unloading more bound and tagged trees from a large pickup truck so heavily loaded that its tires were half-sunk in the spread sawdust. The man put his arms out and a tree would suddenly rise and swing down into them, as if there were some magnetic attraction. But eventually, two other figures appeared in the back of the truck, obscured by the thick boughs they grappled with.

I knew them, just as I knew, once I had recovered from Ezra's sudden stop, what we had come upon. This was the Lums' annual Christmas tree lot, a two-week business competing for seasonal sales with the Boy Scouts (the smoked salmon was probably an attempt to gain a competitive edge). The Lums were not the only Chinese people in town, but they were the most notorious and visible, due mostly to the head of the family, Wing Lum, a potato farmer whose bootlegging exploits against the vegetable marketing boards in the forties and fifties had become local legend. Once, stopped on the Pheasant Island Bridge in the middle of the night by a government inspector, Wing climbed out of his truck and, without speaking, broke the man's kneecaps with a crowbar. No one was quite sure how he managed it, but Wing escaped the incident with just a fine. The rumour was that, though he spoke pidgin English and generally played the role of ignorant Chinee, Wing was a genius who had completely filled one room of his crumbling, unpainted house with law books. Others said that, more likely, he had used some of his long-hoarded wealth to hire a hotshot lawyer from Vancouver to get him off. Whatever he had done, Wing was always in trouble with the authorities for running various businesses without licences, failing to send his children to school, making illegal hookups to water, gas, and other services, refusing to pay property taxes, running a gaming house, or threatening violence against whatever agent or police officer came to question him. As a result, he had become a point of debate in the community. My parents believed that he only acted ignorant and broke the law simply as a way to flaunt the superiority of his intelligence over the system, as a way to entertain himself by getting the better of the "round eyes." Others argued that Wing was nothing but a criminal thug who'd been run out of China on a rail and hadn't changed his behaviour since arriving in Canada in the thirties. "Just look at how he treats his daughters," they'd point out, and the only response possible was, "But that's the way the Chinese are; they don't want daughters, only sons."

Three of Wing Lum's children were now unloading the truck. His son—there were two, but they were both short and dressed so much alike, right down to the dark glasses, that I couldn't tell if it was Nelson or Wellington (and some people pointed to these British names as further proof that Wing was a genius sniggering at the society in which he found himself)—carried the trees from the truck and leaned them against a makeshift plywood fence. Wing's daughters, Margaret and Elizabeth, stood in the back of the truck and wrestled each tree off the heap. Even from across the road we could hear them talking to each other, the conversation loud, coarse, and brusque, peppered with four-letter words.

Their mannish, squat figures were a familiar sight. But in their gumboots and drab, baggy workclothes, the girls blended easily into the background. I had never given them much thought. And when I did, I decided that they were not remarkable, nor were the old widower and his sons. They simply existed as a slightly askew part of the social landscape. They kept mostly to themselves, at least in Chilukthan, but plenty of non-minorities did that, including Ezra, Rod Graveridge, and a dozen other fishermen. The Lums farmed and fished, they owned a small grocery, they sold Christmas trees each December, and the old man had run-ins with the law. As for the daughters, they lived more roughly than other women, with few comforts and no social graces, but that was nobody's business, as my parents were quick to point out.

But now Ezra had paused on the shoulder of the road across from the lot, and the sun seemed to get warmer even as the sky darkened and the snow lost its glittery lustre. The mingled rich scents of sawdust, pine, and smoked salmon drifted over to us and vanquished the apple-fresh smell of the snow. A lone cloud—where had it come from so suddenly?—crossed the sun, and when the dazzle returned to the earth, I looked at Ezra again.

He still hadn't moved. The paper bag hung at his side, and for once he did not look at the ground.

"What's he doing?" I finally said to Jerris, but it wasn't really a question because it was obvious by the way Ezra waited—so unlike him—that we could not even guess what was taking place.

Once the truck had been unloaded, Nelson or Wellington climbed into the cab and started the engine. His sisters, identically dressed in grubby Irish-knit sweaters, lime-green toques, and red-tipped black gumboots flaring wider as they reached the knees, stood and watched as he backed out of the lot and drove off toward town. Ezra, meanwhile, had walked a few paces farther east as the truck came to a stop before the driver put it in gear and continued on.

Ezra crossed the road. The women had gone into the small trailer, and that's where Ezra vanished too, after knocking and being let in.

We entered the tree lot by the neighbouring field, just in case the trailer door swung open before we could take cover. Without discussion, we knew that we had to see inside the trailer. Jerris, as always, led the way, but this time I did not hesitate to follow. Curiosity hurried me over the snowy grasses and onto the sawdust floor at the back of the lot.

The air throbbed so heavily with pine that it was as though we'd crossed the border into another country. Taking a deep breath, I continued after Jerris along a narrow, pungent corridor through the trees.

A minute later, we stood on a mandarin orange crate at the side of the trailer, peering through a small, greasy window.

At first, we couldn't see much, but once our eyes had adjusted to the shadowed interior, we made out three figures seated at a small, linoleum-topped table, their faces in profile to us. Ezra sat across from the women, and was again motionless. He held a coffee mug in his right hand and his skullcap lay on the table beside his left hand. The brown paper bag lay tipped over on one side. It was hard to tell, but Ezra looked to be grinning.

The women were silent as well, too intent on what they were doing to speak. Both were bent forward over paper plates, shovelling what looked like scrambled eggs into their mouths. Disappointed, I considered the interior of the trailer instead. Except for a few chairs, a kerosene stove, some plastic coolers, and a metal strongbox by the door, the cramped, uncarpeted space was completely bare.

Jerris groaned in disgust. "Just eating," he said quietly. "Big deal."

"Maybe when they finish, they'll start talking and we'll find something out."

Before Jerris could respond, Ezra sprang to his feet and bolted for the door. At the same instant, we heard the truck's engine and, turning toward Trunk Road, saw a different pickup spin wildly into the sawdust entrance and slam to a stop against the piled trees.

"Holy shit," Jerris said, jumping off the crate and hurrying around the back of the trailer. I quickly followed.

Then the shouting started, a blur of voices chopping the still, piney air. From our new vantage point, crouched in the close boughs of the pines, Jerris and I saw a burly, pig-snouted man in a plaid mackinaw and baseball cap burst out of the truck, a shotgun swivelling in front of him.

"I warned you, you fucking bastard!" The man's shout broke clear of the women's briefly, then their voices overlaid his again, almost as rough and equally frantic.

"That's him," I whispered in Jerris's ear. "That's the guy from the wharf." I didn't know who the man was, but I certainly recognized his voice. Terrified, I crouched farther down as Ezra's blurred darkness crashed through the rows behind us and the man bore down on the noise, his shouts and the women's jumbled together again.

Then the shot exploded. An awful silence accompanied its fading echo before a peal of laughter flooded in and then a giddy cry of "You missed him! You missed him!"

"Shut up!" the man roared, and followed the direction of his shot, popping the shell out of his shotgun as he went.

"Come on," Jerris said. "I want to see if he gets him."

"No way." I grabbed him. "Don't be stupid! You could get shot!"

But Jerris just scowled. "Aw, I'll be careful. Come on, you don't want to miss this, do you?"

Jerris was too excited to wait for me. He pushed out of the boughs and started to edge along the far side of the lot, keeping out of sight in the trees. Alone, I felt even more frightened, so, heart pounding, I followed.

From the back row of the lot, we watched the burly man stop in the snowy field, take aim, and shoot once more at Ezra, fleeing blackly over the white expanse. He would have been an easy target except that he knew enough to veer jerkingly as he ran. Even so, he seemed to stagger briefly at the concussion of the shot.

"Maybe that'll teach you, you asshole!" the man howled. "It'll be your balls next time!" He stood gaping, the gun at his hip, breathing so heavily that we couldn't see his face.

"Who is it?" I whispered to Jerris.

"Don't know. Never seen him before." He turned to me, eyes sparkling. "But Jesus, he's sure pissed off, eh? And I think he winged him too."

My heart sank."You think so?"

"Yeah, didn't you see him stumble a bit?"

I nodded.

"And the guy acted like he'd got him too."

Again, I nodded. "But what should we do?" I suddenly asked, figuring that we had some responsibilty for Ezra.

Jerris shrugged. "Nothing. Ezra can look after himself."

By now, the man had turned back to the lot. I didn't have the nerve to sneak back to the trailer, so I suggested that we go and see if we could find any blood. As I had hoped, Jerris pounced enthusiastically on the prospect.

Minutes later we found the beginning of the trail, though trail was not the right word to describe the sporadic spatters that led out of the field, over a road, through another field, onto Trunk Road, and back into town. It wasn't a lot of blood—the spots like a scattering of red chess pieces—but it was enough to keep our excitement level high.

Once we had reached the dyke near the harbour, we decided there was no point in continuing. Ezra had probably returned to his boat to fix his wound. So we stood in the sun-dazzle, looking out over the frozen channel. I noticed another blue heron on a piling against the far bank—was it the same one? It was hard to tell, but I took it for the same one anyway. Doing so seemed to heighten the strangeness I was feeling, and had been feeling ever since the first snowfall two days earlier.

But now I just wanted to unwind from all the excitement. There was no point in going to school before lunch, so I decided to make a rare early visit to the bookshop. I asked Jerris to come, but wasn't surprised when he said no. I suspected he was headed back to the tree lot to see if he could learn anything more. We guessed that the scene might have had something to do with the Lum daughters, but the idea was ridiculous to us, and would have been even if we had known more about adult relationships. The Lum daughters were such a far cry from the love objects of comic book heroes that we concluded there must be something else going on. But what? The question lingered deliciously in the chill, blue air, and we arranged to make further investigations later in the day. Jerris was disappointed that I wouldn't skip out the rest of school, but he didn't argue with me.

"I'll meet you at the shack," he said, "and help you get your papers done faster."

We parted at the big willow outside the bookshop. Jerris raced along the sidewalk without looking back, and I stepped into the embracing warmth and must of the stocked shelves. Mrs. Bradlee showed little reaction to my presence, just glanced at the clock on the wall to see whether she'd dozed off for a few unaccountable hours. I grabbed a stack of dime comics, crawled underneath the table in the corner, and was soon calmed by the coloured blur of pages and the far-off ocean hum of classical music on the radio.

six

WE DIDN'T FIND EZRA again that day, though we searched all over town until well after dark. On the wharf, we found no bloodstains in his solitary bootprints as we walked past his silent, black boat. Then we carried on to the *Nautilus*, where I pumped out the water in the cabin. I knew Jerris was disappointed that the shimmering atmosphere of the morning had been lost. Even at the tree lot, where we had hoped for some continuation of excitement, however minor by comparison with the shooting, the afternoon was muted with ordinariness. Every few minutes a car would drive into the lot, its occupants would climb out and walk the fragrant rows, eventually hand some bills to one of the Lum daughters, stuff the tree in the trunk or rope it to the roof, and then drive away.

Yet the cold snap remained true to its promise of perpetual surprise, which was why my disappointment did not equal Jerris's. He had relegated everything but the morning's violence to a trivial status, whereas I had begun to feel an uneasy but pleasurable connection between all the recent events of my life. After all, how could I be certain, given the drama the snow had already occasioned, that the evening newspaper wouldn't solve the mystery of Ezra Hemsworth right on the front page?

I felt a giddy and not unpleasant fear as long as the snow remained, a sense of being on the edge of a precipice, with falling and not falling equally attractive and disturbing possibilities.

Jerris and I had just walked past Mrs. Edmundson's skinny side window in the twilight, when, before I could stop him, he grabbed a paper and ran up on the porch.

"No, not that one," I said.

He paused, his back to the screen door, obviously puzzled by the fact I hadn't signed up both halves of a duplex. "How come?"

"Just moved in. I haven't had a chance." I couldn't say, I couldn't even explain to myself, why I hadn't yet attempted to sign the new resident up.

Anxious to be on Ezra's trail, Jerris was about to hurry back when the porchlight flicked on. He looked stricken, though we weren't doing anything wrong. Our nerves were already strained in expectation of what the rest of the afternoon might hold.

The screen door opened and Mrs. Edmundson's wraithlike figure appeared in the wan light.

Jerris still hadn't moved, but I had stepped forward to the bottom of the stairs.

"Leslie, is that you?" She spoke hesitatingly and softly, as if to herself.

Jerris turned to me for help. I climbed the stairs. "It's just me, Callum, the paperboy."

She leaned a little farther outside and tentatively pushed her dark glasses higher up the bridge of her nose. "Oh yes," she said, "I remember. You're the boy who helped me move in."

I nodded, standing beside Jerris, who was fidgeting uneasily.

"Well," she said with a thin smile, deepening the wrinkles around her mouth, "you'd best come in out of the cold."

Jerris groaned just loud enough for me to hear, but I scowled at him to be quiet.

Mrs. Edmundson, as though sensing our unwillingness, sweetened her invitation. "You look as though you could use some hot chocolate. This weather . . ." Her voice trailed away sadly, then recovered. "It's been a good while since we've had such a cold spell."

Jerris and I remained frozen to the spot. I knew he was impatient to get away, and though I had recognized the opportunity for a new subscriber, I was also less than enthusiastic about accepting the old-woman's hospitality. Who knew how long she might keep us there?

Finally, in a doubtful voice, I began, "We have more papers to deliver—"

"Yes, the newspaper," she interrupted. "I would like to buy a copy from you."

I started to say that I didn't have any extras, that she would have to subscribe, but she had retreated farther into the sallow light, only her heavily veined hand visible, holding the screen door open.

Jerris made a quick motion to me with his head, as if to say "Let's make a run for it."

But I couldn't do that. "Come on," I encouraged in a whisper, "a hot chocolate would be good."

Just then Mrs. Edmundson spoke again, with a little more authority. "Come along, you're letting in the cold."

We followed her in and stood awkwardly on a thickly braided throw rug just inside the door. The room had changed from the time of my previous visit. More furnishing had been done: a few other throw rugs, dark as cellar holes, covered the hardwood floor, the tall lamp with the fringed shade stood beside the horsehair armchair, and nearby, the old wooden radio had been set up on a side table. A deep male voice drifted faintly from the radio, which glowed a pale green. I caught the words "love" and "till the end," but the song came as if from a great distance away, and I soon stopped listening.

Some framed photographs and plates hung on the walls, but I couldn't see them clearly yet. Just to our left, between the side window and the narrow entrance to the kitchen, a large cabinet with sliding glass doors displayed neat rows of bone china all delicately embossed with pastel-coloured flowers. A small box, standing on end and opened like a bible on top of the cabinet, revealed gleaming rows of silver cutlery against a red velvet lining. My gaze drifted through the narrow doorway beside the cabinet where a high whistling had started. Mrs. Edmundson floated into view like steam to hover over a burnished, trembling kettle.

"What are we supposed to do?" Jerris whispered anxiously. I sensed his discomfort was greater than mine, for he had less experience with such situations. Yet, while I had stood in similar, though less shabby rooms, waiting for some elderly widow or widower to return with the money they owed for the newspaper, or even with a glass of milk and a plate of cookies, I recognized that this felt different. The smell in the room wasn't the common, smothering blend of boiled vegetables and meat with cat food and kitty litter, or the equally common and somehow just as unpleasant lemony scent of furniture polish and cut flowers. Instead, a dry mixture of dust and cigarette smoke hung in the air. And apart from the china in the cabinet and the plates on the walls, there were no familiar touches of a lifetime's gathering, no little porcelain knick-knacks, no vases, crystal or otherwise, nothing crocheted or knitted; there wasn't even a bookshelf. Even the framed photographs were few and small, a stark contrast with the galleries that often covered most of the wall space in the apartments of the elderly.

And this was another significant difference: most of my elderly subscribers lived in apartment buildings, and those who still lived in houses were generally not alone. Or, if they were, there was a palpable sense that someone was close by and keeping a watch on them in case they needed help. But at the back of this sagging duplex it was hard to believe that the rest of the world even existed.

Finally, Mrs. Edmundson emerged from the kitchen carrying a tray on which sat two steaming mugs and a plate of chocolate digestive cookies. That much, at least, I noted as familiar. I suddenly realized how strange the radio music also was. Normally, canned laughter or soap opera voices would be emanating from a television set glimmering like a blue aquarium in some dim corner. Or else there would be a silence so deep that the ticking of a clock would eventually swell to a series of small explosions.

Mrs. Edmundson stopped a few feet in front of us, as if puzzled by our presence. My face was burning from the room's warmth, and I unzipped my coat.

The noise and my action roused her to speech. "Yes, you'd be more comfortable if you removed your things." She gestured to a coat rack I hadn't noticed behind me. "We'll go into the living room. I think that will be all right."

Relieved at the chance to cool down, Jerris and I quickly hung our coats, then turned to find that she had already gone farther into the room.

"What about our boots?" Jerris asked me.

I shrugged, then noticed the slushy puddles on the rug where we'd been standing. "I guess we'd better take them off."

A minute later we were seated side by side on a small horsehair sofa across from Mrs. Edmundson, who had settled into the companion armchair. It was hard to be certain, though, whether a person had sat down or a puff of dust had risen from the worn fabric.

Jerris gulped at his hot chocolate and seemed happy to hide his face behind the mug. Neither of us knew what to say, and our hostess did not speak for a few minutes, an interminable time. Where were the usual questions about school and what grade we were in and whether we liked our teacher? Where were the stories about her grandchildren and great-grandchildren, meant to entertain us because children love to hear about other children? This silence was so much stranger and more disturbing than the awkward, brief pauses that occurred when other old men and women sat smiling at me, just enjoying my being there, if only as a break from the television or their own thoughts.

Eventually, Mrs. Edmundson did speak.

"It's very lonely here," she began, looking slowly around the room as though to prove her point. "The days are long, longer than they were." She sat forward and reached for a package of cigarettes beside the radio. Trembling, she fingered a cigarette from the package but did not put it to her mouth right away. She simply held it between the index and middle fingers of her left hand, as if its tiny weight were exactly what she needed to reorient herself. "But you're just boys," she sighed.

Jerris looked at me with widened eyes. I knew he thought she was crazy, but I was just relieved not to be fussed over.

With difficulty, Mrs. Edmundson struck a match, lit her cigarette, and leaned back again. "My son, Leslie," she continued in a stronger voice, "is a good man, a kind man, like his father. But he lacks his father's will." She pointed to the wall beside us, her cigarette smoke trailing like a loose hair. "That's Reginald there, in our wedding picture."

Jerris sprang up, eager to escape the stillness—I knew he had little interest in wedding photographs. I followed, careful not to spill the hot chocolate that I had barely touched (Jerris had almost finished his, and had eaten two cookies).

The black-and-white photograph was ordinary enough, showing a man and a woman posed on the stone steps of a church. The man was stout and amiable, wearing a plain suit with a carnation in the lapel. He held the woman's arm in his own and beamed at the camera. The woman—whom I recognized as our hostess (the face unwrinkled, the hair blond and flowing, but the same pronounced nose and high cheekbones, the same willowy figure)—was not beaming, but she looked content, holding a bouquet of flowers close to her plain but elegant dress, which I recognized as not being particularly bridal. The man's face was vaguely familiar, and I remembered that I had seen it before, reflected in the man who had paid me two dollars to unload the trailer.

Jerris took advantage of our increased distance from the armchair to nudge me and say, "She's loopy, huh?"

I shushed him and looked at another photograph. This one was older, cracked a bit, and showed a different, younger man in a woollen soldier's uniform. His fair hair was slicked and parted neatly in the middle, a contrast with his mouth which he held firmly shut, as if stifling a sob. He had small features and looked almost faunlike. His expression was strange; he seemed sorry for the photographer and every other person who would ever look at his picture. It made me nervous just looking at him, though he resembled a lost girl more than a soldier.

Once again, Mrs. Edmundson's uncanny knack for reading my thoughts broke the silence. "Arthur, my first husband," she explained. And her voice dropped as she added, "He was killed in the war."

Jerris bumped into me in his sudden eagerness to look. "How?" he asked, and the sound of his voice shocked me. I realized we hadn't spoken at our normal level in quite a while.

Mrs. Edmundson did not respond right away, and I was worried that Jerris had offended her. I was also irritated by his lack of knowledge, something that never used to concern me. A little embarrassed, I suspected that he hoped Alfred had been scalped by raiding Comanches.

I turned around to cover for Jerris, but Mrs. Edmundson was not even looking in our direction. "I don't know," she finally said in a fatigued voice. "He was just killed." Her cigarette rose to her lips and the burning end lengthened as she inhaled. Then she began to cough, violently enough that her whole body shook.

Jerris and I looked at each other helplessly. Though he said nothing, I could almost hear him blurt out, "She's not going to die, is she?"

Fortunately, the coughing subsided and Mrs. Edmundson showed no signs of being dead. She raised the hand without the cigarette to her glasses and readjusted them. Then she laid the cigarette in an ashtray beside the radio and, with a prolonged sigh, leaned back in the chair. Once again, she seemed to have forgotten about us. I no longer heard any sound coming from the radio and noticed that the pale green light had faded—she must have switched it off. Now the silence, even without the ticking of a clock, was thunderous.

I studied one of the plates on the wall. It was commemorative of a Royal visit made to Canada decades before, and showed an old, bearded king. I knew about the Royal Family, of course. Each morning at school, we sang "God Save the Queen" (after reciting the Lord's Prayer and singing the national anthem), all grades in unison over the public address system. And my mother often expressed sadness that we (Canada) had broken our ties with the Mother Country, something she blamed on the prime minister, Pierre Trudeau. Many times I had heard her tell Mr. Graveridge how disgraceful it was that we had abandoned the Union Jack as our flag. In fact, this particular speech had become an annual tradition of its own, a substitute for the regal dignity my mother believed we had sacrificed. But I knew little about kings, except for Henry VIII and his wives and gluttony and drumsticks. The king on the plate looked about as far from gluttony as it was possible to get.

"Come on, let's go," Jerris said quickly in my ear.

I could see no reason to stay any longer, yet the silence held me as if it were a thick mud. I managed to turn and face Mrs. Edmundson again, and was about to speak when she sighed, "No more than a boy himself, my Arthur. Just eighteen years old."

And so the silence resumed, deeper and deeper. The air felt fragile, and I had a sudden notion that everything had turned to glass, including the floor on which we stood. Mrs. Edmundson still faced straight ahead to where we had been sitting, as if we had already become ghostly presences for her, the dead who had once been boys. After another minute, when she had not spoken and Jerris had elbowed me in the side and mouthed "Come on," I finally cleared my throat and took a step toward the armchair.

"Thank you for the hot chocolate," I said. "But we have to be going now. We have more papers to deliver."

She lifted her head slowly and gently pushed a loose strand of grey-black hair behind one ear. "Yes," she responded. "Yes, of course," she spoke up a bit, "thank you for stopping. It's nice to have a little company."

Jerris had already reached the door, and was bent over, yanking on his boots.

"Well, bye," I said with an awkward cheerfulness, and walked over to join him. Mrs. Edmundson stirred behind me, but I didn't turn back to her until the knocking on the door started.

"That will be Leslie," she explained, now standing. "Would you mind letting him in, dear?"

I did as she asked. At first, her son just blinked rapidly into the light, obviously surprised to find someone there other than his mother. But a worried look soon replaced the confused one. "Mother?" he queried nervously, side-stepping us. As soon as he saw her by the chair, his body slackened noticeably, as if it were a balloon with a leak.

"Good afternoon, Leslie," she said calmly. "Everything is fine. These two gentlemen have been paying me a visit."

He smiled broadly as he faced us again, no doubt relieved that a cry for help hadn't brought us into the room. "Hello, boys," he said pleasantly, then stared at me, remembering. "Colin, isn't it? You're the paperboy."

"Yes, sir. But my name's Callum."

"Callum. That's right." He rubbed his blunt cleft chin with the sausage-thick fingers of one hand, and still stared at me. "I wanted to ask you something. Now, what was it?"

His mother appeared even thinner and paler beside him. "I was going to buy a paper, Leslie. Perhaps you have some change?"

"That was it," he nodded. "I wanted to ask you to start delivering the paper here."

Finally, I thought, the visit was going to be worth it after all. I took a subscription form from my coat pocket and gave it to him. As he filled it in, I mentioned that I didn't have any spare papers today.

"That's all right," he said. "I brought one with me."

"And I can't start delivering until next week."

He looked up from the form. "No?"

"Um, well, it takes a couple of days for . . ."

"Yes, yes, of course," he nodded, grinning at me. "You have to go through the proper channels." He clicked his ballpoint pen and stuck it back into his inside breast pocket. When he had handed me the form and seen his mother comfortably seated again, he conducted us out onto the veranda.

Jerris blew great puffs of breath as soon as we hit the cold, fresh air. I did the same, exhilarated just to be out of the stifling room. I wanted nothing more than to leap off the veranda and sprint into the increasing darkness. But Mr. Edmundson (he began by finally introducing himself) had something he wanted to ask.

"My mother," he began in a confidential tone, then seemed to reconsider. For a few seconds I thought he was going to tell us all about the first husband and the war and his mother as a young woman. Instead, he took a business card out of his pocket and asked me to call him at the number printed on it if I should ever notice anything wrong. I said I would, not knowing at all what concerned him. Then Jerris and I quickly left, ecstatic to be running through the night toward the mystery of Ezra and the Lums and the man with the shotgun. At the bottom of the alley, I stopped and looked back. The veranda was empty. Only a few skinny black branches from the willow clutched at the yellow light spilling out onto the snow.

Jerris was so happy to be outside that he didn't even comment on our visit, except to say that it was awful and to repeat that the old lady was loopy. I agreed because I also felt a wonderful sense of liberation as we bore down on the final dozen porchlights, the paper sack becoming light as a dusting of snow on my shoulder.

But something else happened before we started our search for Ezra. As we hurried along a side street, whooping at the sky, I noticed Mr. Vreen's car parked in the driveway of Donald Bints's house. Oh oh, I thought, he must really be in for it now. Briefly, I wondered what the next day would bring at the shack. But by the time we had passed the house, I had already started to think about where to look for Ezra.

We didn't find him that afternoon. By suppertime, Jerris and I were standing on another side street, just off the main. We were cold, tired, and disappointed, but the small flakes drifting down lifted our spirits, promising a continuation of the strange and wonderful weather. How still the town was in the snowlight and snowfall, and how different from the stillness we had just experienced in Mrs. Edmundson's room. The night was all motion and vastness. With the snow falling again, it was as though we were part of the current of the nearby river, swept along in the silted depths below the ice toward some even deeper and vaster sea. I looked up at the thin spire of the United church on the corner, and it seemed like the mast of a sinking ship. We were sliding along its black deck even as the waters overwhelmed us, and the stillness, the muffling, regenerative gift of the snow, kept adding to the sense of drift, the sense that no matter what happened the sea would accept us into its chill, salt folds.

I watched the spire for a long time as Jerris and I headed home, until it vanished in the thickening swirl of white, and I finally realized that what I was staring at behind me was no different from the flecked darkness that stretched out ahead.

seven

I DID NOT TELL MY PARENTS about the shooting at the tree lot. My mother would have known that I had skipped out of school, and both of them would have ordered me to stay away from the tree lot, Ezra, and the Lums. I could not do that, and so it was easier to keep quiet. In any case, my father's condition had deteriorated since I'd left the house in the morning, and my mother was even more preoccupied with her nursing duties. "A bad cold," she said whenever I pushed for an explanation, but I suspected she was just trying to shield me from the truth. She did allow me to speak briefly with my father, however. For a few moments, I stood scared by his bedside, looking down into his pale, drawn face, inexpertly shaved by my mother—a few tufts of stubble darkened his jawline and upper lip. He blinked his watery eyes at me, managed a slight grin, and said softly before a spasm of coughing overwhelmed him, "Hi, Cal, how are you getting along?"

Once his coughing stopped, I told him about the snow and the ice on the river and how I was pumping the boat out like he wanted, but he didn't seem very interested.

"All right, Callum," my mother said, and gently touched the back of my neck, "let your father rest."

What else could I do but accept her assurances that he was going to be fine? I believed her because she did not lie except in minor things (what she called white lies, designed to spare people's feelings), and my father's illness was clearly not minor.

So I made the best of it, and left that world behind to explore others. That night, I went with Eric and two other friends to a farm field at the western edge of town. Carrying our sticks and skates in the faint starlight and dusting snow, with Pepper bounding excitedly around us, we hurried along the river road, turned at a treeless farm road, past a lone gloomy house and barn, then jumped a narrow, ice-slickened ditch and stumbled our way over the furrowed, glazed chop of a potato field. Finally we reached the depression where all the autumn rains had pooled; it now gleamed dully as old steel. Some older teenagers had already started a game. We heard their shouts and the smacking of sticks as we approached, and saw, with envy, how they'd parked their cars and trucks around the makeshift rink so the headlights could illuminate the ice. From a distance, they seemed to be moving through a pure, still fog. We skirted them, noting without surprise that they'd taken the smoothest expanse of ice. We considered asking if we could join in, but once we saw how skilfully they played, at high speed and with much contact, we decided we'd enjoy ourselves more on our own.

As it turned out, the starlight and the surrounding acres of reflecting snow allowed us to see the puck and one another quite well. We even managed to find a section of ice that wasn't too rough. Soon, we had paired off into teams and started a shouting and smacking echo to the neighbouring game. Knowing that outdoor hockey was a great rarity that might not occur again for years, we played as though the ice would vanish at any second, throwing us back to the slick pavement and the sodden tennis ball, the sluicing drag of a wrist shot and the revolving spray of a long pass.

We whirled around in the semi-dark, with Eric delivering non-stop, manic, perfect impersonations of famous hockey announcers. For a while, he called out Russian names in Foster Hewitt's high nasally voice—"Yakushev drops to Lutchenko over to Nesterenko who, oh no, twists his ankle, and Shave-a-yak comes in." Then, more faithfully, he adopted Danny Gallivan's wordy extravagance—"Oh it's a Savardian spinarama by Taylor, and he lets go a cannonading drive! Did you see that, Dick?"—and followed it up with Dick Irvin's nostalgic non sequiturs—"Yes, Danny, and it reminds me of the time Doug Harvey, I think it was in the semi-finals in 1948, said to my father, 'How should I run the powerplay, Mr Irvin?' and my father said, 'You do whatever you think best, Doug.' Harvey was one of the greats. I remember another time . . ." Then Eric would switch back to Gallivan— "Those were the days, all right. But we'll pause now for a commercial break while the officials mop up the blood from that brawl and get that naked woman off the ice." And all this patter, punctuated by our own contributions, done at rapid, breathless speed as we chased the puck and banged our sticks on the ice and, heads down, plunged toward the boots we'd turned into goalposts.

Only the cold and our curfews ended the game. We unlaced our skates, yanked the boots back onto our numb feet, propped our sticks on our shoulders, and returned the way we had come, past the other game that seemed as if it would go on until the headlights burned out and the sun pinked the sky above the Coast Mountains. Pepper danced around us as if our skates were bagged pheasants he had just retrieved, his excitement so contagious that we almost returned to the field for just one more goal, winner takes the Cup.

But soon we had reached my house. Eric and the others continued into the darkness of the orchard while I stood in the yard, not wanting to go in.

I was not thinking about Ezra or Mrs. Edmundson, my father, Donald Bints, or anyone else. I stood in the yard, hearing my name in wave after wave of cheers, extending the exhilaration of the game we had just played.

So, when my name actually did ring out through the cool air, I was briefly puzzled.

Jerris burst out of the orchard, yippee-yiiying as snowballs whizzed past him. He flew toward me, his torn, nylon parka unzipped as always and his hands and head uncovered, the furred hood bobbing on his back. Eric and the others shouted as they reached the edge of the trees, but they did not continue the pursuit into the open. I figured that they realized Jerris was uncatchable, or that they were just tired from all the skating.

Either way, Jerris had slowed to a walk before he reached me. His face was shining, a slightly brighter red than his snow-flecked hair, and he kept wiping his snub nose with his bare wrists, one after the other in rapid fashion. Under his parka was a thin T-shirt. And he had sneakers on his feet instead of boots ("I can run better in them," he always said).

"Aren't you cold?" I asked.

"Nah, I'm hot." He flapped his parka, then ran one of his wrists across his forehead. "See? I'm sweating."

He told me he'd been to set some muskrat traps in the ditches. "Had to bust the ice," he said, "and it was pretty thick. I got a soaker when my foot smashed through one time. I almost fell in!"

He giggled at the recollection, then changed the subject. "I was looking for Ezra too, but I never seen him. I thought he'd be out hucking snowballs for sure."

"Maybe he can't throw. Maybe that shot got him in the arm."

"Hey, yeah, I'll bet that's it!" Jerris whirled around toward his house. "My dad's home," he said excitedly. "Come on, I'll ask him if he knows who that guy is with the pig face."

Since I still didn't want to go home, I happily followed Jerris across the snow.

The Elys' house was very different from my family's, about seventy years older, built by one of Chilukthan's pioneer farmers in the 1890s. Skinny and tall, with two storeys and a dozen tiny rooms, except for the kitchen, which was twice the size of the others, it was a crumbling, sagging structure that lacked only plywood over the windows to pass for condemned. Yet a few lingering Victorian touches still preserved some of the building's original grace and dignity. A black iron lamppost at the top of the front yard walk continued to conjure up images of horse-drawn coaches and engraved invitations. About six feet high, with an iron cage around the lightbulb as solid and intricate as a medieval knight's visor, it stood as a beacon to the house's forgotten heritage.

The front door of the house sported a delicate but heavy glass doorknob, grainy as a crystal ball, and when you turned it, you felt as though you were suddenly on the verge of disappearing. The staircase, too, gave the impression that it was a passageway out of the present. Narrow as a ladder, it climbed into the always-dim second storey as if it were climbing into the farthest reaches of space. Only the solid oak banisters, worn smooth by the touch of generations, kept the staircase rooted to the earth.

Jerris and I clumped into the front hall, passed the foot of the stairs, walked along a short, skinny corridor, and emerged into the kitchen, where the high ceiling, another original feature, immediately dissipated the cramped oddness of the entrance.

Mr. and Mrs. Ely sat at a round, metal-legged, linoleum-topped table so covered with newspapers, cigarette packages, beer bottles, milk cartons, hanging needles and spools of twine, even a yawning orange cat, that everything seemed to be floating in the air. Between the table and the stove and refrigerator against the far wall stood a wooden easel on which a pencil sketch of a fishboat hung like a cobweb. The room smelled heavily of oil paint and turpentine, though cigarette smoke and the rank musk of the black Lab asleep under the table contributed to the closeness.

I took everything in, revelling as always in the difference from what I was used to at home. Even though my mother wasn't uptight about keeping house, I entered the Elys' as if it were a bandit cave or pirate ship.

As we came in, Mr. and Mrs. Ely were laughing at Devon, Jerris's four-year-old brother who stood a few feet away, bawling and shouting, "You bitch! You bitch!" He stamped his feet, causing his dirty-blond hair to fall over his eyes, which made him bawl even louder.

Mrs. Ely, a short, brown-haired woman, cheerful as a puffed-up wren, blew a smoke ring up over her pretty, freckled face, and, laughing, said, "That's nice, honey. Thank you very much."

"You little bugger," Mr. Ely grinned. "Get to bed." He was a blocky man with a beer belly who always wore plain white T-shirts a size too small and whose loose-fitting pants regularly displayed the crack between his buttocks when he bent over. His short red hair, snub nose, and high colour made his head look as if it had been wedged off a chunk of cedar. The animated freshness and hot temper of his expression gave him an air of unpredictability. I liked him well enough, but since he was, as my parents put it, "a real go-getter," he wasn't around the house much.

"Go on, Dev," he chuckled, "before I kick you in the keister."

Devon just howled and called his mother a bitch again. Jerris laughed, told him to shut up, and grabbed him in a headlock.

"Oh leave him alone," Mrs. Ely yawned. "He'll wear himself out pretty soon." Then she smiled at me. "Hi, Callum, how's your dad doing?"

"He's still sick," I answered. "Still in bed."

"That's too bad." She blew another puff of smoke and butted out her cigarette in a coffee mug. "Ah but he'll be okay. Your dad's a tough bird. Jerris! Knock it off!"

He had pinned Devon to the floor by sitting on his chest and was blowing raspberries in his face, while Devon shrieked "Fuck you! Fuck off!"

"Okay, that's it." Mr. Ely stirred, leaning forward in his chair. Jerris immediately sprang off his brother, and Devon rolled away, got to his feet, and scrambled for the hall. At the entrance, he shouted "Go to hell!" and then vanished. A few seconds later, we heard him stomping up the stairs.

"Hey Dad," Jerris said. "Guess what me and Callum seen today?"

Mr. Ely reached out, grabbed the cat by the scruff of its neck, yanked it onto his lap, and proceeded to scratch it under the chin. "What's that?" he said with little interest.

As Jerris told the story of the shooting, his parents listened calmly, blew smoke rings, and occasionally raised their eyebrows at each other.

When Jerris finished, Mr. Ely shook his head and addressed his wife. "Jesus, I wonder what in hell that's all about?"

She shrugged. "Who knows? Maybe he owes somebody money."

"I didn't know the guy with the gun," Jerris cut in. "He looked like a pig, didn't he, Callum? And he had a big orange truck."

"Don't know him," Mr. Ely considered, pressing hard on the cat's ears. "You think he winged him, huh?"

"We seen the blood," Jerris declared proudly.

Suddenly, Mrs. Ely looked up at the ceiling and shouted, "Devon! You little bugger!" A trickle of water came out of the floor grate and splattered on one of the newspapers.

Mr. Ely chuckled and then muttered "Jesus," but almost with admiration.

"Devon!" Mrs. Ely shouted again. "You'd better knock it off!"

"He'd better not," Mr. Ely guffawed. "He might want to use it for something else one day."

Jerris turned to me. "He's pissing in the grate again," he explained. "He always does that when he's mad."

I noticed the stains on the ceiling; they were like maps of the continents.

Once the trickle stopped, Mrs. Ely folded the paper, stuffed it into a nearby garbage can, then headed for the stairs. "I'll settle him down," she said to her husband, as if to prevent him from doing it.

When she had gone, Jerris started in on the subject of the shooting again, explaining how Ezra had been in the trailer with the Lums. Then, with increased excitement, he remembered what I'd seen and heard on the wharf the day before. "Callum says the guy said 'You'd better stay away.' What do you figure he was talking about, Dad? Do you figure he meant the tree lot?"

Mr. Ely was stroking the cat so hard that its teeth were bared in a silent snarl. He didn't ignore Jerris but he didn't seem very engaged by his conversation either. Indifferently, he repeated that he knew nothing about it. Then, tossing the cat onto the floor, he reached for another cigarette and said, more thoughtfully, as though to himself, "Maybe he's getting it from one of them. Or both of them." He coughed deeply and lit the cigarette.

Mrs. Ely reappeared. "Asleep already," she grinned.

"Getting what?" Jerris asked, ignoring her.

Mr. Ely laughed. "The business, Jer, that's what."

Mrs. Ely cuffed him lightly on the back of the head and told him to be quiet.

He laughed even harder.

Jerris rolled his eyes at me, and I knew he thought the idea was as ridiculous and unpleasant as I did. We knew, however imperfectly, what the business was, but we couldn't accept that the mystery of the shooting had such an uninteresting solution. Ezra somehow seemed apart from all that, and the Lum daughters hardly even counted as women as far as we were concerned.

I wandered over to the easel and looked at the sketch. Mrs. Ely came and stood behind me.

"Mcalvaney's troller," she explained. "What do you think? Should I start slapping the paint on?"

"It's nice," I remarked without turning around. "I mean, it looks like it."

"Yeah, except she didn't put the whisky bottles in," Mr. Ely added.

His wife ignored him. "The poles were tricky, though. Getting them right."

I nodded without understanding, a little taken aback as always that Jerris's mother was a painter. She received many commissions to do fishermen's boats, but she had told me once that she preferred painting portraits and scenes from nature. In our living room, for example, hung a small study of chickadees perched on a pine bough, a present Mrs. Ely had given my mother. And all around the Elys' house hung paintings of the north coast bays and inlets where

Mr. Ely fished, as well as portraits of family members and others—
my favourites were of a wrinkled old native woman and of Jerris
and his dog. I was greatly impressed by Mrs. Ely's talent. She
seemed good enough to illustrate comic books, but I was too
shy to ask if she had ever considered that.

I stared at the sketch awhile longer and then realized I'd better
go home. Jerris accompanied me to the front door, where we
discussed our next move for unravelling the mystery of the shooting. We agreed to keep a lookout for Ezra whenever we were in
town or around the river, and planned to spend much of the
coming weekend making a more concentrated effort.

"Ezra's not doing it with them," Jerris announced to the cool air
as I looked back at him from the iron lamppost. The heavy
Victorian lamp simmered like a trapped wasp above me, as if the
light were about to whisper a secret it had been keeping for almost
a hundred years. And somehow the secret was about Ezra, which
made no sense at all since he hadn't been alive then. Confused, I
waited another minute before turning away into the swirling dark.

eight

AT NINE-THIRTY THE NEXT MORNING the inevitable happened. I was sitting at my desk concentrating on geometry, with the scritch-scritch-scritch of pencils on paper the only sound in the classroom. Suddenly, the public address system crackled into life and our principal's voice boomed angrily over our heads. "Would Eric Turnbull report to the office immediately! And Callum . . ." Here he paused, and we could hear him speaking away from the microphone. "Taylor," he continued. "Callum Taylor. I want to see you both. Now!"

Everyone stared at me, but I hardly noticed because of the pounding in my ears. Why me? I thought in a panic. What had I done? My teacher, Miss Coronet, looked equally puzzled.

"Callum Taylor," she said teasingly, "what have you been up to?"

"Nothing," I answered in a low quaver, my mouth dry.

Whispers of speculation buzzed around me. Miss Coronet hushed the class, then raised her eyebrows in my direction and said kindly, "Well, you'd better be going."

Trembling, I walked out of the classroom, still in shock that my name had come out of the big box up above the chalkboard. I had served my share of detentions before, but I had never been called to the office, not even by the secretary. And here I was, ordered by the principal himself to report to the office immediately.

I had taken only a few steps down the hall when I heard Eric behind me, half-shouting my name. He rushed up, his black curls shaking violently as he ran.

"I don't know why he wants to see you, Cal. You didn't have anything to do with it."

Eric's words, meant to comfort, didn't have the desired effect. The principal had spoken my name with considerable anger; it didn't really matter why he had done so. I walked as slowly as I could while Eric bobbed in a half-circle around me.

"I'll bet it's because I told Brent Kemmis," he said. "He had a whole bunch of guys gawking and laughing at it after school yesterday."

I could tell by Eric's tone that he was uneasy too. He was often in trouble, but for very minor things. He didn't mind crossing adults as long as his parents didn't become involved. The thought only upset me more, since the last thing I wanted was for my mother to be bothered while my father was sick in bed.

"I'll bet they'd never even have noticed," Eric said scornfully, "until they took it down after Christmas."

"Maybe it's because I didn't tell on you," I suggested, still trying to figure out why I was implicated. "Maybe it's just because they've seen me with you."

"Don't worry," Eric said as we entered the front hall. "I'll say you had nothing to do with it."

"Really?"

He grinned. "Sure. All you did was look, right?"

"Yeah," I agreed, feeling better.

We passed, one by one, the huge, dark oil portraits of the dour-faced prime ministers—Meighen, Bennett, Tupper—a complete gallery that was the pride and joy of our principal. If he happened to catch you standing by one of the portraits, he'd bear down on you, quizzing in a bellow as he approached, "Who succeeded Laurier? What party? What year?" This habit was one of many that made him such a holy terror.

We finally reached the front office, pausing only to see that the Christ-child had been removed from the manger. The sight, while not unexpected, still made all my panic flood back.

The secretary, Miss Templeton, a pretty, sweetly perfumed blonde, ushered us into a smaller office off the main one. "Have a seat," she said cheerfully, as if feeling sorry for us. "He won't be long."

Eric tried to lighten the mood by pretending to sit on the large potted cactus on the desk, but I didn't laugh. Instead, I looked around at the pictures on the walls, most of which were photographs of desert landscapes, the sort of places the Rawhide Kid would have galloped through. The largest picture, however, was a framed and autographed close-up of Lester B. Pearson. In a flowing black hand across his right shoulder was written, "To Ambrose T. Southern. Thank you for your support. Mike Pearson." Underneath this photograph, a two-foot-tall bronze-cast statue of a rearing horse seemed oddly connected to the former prime minister, as if he were about to climb down from the wall and ride off into the sunset.

Following my stare, Eric waved his hand dismissively. "My dad says going from Pearson to Trudeau would be like going from Mackenzie King to Warren Beatty."

I didn't understand. But then, I generally had a difficult time understanding Eric's father, a lawyer whose conversation was cryptic in a good-natured way.

"Pearson wasn't very cool," Eric explained, seeing my confusion.

I nodded, only half listening. The ceaseless typing in the outer office sounded like an approach that never arrived. Just when I thought I couldn't stand it any longer, the door opened.

Mr. Southern strutted in, glared at us without speaking, then crossed the room to face the Pearson photograph, his back to us. He had moved quickly but I still managed to see that he held the Christ-child, though I couldn't tell whose face was on it. For a while, Mr. Southern stood motionless, as if composing himself. As always, he wore crisp, loose-fitting, unfaded blue jeans, a pair of dark leather cowboy boots and a mahogany-coloured leather vest. When he finally turned around, I wasn't surprised by the rest of his attire—a white shirt embroidered in yellow thread with a lasso design, a black bolo tie, and a prominent metal belt buckle in the shape of a horse's head. But I was much more interested in the principal's face as I tried to decipher his mood. Mr. Southern was a small man, no more than five-and-a-half feet tall, but he had the feisty manner of a bantam cock. This feistiness was most evident in his face, which was so rigorously clean-shaven that a few tiny, blood-soaked dabs of toilet paper were always stuck to his cheeks, as though his face had refused to live up to his high standards of smoothness. His black, slightly greying hair was equally controlled, short on the sides but with a few tight curls dangling over his forehead (which, in a good mood, he would happily refer to as his "tumbleweeds"). With a strong nose, a thin-lipped mouth, and tiny metallic-blue eyes, he resembled a sort of cowboy garden gnome.

All of this was frightening because it made him seem like a child himself, one of our picked-on peers who had graduated to a position of power and was enjoying getting even.

Yet Mr. Southern was clearly an adult. What child would care
so much about prime ministers? Who among us drove a white
Eldorado with a steer-horn hood ornament? Most important of all,
who was capable of so much rage when crossed, a rage made even
more terrible by his obvious struggle to control it?

He glared at us now as he sat back on the front edge of his desk,
the wooden Christ-child gripped like a club in his right hand, a
tiny photograph held like a cigarette in his left. I caught a whiff of
his cool, minty aftershave. The redness of his cheeks had spread
down his neck, and for one horrible second I imagined that he was
bleeding from some shaving cut that the toilet paper couldn't
stanch.

He cleared his throat with a deep grumble, opened his mouth
to speak, and then closed it again so quickly that I expected to hear
a snap. Finally, he held the Christ-child out to us, and with his
teeth clenched between each slowly pronounced word demanded,
"Is this your idea of a joke?"

I turned slightly to Eric and saw that he was suppressing a grin.
Oh god, I thought, don't make it worse, please!

"Well!" Mr. Southern raised his voice. "What do you have to
say for yourselves?"

"He didn't have anything to do with it," Eric explained, pointing
at me. "He just looked. I was the one who put the picture there."

At this reminder, Mr. Southern looked at his left hand and grew
even angrier. "Do you have any idea," he shouted at us, his brow
reddening, "do you have any idea of what you've done!"

I tried to stop shaking by concentrating on the Christ-child's
placid face, but it didn't work. I was on the verge of tears.

"Yes, sir," Eric answered quietly.

Mr. Southern ignored him. "Blasphemy. Do you know what
that means? It means going against God! It means going against

the very power that gave you life! Do you understand!" He stood before us, leaning slightly forward, punctuating the air with the Christ-child so emphatically that its placid features had become a blur.

Eric seemed remarkably unaffected. He stared straight back at Mr. Southern without so much as a blink.

His composure infuriated the principal, who crushed the photo in his left hand and tossed it on the floor at Eric's feet. "If I could," he seethed, tapping his belt buckle, "I'd use this. If this were last year . . ." He fell silent for several seconds, and even seemed to be praying to the wooden figure for guidance. Eventually, in a calmer voice, he continued. "How did you do it?" he asked Eric. "I've been here since before the front doors were unlocked and I saw no one at the manger."

Puzzled, I glanced at Eric. He just shrugged his shoulders.

"I asked you a question!" Mr. Southern thundered.

"I did it over a week ago," Eric said calmly. "At lunchtime, when no one was . . ."

"Come now, the truth!" Mr. Southern raised the Christ-child and shook it threateningly.

"I'm not lying!" Eric shouted back. "I did it last week!"

Mr. Southern turned savagely to the intercom on his desk. "Miss Templeton, would you come in here, please?" he commanded.

Almost immediately, as if she'd been eavesdropping outside the door, the secretary appeared, looking overwhelmed. I felt a surge of sympathy for her as she faced her hot-tempered boss, who was pointing accusingly at Eric as he addressed her.

"He says he put the picture on last week."

Miss Templeton appeared even more confused. She put the tip of her pen between her crimson lipsticked mouth and bit down hard.

"Well?" Mr. Southern pressed her, crossing his arms. His tie had fallen like a skinny shadow over the Christ-child's face.

"It's possible," she responded at last. "But no one reported it."

He made a loud harrumphing noise. "Surely you must have noticed it before today?"

Miss Templeton, biting the pen once more, just shook her head.

After an uncomfortable pause, Mr. Southern said wearily, "All right, that will be all."

As soon as the secretary had gone, he returned his attention to us. "This is very serious," he said. "I don't think you appreciate how serious it is."

When we didn't respond, he continued in a stern but somehow wounded tone. "Hallowed be Thy name. The whole school recites that every morning. What makes you think you have the right to . . . to . . . to do such a thing? Who do you think you are?"

"Cal didn't have anything to do with it," Eric repeated, much to my relief.

This time, Mr. Southern actually looked at me. "I've been told that you were seen, along with your friend there, outside the manger on several occasions recently."

I nodded, and swallowed hard.

"Miss Templeton and some of the teachers took you to be interested," he scoffed. "But I see now that you were just having a good laugh at the expense of the Lord." He seemed to soften at my contrite posture, as though mistaking my fear for remorse. "Silence in such a situation is not acceptable. It makes you an accomplice." Then he turned to Eric. "As for you, you're older and should be setting an example. I'm disgusted that any boy could do such a monstrous thing. Obviously, I will be contacting both of your parents."

Eric saw me flinch and so he asked for a clarification. "Um, excuse me, sir, but do you mean by *both,* my mother and father, or my parents and Cal's too?"

"Be quiet!" the principal snapped. I thought for sure he was going to club Eric with the Christ-child. "Any more backtalk and you won't be able to sit for a week, I don't care what the board says!"

He returned to the photograph of Pearson, and that seemed to calm him down. I wondered briefly if the former prime minister had some power that the wooden figure lacked, since staring at it hadn't helped to calm him down at all.

"God, Queen, and Country," he said with conviction. "And in that order. It's what our great nation is built on. It's what the great men of our nation have always fought for." He turned slightly to the photograph of Pearson, as if to say, "It's what *he* always fought for," but he must have thought saying it was unnecessary. Instead, by way of conclusion, Mr. Southern dropped into a more matter-of-fact, disciplinary tone. "I want you here in my office after school every day this week. At which time you'll be assigned some Scripture to write out. Perhaps that will teach you some respect. Now get back to class."

Minutes later, in the boys' washroom, we stood at the urinals discussing what had happened. Eric was laughing and calling Mr. Southern a jerk for the way he had treated Miss Templeton. "Yeah, it's not like he didn't have a chance to look in the manger every day."

"I thought for sure he was going to hit you with Jesus," I chuckled.

"Me too! Hey, that would be a good one. Who gave you that black eye? Jesus did!"

We laughed awhile longer, then soberly considered our punishment. Eric decided it wasn't so bad, especially if our parents didn't add anything to it. With a sinking feeling, I realized that I wasn't going to escape the dreaded phone call. How would my parents react? Washing our hands, we discussed what was likely to happen at home.

"My parents aren't religious," Eric mused. "But my mom's pretty big on respecting other people's feelings and stuff. She'll probably just talk to me." He suddenly smiled out of his concern. "I don't know, my dad might even think it's funny, but my mom wouldn't like that. She's always telling him not to encourage me. Anyway, it shouldn't be too bad. It will probably depend on who Southern talks to." He turned off the tap and banged the paper-towel dispenser with one hand. "He'll probably make my dad mad. My mom's always a lot calmer. How about you?"

"I'm not sure," I answered as we left the washroom. I knew that religion wasn't a big part of our lives, but my mother often referred to God. "The Lord helps those who help themselves." "There but for the grace of God." "The good Lord willing." She'd say such things as naturally as she'd say "Don't talk with your mouth full." And she always described Sunday as "a day of rest," during which we were not allowed to cut our toenails and fingernails, even though we could do just about everything else.

I walked in silence beside Eric, wanting to explain further, but the subject was confusing. My mother had a fat, black leather Bible on her bedroom dresser but I never saw her reading it. I often admired its appearance, all beat-up like a whaler's logbook and stuffed with yellowing telegrams and old letters and birth certificates, even some snippets of hair. My mother once explained that it had belonged to her mother, who had died years before I was born, and that it contained all sorts of family information.

What else? What else? For a few days in the summers of my sixth and seventh years I went to Christian Bible Camp organized by the Dutch Reformed Church. We painted pictures of Biblical scenes, sang "Jesus Loves Me," and drank Ribena. But mostly we played in the big grassy field behind the church, catching grasshoppers and trapping them in Mason jars, then getting in trouble for letting them loose when we went back inside. Jonah and the whale: that was pretty neat, because I'd seen a dead whale on the beach once. And Joseph getting all bloodied and dumped in a hole by his brothers: that was even better than some comic book plots I'd read. Of course, there was also the Lord's Prayer, the words of which we recited daily but never paid much attention to, though Donald Bints occasionally sang "Our Father who farts in heaven, stinky be thy name" out on the playground.

What about my own father? I had heard him say on several occasions that he had no time for religion, but his response seemed more complicated than that. Out on the river, in the middle of the night under the clustering stars, with only the sound of the current sucking at the muddy banks, he would speak from out of the endless dark behind the scarlet nub of his cigarette, telling me about the salmon and the tides with a sort of hushed tone to his voice, as though nature were a kind of god. And yet he would grumble to the Jehovah's Witnesses who sometimes came to our house that he didn't believe in God. My mother would scold, "Oh, Mack, you just have to get a reaction," but he always defended himself with "But I don't believe. Let them go peddle their papers to someone who's interested."

None of this rapid flow of thought helped me to predict how my parents would react to Mr. Southern's phone call. "I guess they'll be mad," I finally said to Eric. "They don't like me to get into trouble."

We eventually separated and returned to our classrooms and to a brief and glorious sort of fame. For the rest of the day I was the centre of attention—everyone wanted to hear why I had been called to the office, what Mr. Southern had said and done, and how I was going to be punished. I had never been so popular, and my head swam with the sensation. By lunchtime I was giddy and beaming, relating for the dozenth time, and with astonishing embellishment, how Eric and I had taped his picture onto the baby Jesus. Everyone laughed, said they wished they had seen it, wondered how we'd thought of it, couldn't believe we had the nerve, etc., etc. I didn't come down off my towering pedestal until Deborah Glavin, a shy girl from my class with whom I sometimes studied and talked, said, "I don't think it's very funny, doing that to Jesus." When everyone else howled at her and teased her until she almost cried, I lost some of the pleasure of my newfound popularity. Just afterwards, back in the hallway, the sight of Mr. Southern striding toward a group of girls who had been caught unawares under the portrait of Alexander Mackenzie made my heart leap. What if he found out that I had been bragging about our practical joke? As he bellowed "Girls, girls, who were the Whigs and who were the Grits? Quick now!" I ducked into a classroom where, alone, I decided to play it cool for the rest of the day.

A few minutes after three o'clock, Eric and I reported to the office and were delighted to learn that Mr. Southern was busy. Instead, Miss Templeton gave us two small Bibles, referred to a note the principal had left, and told us we were to copy out twenty-five verses from "Deutermony" (Eric gave me the correct pronunciation after she'd gone). Once we were finished, she continued, we were to hand our assignments to her and then to think about the verses on our way home.

Since we were both fast writers, Eric and I finished quickly, despite the fact that we talked about comics the whole time we were copying. Even so, the schoolgrounds were deserted by the time we got outside. Eric said he was going home to watch TV before he went to the bookshop. I said I'd see him later, once I'd picked up my papers at the shack.

I had just started my solitary walk toward town when Donald Bints came whinnying up behind me, all teeth and glasses and loud noises. He explained that he'd just served a detention too, for setting someone's book on fire in a Bunsen burner, and I could tell that he was jealous about all the attention Eric and I had received. We laughed for a while, said it was a bugger we couldn't ride our bikes to do our papers, and then I mentioned that I had seen Mr. Vreen's car outside his house the day before.

Bints's reaction took me completely by surprise. He grabbed my shoulder, swung me around, and put his face to within a few inches of mine. "Did you say anything? Did you tell anybody?" He spoke as if we were conspiring to blow up the town.

I was too startled to do anything but shake my head and step back. Bints's breath was unpleasantly hot on my face. Reluctantly, he let go of my shoulder, then made a fist and with his other hand grabbed the front of my jacket. "You'd better not," he threatened, bringing his fist up near my chin.

Though Bints's behaviour shocked me, I wasn't really frightened by it. This aggressive stance was completely out of character. Even he seemed to realize this, so he released my jacket, unclenched his fist, and changed tactics.

"If you don't tell anybody," he wheedled, rummaging in his pants pockets, "I'll give you stuff." He looked down and I noticed a thin white scar on his bristly scalp. "Here," he said, holding out his hand, palm up, "have some spits."

When I declined, he stuffed the sunflower seeds, lint and all, into his mouth, then moved skittishly along beside me as we continued toward town. "What do you want? Chips? Pop? I'll buy it for you."

I had no idea why my silence was such an urgent matter for him, but the prospect of making some easy money was pleasant enough. For weeks I had been saving for a big comic book convention to be held in Vancouver in January, which was why I had been working so hard to sign up new subscribers. Now here was an opportunity to pad my savings without even having to work. "Nah, I don't want chips or pop," I said hesitantly. "But I could use some money."

"Sure!" Bints agreed, bobbing his head emphatically. "How much?"

I wanted to be cagey, but no matter what I thought of Bints, his being three years older was still a bit intimidating. I did suggest, though, that it would be hard not to talk about Mr. Vreen at the paper shack, especially if someone else mentioned him first.

Bints spun around, hang-jawed, and put his arms out as if to keep me away from the paper shack forever. He was breathing so hard that his thick glasses had fogged up, and he tried to clear them with the sleeve of his jacket. "Fifty cents," he spluttered. "Fifty cents a day. But you can't tell anybody! If you do . . ." He paused to pull a soiled white handkerchief from his pants pocket. Then he dropped his glasses so that they hung around his neck on their band, and started to scrub the lenses with the handkerchief. "Fucking glasses," he muttered, squinting. He suddenly looked so defenceless that I almost regretted taking his money.

His unfinished threat hung limply in the air between us. I considered telling him to forget about it, that I wouldn't mention Vreen to anybody. But I couldn't say the words. Bints almost seemed to invite the ungenerous treatment he received. Besides, once he had finished scrubbing his lenses, he fumbled in his pockets again, pulled out some change, and counted it.

"I've only got thirty-five," he said. "But I'll give you the rest tomorrow."

I agreed, and we hurried on toward the shack, our conversation switching to the punishment Eric and I had received from Mr. Southern. Bints was clearly impressed with the joke, but only because it had been so universally admired; I don't think he understood why putting Eric's picture on the baby Jesus was funny.

The snow had stopped falling but was still thick on the streets. The air, though, felt even colder. As we walked, our boots crackled a thin crust of icy snow wherever cars hadn't passed, and each intake of breath was like sucking on a peppermint. Snow had transformed the boughs of the evergreens into fish skeletons, and spirals of smoke drifted out of the chimneys of the houses we passed as though the bricks were gasping. All the way into town, the strange silence continued.

Just before we reached the paper shack, Bints grabbed my arm, leaned close again, and said in a half-plea, half-threat, "Remember, we've got a deal. Fifty cents."

And then he returned to the ceaseless physical and verbal abuse in which he seemed most comfortable, and I retreated to my anonymity, fingering the cold change and no longer even wondering why I had been given it.

I presented Clive Withers with the subscription form that Mr. Edmundson had filled in the day before, and he responded with his characteristic mixture of scorn and appreciation. "Another one? Geez, there must be a new Nancy Drew book out you want or something." He suddenly shouted over my shoulder. "Hey, knock it off, you dorks!"

I looked behind to see several of the older boys spitting up into the beams of the shack to create "hangers." If your spit landed just right, it would freeze into a tiny icicle as it trickled down. The prospect of being ridiculed for failing was greater than the prospect of being admired for doing a good one, so I hoisted my full sack of papers on my shoulder and left the shouting and the spitting and the skinny chandeliers behind. The change Bints had paid me jingled in my pocket and acted like magnetic filings to draw me toward the bookshop, even though I really didn't have time to linger there. But I wanted to hear Mr. Bradlee's and Jamie's reactions to the latest developments in the manger saga; their appreciation was so much more reasoned and philosophical, more concerned with the nature of the joke itself than with its effect.

But neither Eric nor Jamie were in the shop when I arrived. Mr. Bradlee was ringing in a huge stack of Agatha Christies that an old woman with hair like dandelion seed had gathered from the shelves. He glanced up and winked at me, then dove back into the mysteries. An older teenager waited at the counter, and I knew it would be a while before I could tell Mr. Bradlee about the day's events.

I left the shop, planning to stop in again before I checked my father's boat. Maybe Eric and Jamie would be there later, and I wouldn't miss out on the fun of reliving Mr. Southern's response to our joke after all.

The wind picked up as I moved through the streets, shook snow off branches and blew it up off the ground. It was as if a pale twilight had started to fall. I hunched into my jacket and scurried from house to house, apartment block to apartment block, throwing down the papers, folding them, tucking them neatly out of the weather. Black and white, black and white, black and white, the same motion repeated, the soft squares of dark-dappled snow in my hands, and the huge front page I hurried across, night bleeding through the pulp in the sky, inking the pulp on the ground.

I walked down the long, hot hallways of the elderly, shedding the news like an outer skin, and emerged into the always deepening night a little lighter and freer.

I crossed the plywood plank over the ditch to the collapsing duplex and passed through the skinny beam of yellow light falling from Mrs. Edmundson's window. Then I turned up the black alley, the wind numbing my cheeks and earlobes, lifting my canvas sack like a single white wing.

The dusk deepened. I delivered my last paper and headed back to town, deciding against returning to the bookshop. It was darker and colder and the wind seemed to be pushing me toward the wharf. I was suddenly too tired to resist.

On the gangway, I was greeted by the same chain-clanking, wood-creaking music of my previous visits, the same image of vital summer frozen to an unforgiving moor. The boats looked even blacker under the ice and snow. I followed the old bootprints to the farthest point, crunched over the icy layer to my father's boat, pumped out the cabin, and hurried back to the dyke.

Darkness had folded over the earth as lightly as a heron's wing. But the wind was colder, the gust from featherless bones flapping and flapping. It blew upriver and I had to bend into it to keep warm as I followed the curve of the dyke along the channel.

Halfway to the Home Oil sign, in the middle of the silence and darkness, I heard a strange sound rising just above the thrum of the wind. I stopped and peered into the still-faint black over the river. At first, the sound—a creaking and a splashing, repeated—existed without an image. But gradually the outlines of a skiff and figure emerged. Someone was rowing downriver in the narrow, ice-free middle of the current. This seemed such an odd activity that I immediately decided to follow the skiff to see where it would stop.

The tide must have been going out because, despite the strong wind, the skiff pulled ahead of me and I had to walk faster to keep up. A couple of times I paused, almost convinced that my imagination was playing tricks on me. But the creaking and splashing always drifted back, even when the outlines of the skiff and rower had blended into the enveloping dark.

When I reached the Home Oil sign I stopped again, and looked out at the dim orange pier light glowing dully on the river. The creaking and splashing had stopped. Straining, I saw the dark figure step out of the skiff onto the pier. It bent over and tied the bow line, then reached into the bow and lifted a thick black mass up into the faint light. From where I stood, the figure seemed to be wrestling a bear. But after another minute had passed, I saw that the black shape was a fir tree and that Ezra Hemsworth had positioned himself under it. He carried the ten-foot tree lengthwise across his shoulders, which forced him to walk with his chest almost parallel to the ground. He was so dark among the branches that the tree seemed to be moving by itself, as if it were drifting on the current. It rose onto the dyke, drifted through the incomplete reflection of the sign's letters, and then dropped quickly to the road.

I followed at a safe distance, realizing excitedly that here was perhaps another clue in the mystery involving Ezra, the Lums, and the shooting at the tree lot. I thought of how mad Jerris would be that he'd missed out as I cautiously tailed Ezra and his heavy burden of thick branches.

To my surprise, he entered the plum orchard instead of turning west on the river road. Where was he going?

Minutes later, I hid behind a tree at the edge of the orchard and watched as Ezra reached the front door of my house. He raised the tree high over his head as if he was going to hurl it through a nearby window, but then gently leaned it against the front steps. Pepper barked and strained at his chain, but Ezra took no notice. He just straightened his skullcap, rested briefly, and then turned and headed back the way he had come.

When Ezra had almost reached the orchard, I pressed myself tighter to the trunk and tried to breathe as quietly as possible. He passed within a few feet of my hiding place, the heavy fragrance of the fir swirling briefly in his wake before the wind carried it away. I watched him vanish in the orchard, black as a falling branch, soundless as snow. It was eerie the way he dropped out of sight. Only when he had completely disappeared did I step away from the cold wood to move toward his recent burden, shining its rich, dark green at the edges of the window light.

nine

AS I ENTERED THE HOUSE, my fingers fragrant with fir, I wondered whether Ezra's tree had come from the lot and what that might mean in relation to the shooting. The silence and neatness of the house contrasted with the chaos of my thoughts and I suddenly recalled the day's earlier events. I could almost hear the repeated echo of a ringing phone, and the principal's voice beginning, "Your son, Callum . . ."

My mother was in the kitchen washing dishes at the sink. "We've already eaten," she explained, nodding toward my place set at the table. "Angie and Steven were hungry."

"Ezra brought us a Christmas tree," I blurted out, wanting to fill the silence with anything other than a discussion of my day.

My mother turned from the sink, wiping her hands on her flower-print apron. Her dark hair swung loosely, and she brushed a few strands out of her eyes with the back of her hand, warmed red from the heat of the dishwater. With relief, I saw that her expression was lively, the light in her large green eyes softening the fatigue and worry that had been on her face of late.

"He did? Why on earth would he do that?" She left the kitchen and went to the front door. I followed, encouraged by her enthusiasm; it suggested that I might be off the hook.

Cool air blew past her figure in the open doorway, bringing with it the rich scent of fir.

"Oh it's a beauty!" my mother enthused. "It must be from the bog." She turned back, closing the door, and from the way she stared down at the bottom of the apron now bunched in her hands, I knew she was searching for an explanation.

I waited, still anxious that she was about to change the subject to my recent misbehaviour.

But she didn't. She finally lifted her head and spoke as if she were alone. "I'll bet he heard from Rodney that Mack was too sick to go for a tree this year." Then, remembering my presence, she added, "Mr. Graveridge is a good friend of Ezra's. He must have told him about your father."

"Is Dad any better?"

She nodded. "Yes, a little." Then she returned to the subject of the tree, obviously pleased. "What a sweet thing to do. He must have borrowed a truck to get it."

When I told her what I had seen, her eyes widened. "Down the river? And then he carried it here? It must be ten feet tall." Again, she bunched up the apron. "We'll have to do something nice for him," she considered, returning to the sink.

I sat at the table between the clatter of plates and the hum of the TV coming from the living room where my brother and sister were. Minutes passed. Was it possible Mr. Southern hadn't phoned? I finished eating and still the subject did not come up. As I pushed back my chair my mother said, "Go quietly down the hall and see if your father's awake. If he is, go in and talk with him a bit. He misses you."

I had almost reached the bedroom when the phone rang, shrill as gullcry. I froze in the middle of the hall. In the echoing stillness I could hear my father lightly snoring and the faint rise of canned laughter coming from the TV. When my mother called I was so nervous that I didn't even realize that she hadn't had time to converse with the caller. I was so convinced that it was Mr. Southern that I started to prepare excuses as I returned to the kitchen. It was Eric's idea, I reminded myself, forgetting all my boasts on the playground. All I did was look, I repeated innocently, over and over until, by the time I reached the phone, I felt as spotless as a lamb.

"It's Eric," my mother said, handing me the receiver. I must have looked ecstatic because she smiled and added before leaving the room, "My goodness, a person would think you hadn't talked with him in ages."

"So what did you get?" Eric asked the second I came on the line.

When I said I didn't know what he meant, he responded with disbelief. "What? Didn't your parents do anything about it?"

"Did he phone yours?" I asked, my heart sinking.

Eric laughed. "Sure. I'll bet he was watching the house from his car, waiting for them to get home. Then he probably couldn't get to a phone fast enough."

When I mentioned that I had been home for an hour and that my mother hadn't said anything about school, Eric pressed for details.

"Did she say anything suspicious? Did she drop any clues? Maybe she's just waiting for your dad to get home."

"He's sick in bed," I said gloomily, depressed by the thought that I wasn't going to escape punishment after all. But with a sudden hopefulness, I asked Eric what had happened to him, thinking that if he got off easy, maybe I would too.

He lowered his voice and told me the whole story. His mother had taken the call while he was watching a rerun of *My Three Sons*. And the funny thing was that Chip, on that very episode, at that very moment, was trying to lie his way out of a bad report card. Wasn't that weird? Anyway, Eric turned the TV volume down and heard his mother say "I see" a couple of times, followed by "Yes, I understand that," and then, more severely, "Yes, certainly, I am aware of what it means," and then finally, "I appreciate your phoning. We'll have a talk with him. Thank you." At this point, Eric was trying to figure out how to handle the situation. Should he apologize? Should he try to encourage his mother to see the funny side of things? Or should he just lie low until his father got home and hope for more understanding from him?

His mother came into the room, told him she wasn't at all pleased, lectured him a bit about other people's feelings on religion, and then grounded him for a week without TV privileges. All in all, the punishment wasn't as bad as it could have been.

"But then," Eric went on rapidly, "my dad came home. And that's when things got bad."

Apparently, his parents had had a big argument, with Eric's mother saying things like "But he needs to respect other people's views. He has to live in the world," and his father coming back with "He can make his own world. That's what we all have to do eventually," and then his mother arguing "That's nonsense and you know it! He's a boy and you shouldn't encourage him to sneer at others. It will just make life harder for him." Then his father, raising his voice, started in on our principal.

"He called him a horse's ass," Eric reported with delight, and went on quoting verbatim. "That pompous, ridiculous horse's ass is no more of a cowboy than Quentin Crisp, for godsakes! That get-up! And Pearson—Pearson!" Here Eric said his father almost choked with scornful laughter. "The United Nations of the World. Oh my god! I wonder what that pretend cowboy thinks of the time Johnson called his hero a little pipsqueak and grabbed him around the throat and told him to mind his own goddamned business about Vietnam. Hardly the stuff heroes are made of."

And through it all, Eric's mother simply repeated calmly and coolly, "He has to learn to respect different views, and you're not helping."

Eventually the argument quieted down and Eric thought it was over. But then his father burst out with "He has to do what?!" and that's when the fight really took off, with Eric's father railing against "Bible-thumping hypocrites, weekday sinners and Sunday saints," and his mother saying "Oh, for goodness' sake, it won't hurt him any." In the end, his father was talked out of going to the school the next day to "have it out with that horse's ass," and Eric's punishment was reduced so that he kept his TV privileges.

"My dad didn't say much to me," Eric continued. "I think he was worried about upsetting my mom any more than she already was. But he did sort of grin at me when she wasn't looking, so I know he's not mad." Eric paused for a deep breath, and I could tell he was upset by how everything had turned out. "I hate it when they don't talk," he confided. "Especially when it's my fault." Then he quickly changed the subject to my parents.

"Can't you find out?" he urged. "If Southern did phone, you might as well know now." Finally, after Eric suggested a plan, I hung up and went to find my mother.

She was in the bedroom talking with my father. His face was ghostly pale except where a black beard covered the skin, and since only his white T-shirt showed above the white bedsheets, he looked like a folded piece of blank paper onto which some ink had been splotched. He held an unlit cigarette in his right hand, and as I entered the room I heard my mother explain to him in a weary voice why he shouldn't smoke it.

"It would cut some of the smell down in here at least," he argued without much conviction, then nodded toward me. "Hi there, Cal. How's tricks?"

"I'll light a candle," my mother said, patting the turned-down bedsheet as an invitation for me to sit alongside her.

"They're all right," I mumbled in response to my father's question, relieved despite my concerns about school to see that he was recovering from his cold. The house had been unusually dark and dismal without his being "up and about," as my mother put it. But I didn't enjoy my relief very long, since I expected that trouble lay ahead. I answered a few other questions about the boat and snow, questions I feared as the preliminary to the subject of school.

Fortunately, my mother intervened before the conversation came to that. "Ezra brought us a tree," she began, "a real beauty." She explained how I'd watched him row it downriver and carry it through the orchard. My father smiled at her and at me in turn, charmed as much by my mother's enthusiasm as by Ezra's thought-fulness. "Wasn't that sweet?" my mother said now, a planning look in her eyes. "We should do something for him, Mack. Alone like he is, especially at Christmas. It isn't right."

My father sighed. "I'll have my Christmas Eve drink with him down at the wharf. That's enough. Ezra doesn't care to be fussed over."

"Once a year," my mother insisted. "That's hardly fussing. Besides, Doctor Lewis says you're not to go out until after the holidays."

My father made a dismissive sound deep in his throat that set off a fit of harsh coughing.

In the ensuing silence, I suddenly recalled my phone conversation with Eric, and not wanting to let him down, I decided to give his plan a try. Softly, while strolling around the room looking at the family photos on the walls and dresser, I began to hum "Jesus Loves Me." Neither of my parents noticed, so I added some of the lyrics. "Jesus loves me, yes I know, 'cause the Bible tells me so," I sang, putting a slight emphasis on "Bible." But still I drew no attention.

"He could come to Christmas dinner with Rodney," my mother suddenly proposed. "He and Rodney are close, aren't they?"

"I guess so," my father replied without enthusiasm.

I switched to "Onward Christian Soldiers," humming a little louder.

"Well, he'd probably come along if Rodney invited him."

"I don't know. Ezra's not one for visiting."

"But it's Christmas, Mack. And he's been so good about the boat."

"O little town of Bethlehem," I sang, "how sweet I see Thee lie." But I was hardly aware of what I was doing now, since the prospect of Ezra having dinner at our house was staggering. Gradually, I began to think of him and the Lums and the pig-faced man even as I sang a few more carols. If Ezra did come to our house, perhaps I could learn something about the shooting at the tree lot, perhaps the adults would even discuss it. "Away in a manger, no crib for a bed." No, that wasn't likely, at least not until after Angie and Steven and I had gone to bed. "The little Lord Jesus." But Mr. Graveridge wasn't the sort of adult to censor his conversation. He was pretty quiet, though; didn't talk a lot. "Lay down His sweet head. The stars in the bright sky." Still, there was a good chance I'd find out *something* new about Ezra if he came to dinner. "Looked down where He lay, the little Lord Jesus asleep on the hay."

I finally noticed my parents' silence, and looked up to see them staring at me with good-natured bewilderment. Oh oh, I thought, this is it. Away in a manger, I silently cursed myself, too obvious.

But my mother remarked only that it was nice to hear me singing carols, and my father, grinning, added, "Well, you're no Joe Feeney, but it wasn't bad."

I seemed to have escaped. No mention of Mr. Southern or the baby Eric was made that night. A few times, I faked a sneeze and made a sound exactly like "Deuteronomy," but that went unnoticed by my parents too. I finally concluded that for some reason of his own, the principal had decided to let me off the hook. And since I hadn't really been responsible for the joke, I didn't even feel guilty that Eric took the brunt of the blame.

As I lay in bed that night, I returned to thoughts of money—how much I might collect from Bints, how much I might make from new subscriptions, how much I would need for the comic book convention in January. But eventually I saw Ezra rowing downriver again, hoisting the fir out of the skiff and onto his shoulders, labouring over the dyke and through the orchard. Always, he stopped at our house, laid the tree down, and turned back to his own world. No matter how hard I tried, I couldn't imagine him continuing on into the house. Where would he sit? How would he eat? What would he say? I tried to picture Ezra as part of a domestic scene, but as soon as I got him into the house I saw him reeling across the living room, knocking over the furniture, blood dripping from his shoulder, his mouth open in a scream as silent as snowfall. Fir needles shook down off his back, their green mingling with the red blood, and everywhere the smell of diesel and sweat and the river smothered the freshness of the fir. I couldn't shake this image. Frightened and excited, I fell asleep to the silence of that imagined scream.

ten

DAY AFTER DAY the cold persisted, and the snow, in tiny, dry flakes, sprinkled down onto the great depths of the earlier storms like icing sugar onto leavened dough. The ice did not thicken on the river, but it stayed, and the bootprints on the wharf leading to Ezra's boat never entirely filled in again.

I was too busy to do anything but silently cheer the weather as I looked out my bedroom window each morning. I had more new subscriptions to find, and since Christmas was fast approaching I had started collecting my customers' payments for the month of December, about a week earlier than in other months simply because it was a good idea to capitalize on the nicer tips occasioned by pre-Christmas goodwill. So every evening, after I had pumped the boat and biked home to have supper (the roads were passable by then), I would redo my route and try to collect from customers who hadn't been home earlier. Sometimes Jerris would join me, and we would make side trips to various locations where we thought Ezra might be found. We did see him once or twice, but he was just hurrying from the wharf to the diner or from the marine supply store to the wharf—we followed him those times, hoping for something to happen, but nothing did. And yet we maintained our enthusiasm for the pursuit—who else did we know who had been shot?

I went to the bookshop every day, but it was subdued for the whole week that Eric was grounded. My wallet was getting thicker with the mysterious hush money I was receiving from Bints, and that added an extra thrill to being in the bookshop. I could discuss the upcoming comic convention with Mr. Bradlee and Jamie secure in the knowledge that I would be attending as a real collector, someone with buying power.

Meanwhile, my father got stronger and was soon walking about the house restlessly, anxious to go down to the wharf. He sat in front of the TV in the evenings, watching his favourite programs—*The Beachcombers, All in the Family, The Tommy Hunter Show,* and *The Lawrence Welk Show*—or else he read the newspaper and did jigsaw puzzles with my brother and sister. I asked him once if he thought Ezra really would come to dinner on Christmas Eve, and he shrugged and said he didn't know but that somehow he doubted it.

And so the days passed. About a week before Christmas, school closed for the holidays, and I used the extra hours to step up my campaign for new subscribers and to play more hockey and read more comics. Yet there was always something else to do—no part of the day was wasted. It was a glorious, exciting time, made troubling by one small development that, no matter how hard I tried to ignore it, kept gnawing at me.

The first few times I delivered the paper to Mrs. Edmundson, she opened the door as I came up the porch and invited me in for some hot chocolate. Once inside, the same awkward silence ensued, during which she would seem to forget my presence and suddenly sigh so deeply that I was certain she was about to have a heart attack. The oddly glowing radio would murmur something to an old melody and Mrs. Edmundson would switch it off, light a cigarette, and nod to herself slightly before beginning a halting monologue about her past, a monologue that I had a hard time following because I did not know any of the people she mentioned. Gradually I realized that she didn't expect me to respond, so I would sip at my chocolate and eat the cookies and wipe the sweat off my flushed face. Somehow I managed to leave each time, choosing a long lull in her conversation to say cheerily, "Well, thank you for the hot chocolate. I have to go now." And then I would hurriedly pull on my boots and jacket and rush out the door while she sat motionless in the horsehair armchair, the smoking cigarette burning down in her hand.

By the fourth day, I could stand it no longer. I was terrified that she was going to die during one of my visits, a fear that grew when I recalled her son asking me to contact him if anything went wrong. So I tried parking my bike before I reached the back of the house and then sneaking up onto the veranda. This didn't work, because she heard me anyway, and by the time I returned to my bike she was standing in the open door, calling "Is that you, Leslie?" in a voice at once loud and pitiable. I had no choice but to answer and then accept her invitation to come in.

The next day, as I sat in that dingy room, bored, restless, and cursing myself for not being able to avoid the situation, I came to a decision that shocked me. While the old woman spoke of Arthur, her first husband, and his mother who never really liked her because she expected someone better for her son, I decided not to deliver her paper the next day. I could see them stacked on one end of the kitchen table, and it was obvious they had not been read. What did she even need the paper for?

And so, on the fifth day, I took a risk. As I pedalled toward the duplex I thought, "I'll bet she doesn't even notice." But convinced though I was, I still hesitated for several minutes at the front of the property. I suspected that Mrs. Edmundson looked forward to my visits, and I knew that she was lonely; I even knew why she had ended up living there. Her voice came back to me as I balanced on the plywood bridge over the black ditch: "Leslie's a good man, a gentle soul, but he doesn't have his father's will. Reginald would never have let me talk him into doing something that he didn't want to do." As far as I could tell from her disjointed conversation, Mrs. Edmundson had been living with her son and his family since her husband's death a year earlier, but her daughter-in-law had finally forced her out, apparently because she was depressing. But the reason meant little to me. All that really mattered was this feeling of responsibility that I couldn't shake. I kept seeing the old woman standing by the skinny window, watching for me, the kettle probably on the stove and the cookies on the plate. What if I didn't come? Would she open the door anyway and call out for someone? But even worse was the thought of enduring another painful silence in that drab room.

I turned my back on the duplex and pedalled as fast as I could down the street.

For several afternoons afterwards, I wrestled with my conscience for a few minutes, then returned gratefully to the vast pleasures and excitements of the season. Oddly enough, I did not consider the obvious problem: eventually, I would either have to collect the money for papers that I wasn't delivering, or else pay for them myself. But all that concerned me at the time was avoiding the old woman's company.

The first day at the shack after not delivering Mrs. Edmundson's paper, I was afraid that she might have phoned the *Sun* to complain, but Clive Withers said nothing unusual. Soon I stopped worrying at all, and the guilt was restricted to those same few minutes in the late afternoons as the tiny snowflakes sifted down onto the thin ice of the ditch.

One afternoon I arrived at the paper shack to find it in a more chaotic state than usual. Several of the older boys were howling at Bints, who flew around the tiny building in a rage, lashing out at whoever shouted the loudest. "Donny's got a new daddy! Donny's got a new daddy!" the chanting went, punctuated with mock-ecstatic moans of "Oh, Mr. Vreen, oh oh ohhhh!!!" Clive leaned back in one corner, grinning widely, every now and then thrusting his hips forward and shouting, "Are you ready for another delivery, Mrs. Bints?" I snuck through the doorway, and stayed on the fringe of all the commotion.

Bints was in a fury, his glasses dangling around his neck, his nose running, tears streaming down his cheeks as he staggered from one shout to another, swinging and kicking wildly, all the while screaming "Fuck off you pricks!" His jacket was ripped in several places and a bright red streak flared across one cheek, growing brighter as the taunting continued.

"Maybe Donny's getting it too!" someone shouted, setting off a new chant of "Vreen's bumboy! Vreen's bumboy!" Now Bints screamed even louder, his mouth open so wide that I was sure his jaw was going to snap off. He managed to grab one of his tormentors, a much larger boy named Brendan, and tried to wrestle him to the ground. But Brendan, laughing, twisted Bints into a headlock. Another boy came up and, bending over, said directly into Bints's red and gasping face, "Maybe Withers has been giving it to her too." Again, another loud burst of laughter and shouting filled the shack.

One of the younger boys, seeing my confusion, explained in a hurried whisper that Bints's mom and Mr. Vreen were doing it.

"How does he know that?" I whispered back, stunned.

"Dunno. He just said so."

Meanwhile, Bints had squirmed out of the headlock and had rushed for the doorway. Halfway there, someone tripped him and he landed face-first on the hard, spit-stained planks. He got up with his nose bleeding and his forehead scraped, but he didn't even hold his hand to his nose; the blood just gushed out as a new chant of "Gross! Gross!" went up. Now when Bints turned, it was as though he were being jerked by a scarlet rein. He headed for the doorway again, and I shrank against the wall so that he wouldn't notice me as he plunged through the opening.

Even by the high standards of abuse the shack had established, this scene was remarkable. Bints seemed to have gone out of his mind, but the fact only increased the taunting; the stronger he reacted, the greater the push. I stared at the slick blood on the planks. And in the strange, brief silence accompanying Bints's exit, the vivid image of his pleading face came back to me from the day he had promised to buy my silence. I realized now what the money was for, which didn't make me feel any better. I had always sort of liked Bints, and had begun to like him a little more as payment followed payment. He was a goof, but his impersonations of our peers made me laugh, and I admired his nerve. I stood in the shack, alone. Everyone else had followed Bints outside to see what he would do next. When I heard the shouts rise again, I couldn't resist taking a look for myself.

Bints had changed tactics. He had turned his anger toward the bikes propped against the shack. One after the other, he flung them to the ground and stomped on them with his boots, trying to snap the spokes and bend the wheels. Boys were scrambling madly to pull their bikes out of danger. The air was filled with white vapour from all the heavy breathing and shouting, as if a mist had rolled in off the marsh. Bints, bleeding heavily, left a twisting trail of red behind him, vivid as flame on the snow. As my own bike was already safe, lying some distance away because there had been no room for it against the shack when I had arrived, I didn't join the general exodus toward the road. I just stood on the mixed snow and gravel a few feet outside the doorway, poised to run if the violence came too close.

Clive had had enough. He shouted so loud at everyone to knock it off, to come and get their papers, that his veins showed behind the purplish tint of his neck. But his authority meant nothing at the moment. From the way he avoided Bints, I sensed that even he was unnerved by the unprecedented violence.

Bints had not been able to wreck a single bike; each had been pulled to safety as he was easily distracted by fresh taunts. Frustrated, he eventually picked up a large chunk of gravel off the scuffed ground and, holding it high over his head, ran at the group on the road, scattering it like a flock of crows. Finally, exhausted, his tears almost spent, Bints returned for his own bike. His thin chest heaved. Blood trickled from his nose down over his lips, which were smeared as if he'd been biting the heads off chickens. His rasping sobs sounded even harsher in the sudden stillness. He didn't look at me or Clive until he had grabbed the handlebars of his bike and was slowly pushing it away from the shack. After he'd gone about ten feet, he stopped and looked back over his shoulder. His eyes, tiny and squinting without the glasses that still hung around his neck, settled on me.

"You told," he said sadly, all his rage spent.

I was too shocked to respond. Then, once I had realized what he meant, I protested loudly, "No, I didn't! I swear!"

But Bints only repeated in a quieter voice, "You told," before he climbed on his bike and rode away.

I wanted to prove my innocence. If I'd been thinking clearly, I would have pointed out how foolish it would have been for me to tell since he was paying me to keep quiet. But Clive chose that moment to lower his pinched face to mine and say with disgust, "Nice going, Nancy," as if the whole incident had been my fault. Fearing I had earned a reputation as a snitch as well as a book-worm, I responded desperately, "I didn't know about his mom and Vreen! Honest!"

Clive just curled his skinny upper lip and snarled, "Come and get your papers," an order he then shouted at the group slowly pedalling toward us.

As so often happened after someone had been picked on merci-lessly, the atmosphere had become sombre. Far down the road, Bints's coat was just a blip of colour, and as it faded from view, I felt more than my financial prospects diminishing. Bints's wounded, accusing look seemed to hit home, even though I suspected I wouldn't have revealed his secret even if I had known it and wasn't getting money to keep it. But was that true? Maybe I would have told. I stared into the now-empty distance until the surrounding bodies and voices returned me to the cold facts of the late afternoon, the printed news to deliver under a smudged and rapidly setting sun.

eleven

AMAZINGLY, THE COLD AND SNOW and ice persisted, day after day, past the closing of school. "A white Christmas," my mother said, the memory of childhood sleigh rides on frozen sloughs soft in her eyes. Her nostalgia added to the pleasurable anticipation I felt as the winter solstice came and went. Each morning I woke to the white brilliance on the ground and the startling absence of rain sounds, and each night I fell asleep with that radiant silence around me like a shield, keeping the familiar at bay. But even when the familiar did push through, as it did on Christmas Eve, it carried the same trembling and unexpected magic.

"Did you ever hear tell," he said, pausing to lick the cigarette papers he held in the long, dark-haired fingers of one knob-knuckled hand, "of Sweeney Todd, the demon barber of Fleet Street?" A few flakes of tobacco stuck to the moist underside of his thick upper lip as he leaned closer toward Angie and Steven huddled on either side of my father on the chesterfield. The twins' eyes widened as they shook their heads nervously, and my father grinned with contagious expectation. Even my own pulse quickened slightly.

A fire of driftwood bark snapped and crackled in the grate, filling the living room with a capering ruddiness that suffused Mr. Graveridge's face with light, as though his blood had risen to the tiny area of exposed skin below his eyes, which were so large-pupilled that they seemed to be no colour other than black. His beard, almost completely grey, was as full as Ezra's, and he had surprisingly thick and long hair for an old man—it fell well over the finely bristled tufts of his huge ears, which were so gnarled and hard that they resembled conches.

"Well now," he continued, leaning back in the chair, "Sweeney Todd was the worst devil of a man who ever walked this earth, a right brute and no mistake." He fingered a butane lighter from his dun woollen vest and flicked it on. The tiny flame burned dangerously close to the bottom of his beard. "Are you sure you want to hear about him? You might have nightmares." His voice, British only in the occasional phrase and the faintest trace of an accent, was deep but smooth, and resonated with far-away worlds and possibilities that belonged to the pages of leather-bound and snuff-stained books.

Angie and Steven nodded in unison, pressing their pyjama-clad bodies even tighter against our father, who grinned at our mother across the room. She stood in the doorway to the kitchen, absently drying a supper plate with a dishtowel, her mouth slightly open, her attention fixed on our guest.

I looked at the stuffed pheasants on the wall above the mantel-piece, their auburn wings outspread in permanent flight and deep-ened by the fire glow, their glass eyes sparkling; they seemed to have come to life and were about to flap their way to freedom.

Mr. Graveridge lit his cigarette and inhaled slowly, letting it go briefly as he adjusted his position in the chair, lifting one

woollen-socked foot up onto the opposite knee. Whenever he
did this with his cigarette, I wondered if he had fixed it firmly
in the gap between his front teeth, which were as large as the rest
of him. He was well over six feet tall, with shoulders broad as a
barn beam, though slightly stooped, and a capacious chest. I
always marvelled at how he managed to fit his huge frame into
the chair so easily, stretching his long legs beneath the coffee
table as if he was accustomed to being in that position much
more often than the one time each year he was our guest. He
fidgeted briefly, and then, behind a cloud of exhaled smoke,
began his tale.

"It was in the great city of London, more than a hundred years
ago, when there were no cars or electric lights. A dark and frightening place it was, especially in Fleet Street, the part of the city I'm
talking about. A real rogue's paradise. This one black and drizzly
night, a young fellow from the country all wrapped up in a cloak
against the wind and rain with his hat pulled down right over his
eyes . . ." Mr. Graveridge made the motion of jerking a hat brim
down before finishing the sentence. "He stopped outside the old
church of St. Dunstan's. A funny noise made him look up, a kind
of whirring like. And what do you think he saw but a big clock
sticking out from the side of the church. A ruddy big clock it was
too, with two big wooden doors on each side of the face. And the
hour was just striking. The young fellow, he blinks up into the rain
and sees these two gold savages holding clubs come out of the
doors and strike the bells—one, two, three, four, five times!—and
then they disappear again. These were the famous giants of St.
Dunstan's. People came from all around to see them."

Mr. Graveridge took another lengthy drag on his cigarette, and
said teasingly to Angie and Steven, "I even saw them once myself,
when I was just a nipper, not much older than yourselves." He

widened his eyes and spoke in a sort of frightened whisper as he leaned forward again. "And I saw the barbershop too. Just like that young fellow on that rainy night." He scratched at his huge fleshy nose with a broken-nailed finger, then went on in a louder voice to describe Sweeney Todd's evil-looking shop with its dirt-encrusted windows in which hung a sign, almost unreadable behind the grime: "Easy shaving for a penny / As good as you will find any."

I had heard the story each Christmas Eve for several years, and though the telling still gave me a delicious shudder at the scariest parts, I did not share Angie and Steven's rapt attention. I was still disappointed that Ezra had not shown up for supper. "He was pleased to be asked," Mr. Graveridge had told my mother, "but you know how he is." Jerris and I had seen him just the day before, walking rapidly as usual, head down, toward the diner. Through the plate glass, we saw with great excitement that he was seated with one of the Lum daughters. At last, we thought, something is going to happen. We expected the pig-faced man to arrive at any time, waving his shotgun wildly in front of him. But after an uneventful half-hour, we decided to do some more collecting for the paper and then return, hoping that he might still be there. But he was gone when we got back, and we were faced with the unpleasant prospect that the mystery behind the shooting at the tree lot would never be deepened, let alone solved.

"Ah but he was an ugly character," I heard Mr. Graveridge go on. "Loose in the joints, gangly, with this big drooping mouth, kind of cruel like. And hands what were bigger than these here." He extended his own, palms up. They looked as large as the supper plates we'd just eaten from. "And his fingers were stubs with the filthy nails bitten down to nothing. But all that wasn't nearly so bad as his hair. Aaaaghhh." He made a sour face, then paused, as if it was too awful to continue. My brother and sister squirmed with pleasure. "Thick as a ruddy hedge it was, yellow and greasy, and he kept all his combs and scissors in it. So when he moved his head, the whole mess shook and clanked something terrible."

Mr. Graveridge proceeded to describe Sweeney Todd's disturbing hyenalike laugh and his unpleasant squint and his odd way of telling his customers to sit in the chair so that he could "polish them off." Then he described the unusual barber chair, of sturdy oak with a padded seat, positioned strangely in the middle of the shop, away from all the tables and bowls on the counter against the wall.

"And even worse," he continued, "was the unpleasant odour coming from the dad-blamed thing. Bad as a fish hold you haven't cleaned out all summer, only faint like. Our young fellow sniffed at the air and looked up nervously at the barber. He was stropping a razor, back and forth, back and forth, and grinning in a sick kind of way. I'll tell you, the hairs on the young fellow's neck rose right up."

"I'm scared," Angie whimpered, "I don't like it."

My mother went and sat on the other side of her. "Shh, it's okay, honey."

Mr. Graveridge had hesitated for only a second, one shaggy, grey eyebrow cocked mischievously.

I had heard it all before, though with slight differences, but I was curious to see how Angie and Steven would react. Mr. Graveridge had leaned forward again, his cigarette free in his mouth, his hands splayed flat on his massive thighs.

"Sweeney says, 'Oh, begging your pardon sir, I forgot the hot towels. I'll just step into the back room and get some.' And our young fellow, he's so nervous he's started thinking to himself, I'll just get up and leave before this strange barber comes back. But just then," Mr. Graveridge raised his voice, "there was a loud creaking sound and then a big whooooshhhh, and before our young fellow could even move, the floor opened up under the chair and the chair pitched back through the hole, our young fellow tumbling through with it!"

Angie was sobbing now and hiding her head in our mother's apron. Steven was trying to be brave, but I could tell that he wasn't enjoying himself much either.

Mr. Graveridge waited longer this time. Then, with a smile and a shrug, he said, "Oh, that's all right, little ones. I won't tell you any more if you haven't a mind for it."

"I think that would be best, Rodney," my mother smiled gratefully.

He suddenly turned toward me. "Now young Callum there, he always loved to hear of Sweeney Todd." He chuckled deeply and at length. "I can still see him jumping when the chair gave out and another one flipped up from the hole!"

I remembered it well too. For months, I couldn't pass Mr. Hathaway's barbershop without a shudder, and I refused to eat anything remotely resembling a meat pie (Sweeney Todd's victims were chopped up and made into meat pies, which were then sold in the shop next door by his evil accomplice, Mrs. Lovett) for fear of finding a fingernail in it.

"Maybe next year," my father said apologetically, recognizing our guest's disappointment. Mr. Graveridge was never so animated as when he told the tale of Sweeney Todd.

"All right, off to bed," my mother ordered, to Angie and Steven's prolonged but half-hearted "aaaawwws," expressed as if they knew they'd missed their chance to stay up late.

Mr. Graveridge took another drag of his cigarette and looked at me again. "What do you say, young Callum? Are you getting too big for Old Cut-em-Up?"

"No," I protested. "I like hearing it."

But he just grinned as if he knew better. I watched the shadows of the fire flicker at the base of his throat, where great tufts of grey hair stuck up above his flannel shirt. "Getting to be a big lad now," he said. "Be fishing your own boat one of these summers, like as not."

"A ways off for that yet, Rod," my father said, amused.

"Aaghh, what is the boy, eleven, twelve? Hell's bells, I was holding down two jobs at his age."

My father kissed Angie and Steven goodnight before remarking humorously, "Sure, but you were probably a full-grown man by then."

"Right you are," Mr. Graveridge nodded appreciatively, his grey hair swinging loose around his shoulders. "I was a right heifer as a lad, god's truth. My mum always said she couldn't believe summat the size of me came out of her little body."

A chunk of bark collapsed in the grate with a whoosh.

"Where was that when I needed it?" Mr. Graveridge chuckled. "There goes another one for the demon barber, young Callum."

I stared at the fire, equal parts red and black, like a lava spill. The warmth of it almost burned my cheeks, and the smoke hung in pale cobwebs from the ceiling, almost overwhelming the lingering aroma of our roast beef supper.

The night went on. My father and Mr. Graveridge spoke calmly about the prospects for the spring fishing season while my mother finished cleaning up in the kitchen. A wind had come up outside, and intermittently a gust would blow into the chimney and enliven the fire. I sat still in my chair, bored with the conversation, but for some reason unwilling to rise and leave the room. I didn't want to help my mother in the kitchen, but it was more than that. Mr. Graveridge's voice rolled on, deep and smooth, like the sound of the ocean from a half-mile inland, and I waited for something that would equal the promise of that sound. I had no idea of what this might be, though I knew that the excitement of the approaching Christmas morning was only part of it. Mr. Graveridge's acknowledgement of my age seemed to have frozen me into an inarticulate self-awareness. I did not thrill to the story of Sweeney Todd as I had done only the year before, yet I wanted that thrill to return. Where had it gone? The fire and the wind in the chill night, the red and black larger than any room could contain, crackled and gusted, and not even the terrified pheasants, desperate for escape, could tear their nailed bodies from the wall. I watched the firelight flick over my bare hands, and wanted to pull them away. But I couldn't. The moment held me, the voices and elements like shackles that never touched my skin.

And then, just as suddenly, the moment broke. I heard my mother praising the Royal Family, how nice it was for us to have that bond with England and not the States. And Mr. Graveridge remarked, as he always did, that it was nice to be in the Commonwealth where tradition was honoured. "Not like in that land of ruffians," he growled, pointing vaguely southward. And then my father told the story of how, while driving to Ontario one summer many years ago to visit relatives, he had somehow wound up in a run-down section of Detroit, and a Negro fellow, very friendly, had told him that he'd better get out of there because whites weren't very welcome. "Can you imagine," my father shook his head sadly, "a country where people can't get along well enough to share the same neighbourhood?"

I was back in it, the familiar Christmas Eve of my childhood, the adult conversations I couldn't quite follow, the warm fire and comforting aromas of woodsmoke and roast beef, and a toast of hot rum and eggnog to usher in a new year of health and prosperity.

Finally, the time came for me to go to bed. Mr. Graveridge pulled himself to his full height and, dwarfing my hand in his, said with a gravity I always found flattering, "The best of the season to you, young Callum." My father saluted me, and I allowed my mother to peck me on the cheek. Then, with the pheasants firmly settled on their varnished mounts, I left the living room.

Twenty minutes later, too restless to sleep, I crept back down the hallway, drawn forward by the sonorous voices now unconstrained without my inhibiting presence. I had eavesdropped on other occasions when my parents had guests, but what I heard was usually unrewarding, dull in ways I couldn't even imagine. Tonight was different.

I wasn't in the hallway more than a few minutes before the subject of Ezra came up. My mother commented sadly that it was a shame he hadn't come for supper. "A man should be with other people at Christmas," she said.

"He might be," my father said. "You don't know that he isn't."

"What people?" my mother replied, annoyed. "I don't mean that bunch who get their holiday cheer out of a bottle."

"He does have family, you know," my father said almost inaudibly.

Mr. Graveridge made a dismissive sound deep in his throat. "Family!" He almost spat the word. "You ought to know better than that, Mack."

A brief silence ensued, eventually filled by Mr. Graveridge's voice, more conciliatory. "Of course, much of that business was before your time here. Margaret, though, she remembers Ezra's dad."

"I'm afraid so."

"A right devil if there ever was one."

I crept a little farther up the hall, as far as I could go without being seen. The fire threw grotesque shadows against the far wall. I stared at them as Mr. Graveridge spoke.

"Did I never tell you about the time, Mack, that I found Ezra in the shed, damned near starved to death, and more beat-up than a wrapped sockeye? No, didn't think I had. Don't much care to recall it, to be honest with you. Almost killed old Hemsworth over it. Broke a few bones, and no mistake. Begging your pardon, Margaret." He lowered his voice and I had to strain to hear the rest of the story.

Ezra had been only five or six at the time, and Mr. Graveridge had taken a shine to him because he was always down at the wharf, wanting to go out on the boats. "Hard to believe now, I suppose, but he was a cute nipper, all big dark eyes and he didn't talk so damned fast then. 'Course, he didn't say much either. At first, I thought he was a bit off, the way he just stared and hardly spoke, except to ask if he could come out fishing. But there was something about him, I don't know how to describe it. Maybe not having any nippers of my own, and it being just after my good lady had passed over, god rest her, I was just happy to have him around."

Mr. Graveridge paused again, and I heard a spoon clink against a cup. "Anyway, I knew something of his dad, of course. Can't fish the river and not know what a fellow's like by the way he behaves on a drift, eh Mack? You only knew him when he was old, and he'd mellowed by then. But before . . ."

Without going into great detail, probably out of respect for my mother, Mr. Graveridge described Ezra's father as a nasty, greedy man, who, like so many of his kind, was also a coward. "When Ezra," he continued soberly, "started showing up on my float with bruises all over him, and wouldn't say where he got them, I didn't have much trouble figuring it out. So when the little fellow didn't show up for a week—and this was in August, with the fishing going full bore—I knew something wasn't right."

Mr. Graveridge had gone over to the Hemsworth place one morning, and, finding no one there, had decided to take a look around. "Still don't know to this day," he said in an awestruck tone, "where I got the idea to bust into the shed. The Lord's will, you might call it."

He had found Ezra inside, hunched in a corner, as far from his own excrement as he could get. "I'll not forget it till the day I die," Mr. Graveridge went on, a slight catch in his voice. "He was eating sawdust. It was on his lips and he had a handful of it. Good Christ, it was all I could do to keep my wits about me. The poor little fellow whimpered as I moved closer to him, but he didn't fuss when I scooped him up and carried him to my place. Skin and bones he was. I'll tell you, if it hadn't been for some of the others on the wharf that night, I'd have killed Hemsworth, sure as you're sitting there." His voice was firmer again. "As it was, by the time they'd pulled me off, I'd done damage enough."

Ezra had stayed a few days with Mr. Graveridge and then returned home. "I'd not have let him," he explained, "if I wasn't sure that Hemsworth was scared to death of me. And I made a point of reminding him why he needed to be every time I saw him. Oh, he knew, right enough, that if he ever touched a hair on that little fellow's head I'd have taken his own right off his shoulders. Begging your pardon, Margaret. This isn't a fit subject for a lady."

"That's all right, Rodney," my mother said almost inaudibly. "I can't say I'm at all surprised. He was a brute of a man."

"Better to have no family," Mr. Graveridge continued with disgust, "if what you've got is a nest of ruddy vipers." He lowered his voice. "I'm not sure what's been going on lately, but those brothers of his are up to something. Ezra's keeping quiet, as always, but I know when something's troubling him. Just last week I saw him down at the wharf. Hanging a spring net, he was, but he could hardly move his right side. 'Course, when I asked him about it, he just clamped his jaw shut, you know how he does, and I could get nothing out of him but grunts."

I wanted desperately to announce the reason for Ezra's sore side, but I restrained myself: Christmas Eve was not the time to risk my parents' displeasure. In any case, the conversation soon switched away from Ezra, and though I stayed in the hall until my eyes began to grow heavy, he was not mentioned again.

Back in my room, I was too tired to think deeply about what Mr. Graveridge had revealed of Ezra's past. But as I fell asleep I saw one of Ezra's burning black eyes fixed at the centre of the dark, and I could not be sure whether the intense gaze was going to widen or shut and vanish forever.

At first, I took the tapping at the window for another storm. But as I emerged more fully from sleep, I realized that the sound was too loud and irregular to be rain. A staccato burst of taps, a brief pause, and then another, longer burst: the pattern quickly brought me from my bed to the still-dark glass.

As I peered out, a beam of light rose suddenly from beneath the outside sill. I jumped back, my heart pounding. The light swiftly lowered again and brought the tiny moon of Jerris's face into view. He lifted his hand into the light and motioned for me to open the window.

"Come on, hurry up," he said in an excited whisper as soon as I had done so. "Get dressed, come on, hurry." Gusts of earth-rich air blew into the room with his words.

"What is it? What's going on?" I hadn't recovered from the shock of his appearance, though it had certainly brought me fully awake.

"It's Ezra," he answered. But when I still stood there, gaping at him, he burst out with, "He's dead!"

I couldn't believe it. My mouth opened wide and I felt weak with fear and excitement.

"I found him," Jerris went on rapidly, his head stuck through the open frame, the flashlight beam shooting out from the right side of his face and hitting me in the midsection. "Come and see, come on, hurry up."

"It's still dark out," I said weakly, afraid to move.

"So what? I've got a flashlight." Jerris spoke with impatience as he pointed the beam at my face.

I shut my eyes and stepped back. The motion encouraged me to dress, which I did hurriedly as Jerris urged me on. I returned to the window and looked closely at his face; it was half-shadowed in the gloom but I noticed some spots of black mud on his cheeks, vivid against the habitual blushing redness of his skin. The unmistakable odour of the ditches and sloughs rose off his parka, a heavy mix of rushes, muddy water, and muskrat. I knew without asking that he'd been checking his trapline. It was just like Jerris, I thought, to be doing something like that on Christmas morning.

I climbed through the open window and landed with a squelching sound on the ground. Only then did I notice that the air was warmer than it had been in weeks, warm enough to have started melting the snow. I breathed deeply, dazed by the returning earth-smell with its heavy wetness. To the east, a few orange streaks of light, small and faint, undershone the black clouds, the edges of which inked the surrounding night.

Jerris hurried off at such speed that I had to put my head down and follow or else lose sight of him. At the edge of the plum orchard he allowed me to catch up, and then we plunged together through the trees, the beam of light splashing on the slippery earth in front of us.

As we moved farther away from our houses, up the dyke and eastward toward town, my fear and excitement increased. Dead! The word had such weight to it, sounded like the thump of a body dropped on the floor. I could not imagine Ezra dead. It wasn't possible. Jerris might as well have told me that the river had dried up or that the mountains had vanished. Only the speed of our progress kept me from thinking clearly enough about the situation to realize that we shouldn't be involved. Even so, I ran a little to be alongside Jerris, and breathlessly suggested that we should tell someone.

"We will," he assured me, not even turning his head, "but I want you to see first."

Dawn was breaking. The orange strips dissolved into broader swaths just beyond the blue-black Coast range; the faint glow shone dully between the darkness of the peaks and the darkness of the heavy cloud cover. Bird noises rose up from the marsh as we hurried along, and we could see for a greater distance as each minute passed. Without a word, Jerris switched off his flashlight. Soon we had gone by the harbour, the drip of ice off the bows and masts like a miniature, contained rainfall. It was too dark to see Ezra's bootsteps on the snowy wharf, but I looked for them anyway, expecting that his body would rise up from its familiar passage to cackle gleefully at our foolishness. "Goddamnya, goddamnya." I heard the rhythmic echo of his voice behind our breathing and the morning's subtle stirrings. "Goddamnya, goddamnya."

We cut north, over the tiny dyke bridge to the silt island on the far side of the harbour. Here the cottonwoods and poplars reached blackly into the clouds, the branches and the air merging softly. A maze of sloughs angling off from the river's main channel carved the small island into sections. We stayed on the narrow gravel road until we had passed the "shit lagoon," a depressed, rectangular area of flooded marsh that handled much of the town's effluent flow. Just to the west of it, a skinny trail of velvety mulch, made softer by the slushy snow, led farther north through a stand of mossy cottonwoods and sprawling blackberry bushes to the open marsh, an almost level distance of faded bullrushes far beyond which the Coast Mountains were rapidly turning a lighter shade of blue.

But we didn't go that far. Halfway down the trail, Jerris veered to the west through a gap in the trees and bushes. We trudged under the tangled branch cover of the massive trees, a black moisture dripping from them slow as candle wax. The thick trunks, around which morning-glory vines had twisted to a ten-foot height, seemed to close together as we passed them, until it felt as if we were being shut into a room. Birds flew up out of the woods as we advanced, and rabbits, the offspring of abandoned Easter presents, scattered rapidly off the trail in front of us, like kicked snow.

Finally, when we had almost reached the western edge of the woods where they gave way to open marsh and the river, Jerris stopped and pointed at a huge holly bush squeezed in between two blackberry bushes. "There," he said, "that's where he is."

I hesitated, my eyes fixed on the holly, its waxy-green, sharp-barbed leaves and bright red berries stark amidst the softer, surrounding foliage. It was at least ten feet high, crooked, with drifts of snow on the boughs, and dabs, like tiny, pointed caps, on some of the berries. As I stood there, some of the snow, slightly melted, slid off a bough and thumped to the earth. Looking down, I expected to see a dark-clad body sprawled at the base of the bush, but I saw only a deeper whiteness of snow. Out of the corner of my eye Jerris stepped into view, and bent down. "Right here," he repeated, but still I didn't move.

It was lighter now, though sunless and grey. The air was like silted water being slowly cleared. Birds chirped louder in the branches above us and flitted rapidly in the bushes nearby. I could just see the river, thin as a draggled shoestring, through the woods beyond the marsh, and the hazy outline of trees on other small islands.

Jerris lay almost flat on the ground when I finally stepped up to the base of the holly. He seemed to be sniffing the snow. He looked up at my approach, his eyes wide, his mouth open. In the clearer light, I could see that he had mud caked around his jaw and that his jeans were soaked, as if he'd fallen in a ditch while checking his traps.

"He's gone!" he said with amazement. Then, more quietly, disappointed, "He was right here."

I looked to where he pointed. A depression in the snow and some bent lower boughs on the holly suggested that something *had* been there. Jerris was so shocked that he seemed about to dig for a body under the snow. I moved closer. A confusion of boot-prints led back the few feet to the trail, where they disappeared in the marks of general traffic indistinct now that the melting had begun.

I called to Jerris, and together we stood silent over the prints.

"Somebody must have come and got him," he said excitedly. Then, with even more excitement, he added, "The guy who killed him I bet!"

I stared at the scuffed ground, then looked back to the holly. A little group of red berries jewelled the area by the bent branches; I figured they must have been shaken off when Ezra landed in the bush. I looked up at the barbed, shiny leaves, each point sharp as a fish hook, and was about to turn away when I saw a tuft of wool snagged on one of the points. I picked it off. It was dark, a little wet and greasy. A tiny piece of a sweater. Again, I called Jerris.

"See," he said. "I told you he was here."

"I believe you. I never said I didn't."

We stared at each other, as though just realizing the enormity of the situation.

"Are you sure he was dead?" I asked.

Jerris thought hard for several seconds. "Pretty sure. He wasn't moving or nothing."

"He could have been sleeping."

"Out here?"

He had a good point. Why would Ezra sleep in the woods when there were unlocked net sheds not far away? Besides, if he had decided to sleep in the woods, he wouldn't choose a holly bush for a bed.

"Drunk maybe?" I suggested.

Jerris brushed his muddy bangs out of his eyes. "I didn't smell nothing."

I thought some more, conscious of the increasing light, aware that I needed to get home before the day fully arrived. "Was he beat up?"

"I don't think so." Jerris suddenly kicked at the bush, shaking some more berries down, and cursed. "I should have looked closer. But . . ." He paused, embarrassed. "It was dark and . . ."

I nodded, knowing I'd have been terrified too. Even now, I was afraid.

After another prolonged silence, I hit on the obvious solution. "I'll bet he was faking."

Jerris's eyes widened to seal size. "Yeah. I'll bet he was! He was faking! He wants the pig man to think he's dead!"

I nodded, uneasy. Somehow, Jerris's ready agreement made me draw back from the idea. The surrounding silence, the isolated spot we stood in, seemed unsafe and very far from the pages of a comic book. The whole business was too real for comfort, though a part of me greatly enjoyed the danger. But, in truth, I couldn't believe that Ezra was actually dead. I had to raise the possibility, though, if only to keep Jerris from getting too carried away.

"But what if somebody did kill him?" I asked.

We stared at each other, unblinking. Then, after discussing the situation for a while, we decided we should wait; maybe we would find Ezra if we went searching for him. This sounded like the most reasonable plan, and so we turned away from the holly and the scuffed ground, soon skirted the shit lagoon—foul in the ripening day, its generators like mock fountains thrusting up the brown murk—climbed back on the dyke and hurried past the harbour—Ezra's boat blacker and stiller than usual—westward into the absent letters of the Home Oil sign, under the heavy overcast home.

Before noon that Christmas Day a great downpour crashed out of the grey-black, a sky so low and oppressive it was as though a giant jellyfish had clamped itself to the air.

In the afternoon I stood alone in the dissolving white of the front yard, leaning forlornly on a new hockey stick, watching the plum trees drop sheet after sheet of tissue paper and turn blacker by the minute. All the excitement of the past two weeks was leaving with the snow, replaced by a growing sense of guilt and fear that not even the pleasure of receiving gifts could keep down for long.

I had not told my parents or anyone else about the possibility of Ezra being dead. I knew enough about him now, especially from overhearing Mr. Graveridge's story of the locked shed, that his mystery was no longer so impersonal. And I still believed, or at least tried very hard to believe, that he could not have been killed. But the effort to believe had begun to trouble me. What if he *had* been killed, and it came out that I knew something about it but had kept quiet? And yet I could not bring myself to tell my parents. Maybe I'll see Ezra today, I reasoned hopefully, anxious for the problem to resolve itself.

But the days passed, wet and dark, and though Jerris and I searched for hours we did not find Ezra. His boat remained black and still. He did not show up at any of his regular haunts. One more day, Jerris and I told each other, just one more day.

Meanwhile, I tried to allay the guilt by ridding myself of any that came from other sources. To my surprised relief, Mrs. Edmundson had not phoned the *Sun* to complain about my week-long failure to deliver her paper. A kind of gratitude made me reconsider my decision to avoid her. And so, after Boxing Day, when delivery resumed, I paused on the plywood bridge above the brimming ditch then forced myself to ride around to the back of the duplex.

It was even drabber in the rain, soggy and peeling as a wet card-board box. Steady drips off the sloped roof made a bead curtain over the veranda, whose leaky roof allowed puddles to form on the mossy planks. Even the nearby willow moaned miserably, rain like oily rags in its branches. I leaned my bike against the trunk, hopeful that I could run up the steps, plop the paper in front of the door, and run off again before she could appear. But the door creaked open just as I dropped the paper and returned to the steps.

"Who is it? Who's there? Leslie, is that you?"

Her voice sounded frailer than I remembered, more brittle; the words trembled under the weight of the rain.

I turned back and shouted into the weather. "It's Callum! The paperboy!"

The door slowly opened wider and her thin figure appeared. She leaned her kerchiefed head forward. The dark glasses were a shock in the black afternoon.

"Who?" she said, almost whispering, then raised a trembling hand to her throat, as though to force the word out.

I repeated my name, which she greeted with a prolonged silence. Finally, she dropped her hand listlessly to her side, and said, as if to herself, something about the kettle. Then she turned back into the room, leaving the door wide open.

Little had changed from my earlier visits. The wooden radio played softly, glowing eerily with the yearning music, and the air was so stale and warm that it felt solid, as if a wet towel had been applied to my face. From across the room, Mrs. Edmundson's long-dead first husband stared mournfully at me, until somehow I began to imagine that the song on the radio was coming from his cold lips.

A sudden crash from the kitchen snapped me out of my drowsing reverie. It sounded as if a cup or plate had broken, but Mrs. Edmundson said nothing.

"Are you okay?" I finally asked into the unnerving silence. When she did not respond, I asked the question a little louder, already wondering if I should run and get help. Instead, I walked anxiously past the china cabinet and peered through the doorway into the kitchen, a room even darker than the one behind me. Mrs. Edmundson stood trembling above the shards of a plate scattered over the peeling linoleum. She was staring into her upturned hands, which she held out from her body as if they too were something she might drop if she wasn't careful.

"Mrs. Edmundson?" I said cautiously.

She did not seem to hear me. Just then, the kettle on the stove began to whistle, but she took no notice of it either.

After a long pause, she lifted her face to me and, raising her hands a little, said weakly, "It fell."

The kettle whistled at a higher pitch, but she did not turn to it. She just went back to staring at the broken plate on the floor.

"I'll pick it up," I said, anxious to do something. Mrs. Edmundson didn't move an inch as I crawled around her, gathering the shards of plate in my hands. Now the kettle screeched, and I was about to rise to move it from the burner when a loud male voice cried out behind me, "Mother! Are you all right! Mother!"

I heard a heavy, rapid tread, and turned, still on my knees, toward the front room. Mr. Edmundson, stricken and pale, his tie flipped up over his shoulder, stood gaping at his mother. He didn't notice me. In a trembling voice, he said, "Oh Mother, Mother," and his large hands twitched spasmodically at his sides, as if moving for hers, which had remained motionless. I watched as he swallowed hard, the tears welling in his eyes, deepening their brown until I thought the colour was going to flow down his cheeks. "Mother," he repeated weakly.

I looked back at Mrs. Edmundson. She hadn't moved from her position, but she had lifted her eyes to her son and blinked at him in a kind of wordless plea. I felt trapped in the space between them, as if I were somehow keeping them apart. The fractious cry of the kettle filled the air around us, a thin, piercing scream that seemed to come from both of them, from the photos in the other room, the walls, everywhere, even my own mouth. I rose quickly and lifted the kettle from the burner.

The motion woke Mr. Edmundson from his panicked state. Slowly, he took in the rest of the kitchen, his watery eyes eventually settling on me where I waited, between his mother and the stove, clutching pieces of broken plate in both hands. Embarrassed, I placed them carefully on the counter.

"What happened?" he asked dully, with no surprise at my presence.

"She dropped a plate," I answered, nodding toward the counter. Then, guiltily, I added, "For the cookies, I guess."

My guilt didn't seem to register with him at all. I had the odd sensation of being invisible, since he gave no indication that he remembered or cared who I was. He looked at his mother again, and swallowed hard. Then, with a suddenness that startled me, he cast a helpless, desperate look in my direction, a look that, along with the tears, I had never seen in a grown man before. I didn't know how to respond. I just returned his gaze, dumbly, unsure of what he expected me to do.

Fortunately, his helplessness didn't last long. Rousing himself, he stepped across the kitchen and, bowing his head to hers, took his mother gently by the elbow and steered her into the main room. I followed, but stopped several feet behind while he settled her in the armchair, kneeling at the side of it to place a blanket over her lap.

"It fell," she said suddenly and helplessly, her dark glasses level with his eyes.

"I know, I know," he comforted in a low voice. "It's all right, there's no harm done, it's all right."

Just as I was about to make a quiet exit, he turned and asked if I had seen her cigarettes.

When I answered that they were on the kitchen counter, he asked me to bring them to him. I did so, and then stood awkwardly by as he lit a cigarette and held it to his mother's lips, while she inhaled slowly.

"There now, that's better," he said in the same soothing voice, and pulled the cigarette away as she leaned back in the chair behind a thin web of smoke.

For a half-minute, only a soft, wordless melody emanating from the radio disturbed the patter of the rain against the windows and on the roof. I could hardly breathe in the almost-silence. The smoke, warmth, and plain discomfort of the situation made me desperate to be back in the fresh air.

But Mr. Edmundson rose to his feet once more, and with a subtle motion of his hand, directed me to the mahogany dining table between the screen door and the kitchen. We sat on opposite sides and looked blankly at each other.

"Colin, isn't it?" he finally asked.

"Callum," I answered softly.

"Yes, yes, of course." His face was as flushed as mine felt, but his large features looked blurred, washed out, and his eyes had pooled to an unbelievable depth. With a giant, silent heave of his chest, he awkwardly removed his brown suit jacket and sat facing me again, in his white shirtsleeves, large sweat stains spreading out from beneath his arms.

Almost mechanically, Mr. Edmundson pulled his tie into a straighter position. Then he drew another great breath and, after exhaling, said simply, "She's slipping."

I nodded, and turned away briefly to where his mother's thin figure sat in front of the faint green radio-glow. Again, I felt as though I were on a ship anchored to wait out a storm; the rain washed in a steady rhythm around us, and I would not have been surprised if the china started sliding along the shelves of the cabinet.

"Old age," Mr. Edmundson said suddenly, his eyes wet and unblinking, "is a terrible thing."

When he spoke again, there was more resolve in his voice.

"Callum, I wonder if you'd do me a favour?" He took his wallet from his back pants pocket and opened it as he continued. "If I gave you, say, five dollars a week, would you check in on her every day, just to make sure she hasn't fallen or left the stove on or anything like that?"

I must have looked terrified, because he hurried to reassure me.

"I'll give you my number at work, and if anything's wrong, just call and I'll be over in five minutes."

I could think of no excuse for not doing what he asked, apart from the truth, which was a fear of the responsibility along with an aversion to the potential boredom that would accompany it. But he had already addressed the fear, and I couldn't bring myself to mention the aversion.

"It would be a big help to me," he added by way of subtle pressure. "I can't keep coming in the afternoon. I can be here in the mornings before work, and on my lunch hour, and after work. So if you could just check on her in the afternoon?" He pulled a five-dollar bill from his wallet and placed it on the table, not pushing it toward me, just gently laying it down between his large, fleshy hands, even paler now against the tabletop.

"Okay," I said, the money a definite prod to my decision. Yet I did not reach for the bill. Instead, I pushed my chair back and got to my feet. "I have to go now," I explained. "I have to finish my route."

Mr. Edmundson rose immediately, and slid the bill across the table as he did so. "Oh, and I'll give you a key to get in as well. You can knock, but if she's fallen or . . ." The idea seemed to weaken him again, and he looked back at his mother with such quickness that it was as though he feared she had already hurt herself.

I picked up the money and, a few seconds later, accepted the key out of his sweaty, suety palm. He stared at me with such gratitude that I blushed, more anxious now than ever to be outside.

"Thank you, Colin," he said as I opened the door.

"That's all right," I responded, and kept right on going.

And so the rain fell to the end of the year, into Mrs. Edmundson's dark willow and the dark willow outside the Haunted Bookshop and all the dark willows of Chilukthan. I rode past them, their high, swaying branches like empty cradles being rocked and rocked in stricken disbelief. I rode past them in the cool, grey days, my skin pressed with rain just as the pages I carried had been pressed with ink. I pedalled down the sluicing, burbling streets, bringing people the news I could read but not yet comprehend. And at night, the snow and ice long melted, only a rare star shining out of the cloudy gloom as a reminder of that lost brilliance, I rode from porchlight to porchlight, ringing doorbells to cry "Collecting for the *Sun!*" I stood before apartment intercoms, waiting to hear the staticky, frightened voices of the elderly say "Yes?" before I could give out the prepared phrase, the password. "Collecting for the *Sun!*" I'd announce firmly, my clipboard of subscription sheets in hand, my hopes set on large tips. And the faces, the kind, scared faces, would look down to the saved coins in their trembling hands, saved up in old jars on windowsills and mantelpieces, and then smile up at me, travelling over some vast, incomprehensible distance, and bid me on my way again.

twelve

ALL THROUGH THE HOLIDAYS, Jerris and I were keyed up with the pleasurable anxiety of knowing something that no one else knew, except for Ezra's killers, of course. For me, it was just like being a character in a comic or in one of the many Hardy Boys books I was then reading. Sometimes I even dreamed up titles for our own mystery—*The Case of the Vanishing Fisherman,* or *The Clue of the Great Blue Heron.*

Jerris and I would discuss the drama as we waited out the heaviest of the almost constant rains in one of our favourite spots, fifty feet up in a plank-and-driftwood tree fort in a riverside Douglas fir, or in an abandoned Plymouth in a vacant lot of waist-high grass near the centre of town. The storms would wash around us, their mournful hush insistent beyond our lowered voices and dampened faces, the days blackly roaming, like heavily panting dogs, toward the even blacker nights. What if it's true, we'd ask each other again and again, what if he really is dead? Should we tell someone about that morning at the holly bush? And we would cut another slice off the big chunk of bologna we'd bought, or take another handful of ketchup potato chips and another swig of grape Crush, and stare out through the dripping branches or blurred windshield, feeling a thousand miles away from the world we talked about with such fervour. At night we'd burn a candle or shine a flashlight and feel even more distant, snug as astronauts in a capsule whirling through space and time. And always the talk was of Ezra, of what we thought he'd been killed for, of what we knew about him. I related Mr. Graveridge's story about the locked shed and the beatings, while Jerris repeated his dad's belief that Ezra was fooling around with one of the Lum girls.

"Which one?" I asked, trying to think of some difference between them.

Jerris shrugged and stuffed another slice of bologna into his mouth. "I'm not sure," he said, chewing. "The one who doesn't talk, I think. You know, at the tree lot, the one who didn't say nothing."

We then considered the likelihood of Ezra being involved with her in that way, and decided that, while it was possible, it also wasn't very important. We finally concluded that Ezra's murder had to be about something much bigger than women or even money. We didn't know what that "something" was, but Jerris immediately warmed to my idea that the Lums and the pig-faced man were just a small part of a worldwide, maybe even cosmos-wide criminal organization plotting to take control of the planet.

"Sure," Jerris enthused, "and Ezra's hiding out, thinking up how he's going to stop them."

"Maybe it does have something to do with money," I reconsidered, remembering how many villains in the comics lusted after it. "You need money to take control of things. You have to pay people to work for you."

I could relate easily to the heightened emotions that swirled around money from my experiences at the paper shack and bookshop. And Jerris, who trapped and hunted and fished to earn an income (mostly spent to buy better equipment for trapping, hunting, and fishing), also knew the blood-rush that accompanied the handling of dollar bills. "How much?" was almost a mantra for Eric and me, though Jerris always seemed more interested in the activity that produced the money than the money itself. But sometimes I was coldly aware of the feel of the bills and coins, coldly and dimly aware of the power they represented. What else, besides money or violence, could a boy like Donald Bints use to protect himself? The two things were obviously connected. And so Jerris and I speculated endlessly on how money might be behind Ezra's disappearance—had he discovered some planned theft the Lums had masterminded? The more we thought about it, the more convinced we became that Ezra had disappeared because he wanted the Lums to believe he was dead. That way, he could buy the necessary time to figure out a way to stop them.

Yet I became less and less convinced as the days passed and as Jerris continued, with great enthusiasm, to keep a watch on the Royal Bank on the main street. The more he believed my theory, the more I considered the possibility that Ezra had been killed. If the Lums and the pig-faced man were criminals, maybe they *had* just beaten him to death and disposed of his body. The situation was serious enough that we could be in real trouble if we didn't talk, and I knew Jerris wasn't going to; he was having too much fun. But my worrying increased, until I reached a point where I just had to tell somebody all that we knew.

Fortunately, I didn't have to say a word. One blustery late afternoon I was riding my bike toward the bookshop after finishing my papers when I saw Ezra, head down as always, scurry up the main street. At first I thought I was imagining things.

But there could be no mistaking that figure, distinctly feverish in its movements, like a greased piston that kept the day turning over. In his grubby canvas jacket, red-soled gumboots, and tight skullcap he might have been any fisherman, but his ceaseless forward energy belonged to no one else. I stopped my bike on one side of the street and watched him come up the other. He barely raised his head, and I wondered again how he managed to see where he was going. He rushed closer out of the ash-grey, murky background. Three seagulls wheeled and cried high above him, their white the only brightness to the scene, their cries so harsh and constant that they seemed the result of Ezra's motion, the ungreased chafing of his limbs. I watched his approach, shocked at first. Then I felt a great relief, and, soon after, elation. He looked exactly the same, untouched, feverish as always. I felt silly that I had ever doubted his ability to survive. How could he be killed? It was inconceivable. I watched him veer into the diner and almost shouted "hooray!" as if he'd won some sort of victory, not only for himself but for me as well.

But this feeling quickly passed, overwhelmed by the rush of adrenalin that seeing him had produced. Wait until I tell Jerris, I thought, jumping on my bike and pedalling across to the diner. Staring through the plate glass as unobtrusively as possible, I saw Ezra sitting alone on a stool at the counter, no doubt waiting for a meal. It was exactly as if he'd never been gone at all. I stood there until the waitress brought him a plate of food, and then I decided I might as well go to the bookshop as planned. Why not? Ezra was back, and Jerris and I would be able to follow him whenever the opportunity arose. It never occurred to me that, if he vanished once, he could vanish again.

Those grey, blear winter days of the early new year, underlit by the stormy darkness of Ezra's life, were not completely unleavened. Always there was the vivid colour of the comic books and of Eric's hilarity and Jamie's wit, the light of limitless imagination, stories, and jokes. In school and at the bookshop there seemed no limit to the sheer involvement with the world of creation, to the delicious risks of testing the boundaries of authority.

Our principal, Mr. Southern, had begun his annual after-Christmas homage to the prime ministers, especially Lester B. Pearson and his role in founding the United Nations. Public duty, citizenship, international relations: these were the sturdy pillars on which he constructed his educational philosophy. "You children are the citizens of a great nation," he would routinely announce to us in the mornings over the PA system or in afternoon assemblies in the gymnasium. "Prime Minister Laurier believed that this century would belong to Canada, and it is your responsibility to ensure that his prophecy continues to be true." But whenever he mentioned a prime minister, all I could think of was "Whig or Grit?" "After who and before who?" in a panic inspired by the principal's mania for such facts.

Yet the whole school, from kindergarten to grade seven, was soon caught up in Mr. Southern's enthusiasm. The way he entrusted us with a special place in a glorious heritage and called us the "torchbearers of a shining legacy of humanitarian values" was infectious. Sometimes we rolled our eyes and snickered at his almost giddy passion, his boisterous leading of "Frère Jacques" or some voyageur paddling song he'd mimeographed for us to learn. But he also occasionally replayed Foster Hewitt's call of Paul Henderson's spine-tingling goal against the Russians in the 1972 Super Series. On a gloomy, wet morning the PA system would suddenly crackle to life and we would hear that familiar nasally whine: "Here's a shot. Henderson makes a wild stab for it and falls. Here's another shot. Right in front. They score! Henderson has scored for Canada!" It was hard for us to dislike or dismiss entirely a principal who appreciated the importance of hockey, even though he took no real notice of the NHL, except to mention, every now and then, how Maurice Richard had been the cause of a great riot in Montreal in the 1950s, a riot that helped explain our relationship with French Canada—quick! What year was the battle on the Plains of Abraham?—which was behind that silliness of a few years ago when some troublemakers thought the laws of the country didn't apply to them. Often we had only a vague idea of what he meant, but we were alternately impressed, intimidated, bored, and amused by him nonetheless. Even Eric, who mostly scoffed at Mr. Southern, enjoyed the frenzied atmosphere of what the principal called "United Nations Month."

Two highlights of this period were the "Choose a Country Project" (for upper grades) and the school-wide public-speaking contest, the finals of which were held in a big evening performance at the gymnasium with families attending and even a reporter and photographer from the *Chilukthan Clarion*, the local weekly paper. The spectrum of flags of all UN members hung everywhere, the band played as many anthems as they'd been able to learn, and Mr. Southern gave a rousing speech about Lester Pearson's great gift to the world, his visionary commitment to peace and diplomacy.

But before any of that happened, each student in each class of the upper grades had to choose a country on which to do a major research project. And the reward for having earned top grades through the fall was that you had the first choice of countries, Canada being excluded since we were expected to study it all year long. The British countries and the United States usually went early, followed by the countries of more specific student heritages (Greece, Yugoslavia, China, Italy). And several countries were popular either because they were newsworthy, like the Soviet Union or Vietnam, or because they were quirky—Australia with its kangaroos and koala bears always fared well, as did Egypt with its pyramids and tombs. Less successful were countries like Romania, India, the Philippines, and a whole host of others that just seemed blandly foreign.

I was in grade four and facing my first choice. On the morning of the selection, before school started, Eric and I were discussing what we planned to do. We stood against the brick wall in the undercover area, a roofed, cemented square with three sides unwalled and open to the playground, and indifferently watched a game of farthies (in which hockey cards were flung against the wall, the one coming closest without actually touching being the winner). It was windy and cool, and the flung cards kept fluttering short of the target like exhausted butterflies. A few feet away on our other side, some small girls were tossing their charm bracelets into hopscotch squares and giggling as they bent down and tried to pick up the charms without stepping out of the square.

"I think I'll go for Germany," Eric mused, pushing his thumb against his upper lip. "But I think Becky Glaboff might be German. She might try to get it instead."

"But won't you pick ahead of her?"

Eric shook his large head. His thick, black curls crashed like a wave. "Nah, I'm not doing so good with my marks. Too much horsing around, my mom says. Anyway, Becky's pretty smart."

I considered the problem for a minute, then had a brilliant thought. "Hey! You're not allowed to do the same country that you did before. Maybe she already did Germany!"

"Nope," Eric frowned. "She wasn't even in our school last year."

"Oh."

"But she might not be German," Eric said, perking up. "She's a redhead."

We chewed this over for a while as the shouts and giggles swirled around us.

"She doesn't look German," Eric finally continued. "Does she?"

"I don't know," I admitted. "What do Germans look like?"

"Like this, *mein Führer!*" Eric suddenly barked out and began goosestepping around in a tight circle. All we knew of Germany came from TV shows like *Hogan's Heroes* and *Monty Python's Flying Circus,* or from war movies and the war plots in comic books like *The Avengers.* Stormtroopers and serious commandants with heavy accents who said things like "Vee vill make you talk. Vee vill zee the documentz."

After a while Eric stopped clowning, and I asked him, seriously, why he wanted to choose Germany.

Breathing hard, and leaning back against the brick wall, he gave the Nazi salute and gasped "For zee Fatherland." Then he quickly added, "I don't know. It's just sort of interesting. That we've had two wars with them, I mean. You know how Sub-mariner's always swimming into U-boats and fighting Nazis? Well, what was it all about anyway?"

I shrugged, not sharing his interest but still recognizing the point of it. Eric was sometimes so serious in his curiosity that he left me behind. I still had no idea what country I would choose, though I expected to have either second or third choice in my class. But now, given Eric's considered selection, I felt some pressure not to be frivolous.

"What are you going to pick?" he asked, leaning toward me.

I wanted to tell him the truth, that I just wasn't very interested in any country. I was too busy, too preoccupied with my paper route and comics and Ezra to have much motivation or energy for school work. Nevertheless, I almost answered Vietnam, just because it had been on TV and on the front page of the paper so much. I figured that if war was important enough for Eric, then maybe it should be important for me too. But Vietnam seemed like it would be too hard, precisely because it had been so much in the news and adults would be bound to have lots of opinions on it.

"Luxembourg," I replied, straight-faced. It certainly sounded like the last country that would ever be in the news.

Eric guffawed. "Oh no, not those crazy Luxembourgers."

"Yep. It's pretty interesting. The Great Wall of Luxembourg and all that."

"Sure, the Sphinx and the Pyramids, I know about Luxembourg."

We chuckled ourselves into another brief silence. The two boys playing farthies were arguing about whose card was closest to the wall. A Frisbee rolled end-over-end past us.

"What *are* you going to do?" Eric finally asked again.

The joking had lightened my mood and lessened Eric's influence, so I admitted that I really didn't care.

To my delight, Eric responded to my ambivalence with great enthusiasm, confirming my affection for him: despite his intelligence, or maybe because of it, he understood the virtue in slacking off and could sense its presence from a mile away.

"Hmmm, let's see," he pondered, rubbing his chin and looking up to the roof above us. "What would be easiest? You wouldn't want something too big, like the States."

"No, not the States."

Eric squeezed his cleft chin between his thumb and forefinger.

"England?" I suggested. I knew my mom would be happy with that choice, and would probably give me lots of help, especially if the work involved kings and queens.

"Maybe. But that's a kind of tricky flag. There's a lion on it. How about Japan? I think their flag is just red and white with a big circle."

I wasn't the least bit interested in Japan, and couldn't mount any enthusiasm for it. It had been in the war (I had seen *Tora! Tora! Tora!* on TV), but the superheroes didn't fight the Japanese as often as they fought the Nazis.

Eric read the indifference on my face, and suggested Africa. "One of those little countries right in the middle. The map would be easy, especially if you picked a square one."

"Nah."

"Peru?"

"Peru? How come?"

"It's got lllllaaaammmaaaas," Eric drawled with a grin. "They know how to spit."

"That's true, but nah."

We stood unspeaking while the wind gusted rain onto the cement square, darkening the edges like a creeping shadow. Shouts and bodies hurled around us.

"Maybe I should just make up a country?" I said.

"Hey, that'd be fun," Eric nodded. "But I don't think Southern would go for it." Suddenly, his whole face beamed and he sprang forward, punching me on the shoulder. "Indonesia!" he shouted.

I thought he was joking, but I couldn't think of anything funny to say about Indonesia.

"It's perfect," he continued. "I don't know why I didn't think of it right away."

"Indonesia?" I said, wrinkling my brow. "What's so great about Indonesia?"

Eric's face gleamed with satisfaction. He leaned closer, as if to whisper in my ear, then straightened up and shouted "I did it last year!"

I must have looked perplexed because he immediately added, "Don't you get it? You can just copy what I did. Hey, you can even use my flag and my map. Who's going to know? But you should probably write out everything in your own writing, just to be safe. Besides, some of my pages will have the teacher's marks on them."

I began to get excited by Eric's plan, though copying somebody else's entire project seemed like too huge a crime to consider.

"How is anybody going to know?" Eric read my thoughts again. "Different teachers, right?"

I nodded.

"And I got an A too. I had all these different spices taped to a page to show what the big exports were."

"No kidding?" Then the obvious question sprang to my mind. "What did you choose Indonesia for anyway?"

He rolled his eyes. "I picked first last year, and I was going to take Egypt, you know because of the Pharoahs. But just as a joke, goofing around, I said Indonesia, and that old crabapple Burnley made me take it. She never liked me, the old bat. So I decided I'd do a really good job just to show her."

While Eric spoke, I considered the plan. It seemed risky. But I doubted anyone would bother to cross-check all the choices from the year before. Besides, since I was in grade four, my first year of choosing, no one would likely bother to check my choice against any of the older kids. And even if they did, how could they prove that my report was really Eric's? Surely Mrs. Burnley wouldn't remember. Nonetheless, the scale of the cheating terrified me. But the benefits—all that time I would save. I looked at Eric and he was intensely reading my thoughts.

"You're home free," he declared. "Don't worry, it's a cinch. They don't expect anybody to keep their old projects anyway. I've got mine stuck in my desk at home somewhere, though."

"Why?"

Eric smirked. "I guess just because that A made me feel so good, since old Burnley pushed Indonesia on me."

The schoolbell clattered behind his words, and the bodies around us began to scatter in various directions. Rubber balls bounced off the cement and brick, shouts and screams intensified, and we were suddenly at the edge of a flood of colour, as several hundred jackets and coats and sweaters streamed past toward the main entrance. All at once someone yelled "Scramble!" and flung a huge bunch of hockey cards high into the air; they flapped down like pigeons to the cold cement. Eric and I instinctively plunged into the mad circle of our peers reaching and pushing and yelling as they tried to scoop up as many cards as possible.

"Aw, they're last year's," someone groaned, looking dejectedly at his booty.

"Yeehaw!" the boy who had tossed the cards whooped, running off into the rain. Two others chased him, flinging cards and curses at his back.

Eric and I watched the pursuit for a while, and then realized that the playground had almost emptied. If we didn't hurry, we'd be late.

"Jude Drouin," Eric read off the card in his hand. "Hey Jude, whatcha Drouin?" he said with another wide grin, then broke into a mock version of the Beatles' song: "Hey Jude, I like you nude, I'd like you better, without your sweater."

I grinned back, but my thoughts had already returned to Indonesia. Could I really choose it?

We ran into the black rain, our nerves tensed for the second bell. High above us, on a steel pole angled out from the building, the Maple Leaf flapped like a frightened bird. We passed under it into the musty, rotted apple-core air of the hallways and the dour expressions of Mackenzie, Bowen, and Meighen glaring at us as if their country had no room for the antics of schoolchildren.

That afternoon I screwed up my courage and chose Indonesia, much to my teacher's and classmates' surprise (not lessened much when I explained that it seemed like an interesting country, and that I liked its name). Afterwards, the whole school assembled in the gymnasium to listen to our principal's "United Nations Month" speech.

Our gym was tiny, hardwood-floored and brick-walled with a raised stage recessed into one end, its grey, plastic curtain scrunched up at opposite sides like an accordion. All along the two side walls of the gym, basketball hoops and backboards stuck out toward the open court. That day the hoops were hung with tiny flags while larger, fancier cloth flags of Canada and the United Nations were attached to the walls at regular intervals. To the right of the stage the school band had gathered, about twenty-five students of all ages seated on chairs with crow-black metal music stands perched in front of them. The rest of the gym was crammed with students sitting cross-legged on the floor and teachers either sitting on chairs or standing along the side walls and at the back. A solitary wooden podium stood in the middle of the stage, near the front. A small United Nations flag and a small Canadian flag stuck out like antennae from each side. Beyond this, in the dim light of the stage's depths, the oil portrait of Prime Minister Pearson that normally hung outside the principal's office now glowered out at us. Beside it on one side was a portrait of the Queen, and on the other, of Prime Minister Trudeau.

A constant chattering roar, as of seabirds gathered by the pounding surf, filled the gym. Everyone was excited to be out of class, and our voices swirled and clashed and rose to the ceiling while we waited for the assembly to begin.

Suddenly, Mr. Southern was there behind the podium, as though he'd materialized out of the air or stepped right out of the portrait of his hero. He wore a plain dark suit and a black homburg, a great contrast to his usual western style of clothes. The only splashes of colour on his person were a vivid red bow tie and a Maple Leaf pin stuck to his lapel. Even from the floor of the gym I could sense his excitement, the nervous way he kept adjusting his tie, the way he looked rapidly over the crowd, seeming at once intimidated and inspired by the occasion.

After thirty seconds of adjustment, during which we all hushed, Mr. Southern cleared his throat into the microphone, then ordered us to rise for the singing of the national anthem and "God Save the Queen." The band launched into a brassy, squeaky, though adequate rendition of the two familiar songs. We sang along, led by our principal's lusty example and his bandmaster gestures of punctuating the beat with a raised hand even as he stood so stiffly that it seemed he had gone into shock. "Long to reign oooooover us," we sang, and, as always, I had the strange notion that Queen Elizabeth was somehow responsible for our wet climate, that our relationship to England was so natural that it even influenced the weather. But when I really thought about the Queen, I pictured how some of the older boys at the paper shack liked to make her bum out of the dollar bill by folding it in a particular way that I could never quite replicate. I often wondered what Mr. Southern would say if he ever caught someone doing that. Thinking about the Queen's bum made me smile because my father often referred to the toilet as the throne and to the bathroom as the throne room, something my mother pretended to be annoyed by.

Now, with the band finished and everyone seated again, Mr. Southern, his small, pale, jewelled hands gripping the sides of the podium, began his speech.

"Lester . . . Bowles . . . Pearson," he intoned, each name given its special status with a brief pause. "Sportsman, soldier, scholar, diplomat, statesman, leader." Another, longer pause. "But most of all, Mike, a decent, everyday Christian gentleman, no different from the rest of us. Yet he was the very best of our national character, a man who presented our best face to the world. Why do we celebrate him today, at the start of United Nations Month?"

At this point Mr. Southern turned slightly, as if letting an unseen ghost sidle past, and, with his right arm extended, pointed back to the oil portrait of Prime Minister Pearson. In a deeper, stronger voice that echoed through the packed gymnasium, he answered his rhetorical question: "Because, of all our nation's great leaders, Lester Bowles Pearson, more than any other, demonstrated how the Canadian values of tolerance, freedom, decency, and old-fashioned Christian fellowship can make a difference in the world! Mike, plain old Mike from Peterborough, was always there among the world leaders, fighting quietly for peace, for a world order which promotes freedom, well-being, and security for all. He gave us a presence, an honourable presence, among all the other nations!"

Slowly, Mr. Southern's voice and demeanour gained power, until, as always, it seemed that he had actually become Lester Pearson addressing an assembly at the UN or NATO. The portrait behind him seemed to blend right into his features. Mr. Southern went on, speaking briefly of his hero's triumphs, the sending of an emergency UN force to end the Suez Crisis in 1956, the legislating of Medicare, the creation of a new flag, the glorious celebrations of our Centennial Year when the whole country realized at once, in Mr. Pearson's own words, that Canada is "greatly blessed among the nations of the world. Everything that is possible in this world is possible here." Finally, as the big send-off, Mr. Southern,

in a more intimate tone that brought him back to us as his familiar self, mentioned education, which he called, quoting one of Mr.
Pearson's speeches, "the creation of finer human hungers."

"You have a great responsibility," our principal challenged us,
"and also a great opportunity. Our nation's greatness is still new,
and it's up to each and every one of you to make an important
contribution, to work hard, to learn all you can about your
country and all countries, so you can help build a world of peace
and harmony, and by doing so honour the memory of one of the
twentieth century's true visionaries."

He then instructed us to put a lot of time and effort into our
choose-a-country and public-speaking contests (I felt abashed at
this point, as if my cheating were naked to the whole school).
At last, Mr. Southern motioned to the band and told us to rise. In
unison we sang the anthem of the United Nations with its stirring
lyrics about all the nations of the world unfurling their flags and
getting together in peace and understanding whenever there's
trouble brewing.

When the song ended we sat again, waiting for Mr. Southern to
direct us out of the gym grade by grade, as always. So far, everything had been as expected, a straightforward assembly meant to
endow us with purpose for the month ahead.

A strange hush had settled over the gym in the brief pause after
we had sat down and before Mr. Southern started to call out the
grades. Suddenly our school janitor, a sullen, heavy-set man
named George, strolled across in front of the stage carrying a flag
that I didn't recognize. It was blue and white with a sort of flower
in the middle, and George had it neatly attached to the handle of
his broom. The flag wasn't large, but he had to move a little faster
than his usual slow gait to keep it unfurled. There was something
surreal, yet also stately and dignified about his progress; he puffed

his chest out and held his head high, his jaw firmly fixed. It even seemed that his thick, droopy moustache—which, along with his physical bulk and gruff manner, had earned him the nickname "Grumpy Walrus"—had stiffened to a new life.

At first no one reacted at all. The janitor had timed his appearance so perfectly, had stepped into such a natural lull in the proceedings, that we had no choice but to pay him close attention. For several long seconds the gym remained almost completely silent, with only a few uncomfortable coughs emanating from one or two teachers along the walls. I turned around quickly. Obviously someone understood what this was all about. By the time I turned back, the janitor had stopped directly beneath Mr. Southern at the podium. He raised his broom with a kind of haughty flourish, stared briefly at the principal, and then completed his progress across the stage and out one of the side doors of the gym.

Once he had gone, a buzz of curiosity rose up among us. There could be no mistaking the fact that we'd seen a dramatic gesture directed at our principal. George? The Grumpy Walrus? We were all perplexed. He hardly even lifted his eyes while doing his janitorial work, and only spoke occasionally, usually to correct us when we called him by name. "Georges," he would insist, almost snarling, "Georges." And we would repeat the soft Gs to ourselves, amused by his annoyance, which seemed a gross overreaction. But mostly we just kept out of his way. He was new, having replaced Mr. Janzig after his retirement the year before, and we still weren't sure what to make of him.

Meanwhile, Mr. Southern had turned a shade of angry red, bright as his bow tie. It looked as if he had swallowed his Adam's apple and was choking on it, and I swore I could see the blood pounding in the swollen veins on his neck and forehead. "Holy geez, *look* at him!" someone nearby whispered, and we all shrank back instinctively. For a moment it seemed that he was going to leap off the stage after George. But then he returned his gaze to us and, just when it appeared that he was going to deliver a passionate response to what we had witnessed, he calmly removed the homburg from his head, smoothed back his wavy, gelled hair, and took several deep breaths. Then he barked out "grade ones!" and the poor little kids immediately scrambled to their feet and filed wide-eyed out of the gym. "Twos!" the principal barked, and the same hurried exodus occurred. By the time my grade was called his voice was a little calmer, but the red flush on his skin remained. As I passed in front of the stage I was too afraid to stare straight up at him, but I did look in his direction. On each side of the podium, the Queen and Prime Minister Pearson, their oily, dreamy eyes far away, were completely composed in the midst of all the chaos. My look was so fleeting that I left the gym with the strange images of a bow-tied man wearing a crown and of a crowned woman wearing a bow tie flashing repeatedly in my mind. Somehow, I did not even find these images amusing.

Hours later, just before school let out, Mr. Southern's voice crackled over the PA. In a calm, steady manner, he announced that he was going to read part of a speech that Prime Minister Pearson had delivered as his farewell to active political life. "When troublemakers insist on destruction," the principal explained with a sigh, "it is important to remember these inspiring words of strength and wisdom to give ourselves courage and to keep our national dream alive." He then cleared his throat and recited the following:

"A destiny that takes Quebec outside Canada means, simply and starkly, the end of Canada, the end of our forefathers' dream, and of our dream of a great confederation of people from coast to coast developing, for the common good, resources unsurpassed in any country, showing the world how a state of many provinces, of two basic language groups, and of many races and cultures, can combine their efforts, their talents, and their ideals to make Canada a land of hope and happiness and equal opportunity for all."

Mr. Southern read further, explaining how it was up to us to keep our country together despite those who would make separation a reality, the bigots and all those "good, grey men and women in the middle who, by their indifference, could let it happen."

Then, raising his voice to an impassioned flourish, he concluded:

"So we who believe in our country must work with a passionate intensity to see that this doesn't happen, that the Canadian dream does not end but is realized in a Canadian destiny worthy of those who have brought us so far in our first century."

A few seconds of muted, hand-over-mike dialogue followed, ending with Mr. Southern's weary last words for the day: "A reminder for grade five students. This Thursday is Hot-Dog Day. Please let your teacher know in advance whether you want plain or mustard."

thirteen

ALL THAT MONTH, my relationship with Mrs. Edmundson grew more intimate even as the opportunity for real contact drifted away. Faithful to the arrangement I had made with her son, I checked on her in the duplex every day when I brought the paper, always a little frightened by what I might find. But as the weeks passed, nothing more dramatic occurred than a kitchen faucet left running, and I soon grew accustomed to the odd vagaries of her conversation. On most days she was quite lucid, and would answer my knock at the door, greet me pleasantly by name, and then go slowly about the business of bringing me hot chocolate and cookies. But in the living room we soon entered those long, strange silences, punctuated only when, out of discomfort, I would say "It sure is raining" or "I think it's stopping," to which she would respond with a smile and a distantly cheerful "Oh, yes."

Every fourth day or so she would be more talkative, and would discourse pleasantly and sensibly enough on something that had happened years before—a trip she had made to Montreal to see an old friend, a banquet and dance she had attended with her second husband. On these occasions I simply listened to her calm, gently animated voice, soon realizing that she did not particularly expect any response. After a while I felt comfortable enough to offer to make the hot chocolate. In truth, it speeded things up. I came to know every grainy detail of the old photographs on the wall, every intricacy of the patterns on the collector's plates, every melodic shift in the faint songs flowing from the wooden radio's watery green light. At some point during these wanderings, Mrs. Edmundson might suddenly say "Are you there, dear?" to reassure herself, even though it never seemed that the "dear" was specific to me. Otherwise, I might as well have been alone.

I did not enjoy these visits, but I was surprised to find that I did not dread them either. If not for the other, more disturbing days, I would have relaxed a great deal more, my boredom more than compensated for by the thoughts of the extra money I was earning. But it was more than just that. There was a slight bookshop quality to that small room, dingy and musty as it was, and sometimes completely silent but for the low music and the ticking of a clock on a side table. At times, turning from the wall in a kind of warmth-induced reverie, I almost expected to see Mr. Bradlee hunched over in the radio's green light, muttering paperback titles to himself as he scribbled away at a mustard-splattered piece of paper. If only Mrs. Edmundson had been slightly less distant and lost. I was accustomed to both silence and sustained monologues from adults, but I had no experience of how to handle conversations that followed no logical pattern.

On these rare occasions, Mrs. Edmundson still spoke calmly and cheerfully about the past, but in disjointed bursts, moving from one story to another without logic in a way that was more chilling because she did not lose her outward sense of control. Yet the fact that she "seemed" normal, just like herself, mitigated the panic I might otherwise have experienced. She spoke quietly, remained seated, and generally seemed content. Eventually, I came to expect that she would call me "Leslie" or "Arthur," and I learned to just nod and then make sure she was comfortable in her armchair before I left.

Of course, the first time she rambled disjointedly I immediately reported it to Mr. Edmundson, pedalling over to his place of business near the centre of town (he was a notary public, a job that suggested nothing to me) in a breathless panic and blurting out what I had been through.

Finally, in a calm voice, in which the inflection of his mother was oddly present like a sort of ghost-tone behind the words, he said, "She's just a little confused. It will pass. It's not unusual when people get old for them to wander in their minds a little every now and then."

I stared blankly at him, sensing somehow that he was wrong but not knowing what to say about it. I left after agreeing to let him know if his mother ever became upset.

I wasn't reassured enough by his words to keep the day's events a secret. At home, I quickly explained the arrangement and how it was going to my mother.

"Vera Edmundson?" she said, raising her eyebrows. "Does this lady have beautiful long hair, Callum? Does she always wear dark glasses?"

When I answered yes, my mother put down her teacup and sighed. "Now that's a shame, a real shame. You say she's living where, in that old duplex on Finley?"

Again, I said yes.

"I wonder why," she mused to herself, then seemed to forget the speculation in favour of the cold facts. "Well, that's a pity. I always liked her. Such a dignified person, so polite. And such beautiful manners. She used to come into the drugstore when I was working there, this is before you were born, and she was always very nice to me. Not everyone was, I'm sorry to say. But she was always kind, a real lady." My mother stopped talking and looked firmly at me across the kitchen table. "And you say she's wandering in her mind?"

"That's what Mr. Edmundson calls it," I replied.

"Well, what sort of things does she say? What do you mean by wandering?"

After I had related some of the recent rambling monologue, my mother leaned forward and laid her hand over mine. "Callum," she said softly, "how long have you been visiting her?"

I blushed uncomfortably. I knew my mother was proud of me, but I also knew that I wouldn't tell her about how I had avoided Mrs. Edmundson over the holidays by not delivering her paper. "A couple of weeks, I guess. But she was never this crazy before."

"Don't say crazy, Callum. That isn't nice. Say confused or muddled." My mother studied me carefully, then broke into a smile. "You just keep on visiting her. That will do her a world of good, poor soul."

"But what if she goes all cra . . . confused again?"

"Then you just get in touch with Mr. Edmundson right away. He'll know what to do."

I wanted to argue that my trip to see him hadn't left me feeling very confident, but I realized that my mother was right. What other choice did I have? If Mrs. Edmundson was worse the next day, at least now I also had my mother to confide in. I felt greatly relieved.

As it turned out, Mrs. Edmundson was much better the next afternoon, and the one after that, and I soon relaxed again into the routine of silent listening. The next time her speech became disjointed, I was much calmer; it was almost as if I had developed a sixth sense tuned to the rhythms of her condition, and could almost predict a more confused episode. This time I made sure she was settled, and then pedalled over to Mr. Edmundson's office in less of a panic. He took in the information just as he had done before, with a reassurance that sounded more hollow than it had the first time. He was also sweating profusely and hardly seemed to consider what I said; he kept looking around the office as if expecting someone to step out from a corner. I felt even sorrier for him, knowing how much my own mother meant to me. And I was able to feel this sympathy now because I knew I had my mother's support. She told me just to keep on visiting, to be kind, and to pay close attention to what was going on. "Be sure to check the house before you leave," she cautioned, "especially the stove. And Callum, don't worry. She's confused, but there's nothing for you to worry about." And then my mother told me that she planned to get in touch with Mr. Edmundson herself, not to pry or anything like that, but just to make sure he understood that I was only ten years old and shouldn't be expected to handle too much. "But you're doing wonderfully," she assured me. "Your father and I are very proud of you."

So the visits to Mrs. Edmundson were incorporated into my routine without much difficulty. Under the scudding, wet winter skies, I washed into the paper shack, the bookshop, the duplex, school, and home, always half-listening for that other, colourful reality of what I could imagine, not only from books but from my own growing sense of possibility. I knew I had to be certain places at certain times or there would be dire consequences, and yet all I really felt was this broadening awareness of power and freedom, an awareness always intensified by anything that seemed even a slight threat to my not burdensome routine.

So my parents' pride in my dealings with Mrs. Edmundson did not shame me into working harder at school. I should have been paralyzed by guilt for cheating on my big UN project, but instead I was overjoyed at the prospect of actually going through with it. I was dimly aware that at some level I couldn't accept myself as uniformly well-behaved. More and more, certain questionable actions—when Jerris skipped school, when Eric taped a picture of himself on Jesus, when George waved his strange flag at Mr. Southern, but most of all, when Ezra did almost anything—inspired me. I still felt pleasure when I got an A on my school work, or when I signed up new subscribers for my route, or when I scored a goal in soccer or hockey. But these were things I could predict; I could even see the pleasure in the eyes of adults. By contrast, skipping school with Jerris to follow Ezra, or accepting Eric's help to cheat on a school project, contained mysteries and risks to which I was increasingly drawn.

Indonesia. How was I supposed to predict that an island thousands of miles away would throw me deeper into the mystery of Ezra Hemsworth and the Lums?

I had taken Eric's old report and smuggled it into my bedroom, feeling thrilled and edgy. There it was, ten whole pages, a map, a flag, both beautifully unmarked by the teacher, graphs showing climate and economic production, small sections on the history, the economy, the geography, and, the *coup de grâce* (clever old Eric, I thought), the page of exports complete with spices taped right on it. No wonder he had gotten an A.

But much to my disappointment, one of the spices was missing. Right above where Eric had typed "Cloves," there was a blank space. Oh well, I thought, I'll just have to get some more.

I couldn't find any in my mother's spice rack, and Jerris couldn't find any in his house. Or at least we couldn't find anything with that name on it (we didn't know what cloves looked or smelled like). I had told Jerris about what I was doing, and had sworn him to secrecy. His reaction, not surprisingly, was to ask if he could have the project next year so that he could cheat too. By saying yes, I immediately won from him any support I might need, such as looking for cloves.

But we couldn't find any. When I mentioned the problem to Eric, he scratched his head for a while, and then remembered. "Oh yeah, my mom needed some, and she was going to get it at the store, but I took it off my project instead." He then said he'd look to see if she had any more in the cupboard. She didn't. By now, I was becoming annoyed. I figured I'd have to buy some at the store, but when I went to the Shop-Easy to look, I couldn't believe how expensive cloves were! A dollar for a tiny packet! Of course, I couldn't ask my mother to buy them, because then I'd have to tell her about my project and she might want to see it when I was done. So I was feeling deflated by this turn of events, and was even considering redoing the exports page and just leaving the cloves off it, when Jerris had a simple idea.

We were biking home from town one night in a light rain, talking things over, and had just about reached the big, round, clown-nose red Coca Cola sign above Lums' Grocery, when Jerris said, "Hey, let's just go in and steal some."

I wasn't comfortable with shoplifting. The fear of being caught and of my parents' embarrassment and disappointment was so great that I panicked just thinking about it.

But Jerris had already stopped his bike under the streetlamp's drizzly glow and was leaning over the handlebars, scowling at me. "Aw, come on, it's easy, I do it all the time."

I pedalled back a bit, shaking my head. "No, I can't."

Jerris shrugged. "It's no big deal. I'll do it for you."

I wasn't entirely comfortable with this either, but I really wanted the spice. "Well, I guess so."

"But you got to come in with me."

"Why?"

"Duh," Jerris groaned. "So you can buy something else. And when you're at the counter, and they're not looking, I'll stuff it in my coat. No problem."

It seemed unfair for me to protest when Jerris was willing to do the actual shoplifting, but I already felt my throat getting dry.

He didn't give me a chance to back out. "Come on," he urged, leaning his bike against the stuccoed wall beside the dimly glowing glass window of the grocery.

"Wait, wait up," I whispered urgently, following the shadow he cast over the loose gravel.

Just as he pushed in the door, causing the little bell over it to tinkle, I caught up to him. Together, we stood blinking in the warm, confined, oddly pungent entrance. It was a small store, not much larger than a shack, but it was so crammed full of items that it gave the curious impression of a tinyness and vastness. We could hardly move without brushing against something, and yet so much stuff surrounded us that we believed the walls had to extend farther than they did in order to hold everything. Just to our right was the wooden counter, so covered with displays of candy and cigarettes and cheap little plastic toys that its surface barely showed. The wall behind the counter was covered with advertising posters, mainly for pop and cigarettes, though there was a large picture of a cow promoting Dairyland milk products and a slightly smaller one of gleamy-smiled young lovers attesting to the breath-freshening qualities of Certs. All these posters wore a yellow grime of smoke, and one or two were torn in places. Between them and the counter sat a bare wooden chair on the bare wooden floor.

Straight ahead of us over the same scuffed, unswept wood was a narrow curtained entrance to the back of the shop. The dark green curtain was usually slightly parted, and through the gap we could sometimes hear Chinese voices speaking in their low, guttural way and see clouds of yellowish, sickly-sweet-smelling smoke drift out. To our left, four thin, short aisles of plywood shelving seemed to creak under the weight of goods, everything from tinned food to fresh fruit to rubber gumboots to laundry soap. Against the far wall stood a tall glass case for refrigerated cheese, milk, and meat, and also a Coke ice chest filled with pop bottles.

On the left was a high wooden rack displaying a wide-ranging mix of magazines, heavily weighted to the pornographic and auto-motive but also containing such publications as *Mad, The Ladies' Home Journal,* and *Outdoor Sportsman.* It was almost impossible to browse, since the person sitting at the chair behind the counter was so close, and besides, whenever the door swung in it was apt to hit you.

But Jerris and I stood there now, unmoving, stricken by the emptiness of the shop and its unnerving silence. All we heard at first was the buzzing of a fly trapped in one of the cracked, dusty overhead fluorescent lights. The bell over the door seemed to echo right into the buzz, as did the faint hum of the refrigerator case. Why wasn't there someone behind the counter? Or why hadn't someone come out from behind the curtain at the sound of the bell? Usually one of Wing Lum's quiet, unsmiling daughters-in-law sat on the bare wooden chair, looking out suspiciously but with considerable boredom at us as we scurried into the aisles. Or else one of them glided through the curtain and behind the counter with astonishing speed and fluidity.

The buzzing of the fly grew louder. It was a huge blowfly, large enough that its attempts to escape the lighting became audible bumps punctuating the ceaseless low drone. I looked up at it and felt an immediate sympathy.

"Let's just grab some," Jerris whispered urgently, making for the aisles. But before he took more than a few steps, we heard a sudden harsh cough, almost a retching, followed by equally harsh-sounding words spat out rapidly in a man's voice. We froze. A few seconds later, another male voice, less broken and angry, spoke some equally unfamiliar words in what sounded like a pleading tone. The first voice made a deep, grunting, disgusted noise, then fired off a long volley of what sounded exactly like curses. A woman's slight figure crossed the parting in the curtain, and then I heard her speak very softly. I moved a little toward the counter so that I could see farther into the opening. Just as I did so, I heard a familiar voice rise above the woman's.

"Not-gonna-buy-Wellie-eh?" Ezra cackled gleefully. "Old-man's-still-the-boss-goddamnya-goddamnya."

"You shut up," snapped the male voice that had been pleading a moment earlier. "It isn't any of your business."

Ezra's grin broadened in the silence that followed. I could see his long, angular nose and his thick, fleshy lips looming out from his full beard. His head glowed oddly in the yellowish shadows, and looked as if it were severed since I could not see his body. Suddenly, still grinning, he turned toward the curtain and seemed to stare right at me. His expression did not change. I felt my whole body shiver. Ezra was looking right at me but I could tell that he wasn't seeing me.

"Come on," Jerris whispered again. "Before they come out."

Just then, the door swung in heavily and thumped against my leg. The echo of the struck bell pealed violently into the silence.

"Sorry about that!" a deep voice boomed. I turned around to see a heavy-set man in a plaid hunting jacket, a fisherman I recognized from the wharf.

"That's okay," I mumbled, blushing. By the time I turned back, the green curtain was closed, shivering slightly, and one of Wing Lum's tiny daughters-in-law was perched stiffly on the bare wooden chair, glaring at me out of a pursed mouth and thickly mascaraed eyes.

I grabbed a Wig-Wam out of the chocolate bar box on the counter and started fumbling in my pocket for change.

"That it?" the woman said in heavily accented English. "No pop for you?"

I shook my head and laid the change on the counter.

"Five more cent," the woman scowled, scooping up my dime and pennies. At the same time, she leaned slightly to one side, keeping an eye on what else was happening in the shop. I had no idea where Jerris had gone.

"You out of root beer?" the fisherman bellowed from in front of the refrigerator case. "I can't see none in here."

"Just wait, please!" the woman raised her voice thinly. "I be right there." She gave me a swift look that said what I had often heard before: "You finished boy, okay. See you." Under the cutting edge of that look, I lunged for the door, pulling it open and almost sliding down on the loose gravel outside. I jumped on my bike and pedalled several yards away, just out of the shop and streetlamp glow.

In the drizzling dark, I waited. My heart pounded with the combined excitement of the shoplifting and the resurrection of the mystery surrounding Ezra and the Lums. That blank stare through the curtain: I couldn't be entirely sure that Ezra hadn't seen me. I felt as if I had looked into a mirror and there was nothing there except a pair of black eyes that questioned everything I was doing yet didn't care to hear the answer.

Trembling, I watched Jerris walk casually out of the store and then clamber for his bike, jump on, and pedal feverishly through the streetlamp's glow.

"Got it," he gasped, braking beside me after I had half-shouted his name. He pulled a small glass jar out of his grubby parka and handed it to me. I couldn't see his face clearly in the dark, but I could tell how excited he was by the plumes of breath between us. "It was easy. I snuck out when she was looking for the root beer."

"Thanks," I said, feeling strangely deflated. All that risk for some spice to tape to a page. I thought how much more worthwhile it would have been if Jerris had grabbed some chips or a *Mad* magazine. Then we could have headed for one of our cozy hideaways and enjoyed the fruits of our thievery. As a substitute, I unwrapped the Wig-Wam and offered Jerris a bite.

"Nah," he said, his breath thinning a little. "I got lots." One by one, he started pulling items out of his coat: suckers, gum, chocolate bars, chips, and a pack of candy cigarettes. "They were right there," he explained, "so I just grabbed them as I went by."

We decided to go to the tree fort, where we kept a flashlight. On the way toward town, as we passed the Lums' blackened potato field and then the dim neon of the Home Oil sign, we speculated on what had happened at the store. Neither of us had a clue what the back-room conversation had been about, since most of it had taken place in Chinese, but we could tell by the tones of the speakers that it had been an argument. But this time, I kept something back from Jerris. I did not tell him how Ezra's look made me feel, except to say that I knew something big was going to happen soon.

"How do you know that?" Jerris asked, so excited that he stayed standing as he pedalled.

"Just a feeling," I said, a little embarrassed. I knew Jerris wouldn't have understood anyway, and that made me even more aware that we weren't as close as we had been.

But I wasn't about to let the excitement die. More than ever, I wanted to keep the mystery surrounding Ezra at a fever pitch.

We pedalled rapidly toward town, the rain almost a mist now, our cheeks fringed with it as our tires sluiced through the puddles, throwing up skunk tails of spray. The streets were empty and dark. We didn't speak, just leaned far over our handlebars and pressed into the soft air, knowing without words what turns to take, moving in tandem down streets we knew by landmarks more than names. But it was Laidlaw we finally reached, a short street of few houses and several vacant lots overgrown with blackberry bushes and unpruned, wildly tangled fruit trees. Here, close to the harbour and the centre of town, in the middle of a vast vacant lot, stood our Douglas fir, a hundred footer whose branches started about ten feet up the scaly trunk and thickened toward the top. In some generation before ours, small boards had been spiked in the base of the trunk, enabling a difficult clamber to the first branch. Halfway up the tree, where the branches were still wide enough apart to allow for easy movement, a small fort had been built out of plywood, mandarin orange crates, and drift bark. Blackened with rain over the years, moss-crusted, its spike-heads ochre, the fort was nevertheless so solid that we saw no reason to improve its basic structure.

For Jerris and me it was the most sacred place, and the only one we would consider going to after the excitement at the grocery store. As we climbed into the soughing branches, carefully, hand and foot, hugging the old wood, Jerris just above me, as always, and moving faster, as always, I trembled with the sudden thought that what we had just done would make us fall. I tightened my grip and prayed that Jerris's sneakers, two dirty white marks in the air over my head, would remain in place, sure as gull flight.

After what seemed like hours we found ourselves gasping in the boxlike fort. Sitting cross-legged, our knees touching, we grinned as we gulped in great breaths of the rich air. Then I looked out through the rough-cut windows on three sides. Without getting up, I could see only the black night; the rain had turned to a mist not even audible in the boughs. Jerris, anticipating me, slid out the detachable west-facing wall. It was only a thin piece of particle board that, once removed, gave us a broader view when we didn't care about keeping the weather out. Jerris laid the board along an inner wall and then sat on the open edge, his legs dangling over. I joined him there, and together we stared down at the wild, always-shifting edge of Chilukthan, the unchurned earth of the potato fields stretching out to Pheasant Island, the salt marshes, the muddy, silty river, a hundred sloughs, a thousand ditches, and finally the clearer waters of the Pacific. But we couldn't see any of this now; we just felt it all there, sensed the fluid heaviness under the lighter atmosphere we had reached. All we saw was thick darkness sporadically punctuated by the minuscule lights of houses and streetlamps and docks. It seemed as though we were gazing into a handful of wet black sand out of which a few glittering crystals had emerged. I turned slowly to the south and took in the clustered lights of the ferry terminal and the coal port glowing in an orange and white blur at the farthest reach of my vision, out along the salt tang of the gulf, past the Indian reserve curled in at the base of the bluff.

Jerris shifted away then, announcing that he was going to empty his pockets. The sound of his voice pulled my gaze closer to home. Down there, spaced in no discernible pattern, the streetlamps shone fuzzily in cone shapes, their light barely visible. Along the dyke, so faint that I wasn't sure whether I saw them or just put them there because I knew they existed, the letters of the Home Oil sign limply spent their fading neon against the oil tanks. And the wharf lights where my father moored his boat—did I imagine them too because I knew they had to be there? Was this also why, hearing Jerris tear open a bag of chips and begin chomping, that I leaned forward dangerously, straining to see better, convinced that I had caught a blurred figure pass under one of the streetlamps between Lums' Grocery and the dyke? From this perspective, more than any other, the town belonged to Ezra; I could imagine no other person for whom the light would be a hindrance rather than a help. And he had to be there, he had to get from where we had last seen him to that narrow, oil-thick cabin I could also conjure up just by staring at the exact spot in the harbour. I could even see his body hunched over in the smoky haze, his thick-fleshed mouth hanging open, and hear the nasal laugh and the rapid words, each of which I could decipher individually, and none of which I could pin down to the vague meaning underlying them.

Jerris spoke again, mumbling through a mouthful of chips, and his unmysterious voice broke the spell. I pulled myself back from the edge, all the strangeness evaporated with the view, and my easy appetites returned as I knelt over the pile of candy and brought the stolen sweetness to my mouth.

fourteen

JANUARY CAME AND WENT. I spent twenty-seven dollars at the comic book convention in Vancouver, all of it on old issues of *The Amazing Spiderman*. These purchases were kept secret from my parents, for though they encouraged my love of reading, they regarded twenty-seven dollars as a lot of money, far too much to spend on something as trivial as comic books. But I was elated by my finds, and by being in the company of so many fellow comic enthusiasts. The hours flew by. It was a glorious, exciting day, and the rush of it carried over into much else that we did that month, especially for Eric.

His speech at school had been an overwhelming success. As I heard from several of his classmates on the playground before Eric himself told me about it, he had stood quietly at the front of the classroom for half a minute. Then, with his left hand, he made the shape of a pistol, raised it to his wide-open mouth, pointed the finger barrel straight down his throat, and made a loud banging noise by dropping a heavy book on the desk in front of him. In the echoing silence, very dramatically, he began: "In April 1945, in a bunker in Berlin, Adolph Hitler, Der Führer, Leader of the Third Reich and the Nazi Party, shot and killed himself. His body was never discovered." From that blunt opening, Eric proceeded to discuss Hitler's early life, his artistic ambition, his rise to power, his military strategies, his fatal mistakes, the Night of the Long Knives, and his hatred of the Jews. The speech was lengthy, but intense and compelling, and I was told that there was hardly a sound in the room when Eric formed the pistol again, dropped it limply to his side, and suggested that Hitler might actually have escaped to Brazil.

Later, on the playground, opinion was divided over the speech. Most of Eric's classmates were impressed, even stunned, by it, and thought that Eric must be the smartest kid in the school. A few others, though, considered the speech dumb. Adolph Hitler, they shrugged, who cares? Besides, Eric was just a hot dog, always exaggerating and making everything more dramatic than it was. These were the same classmates whose own speeches included The 4H Club: Why It's So Much Fun; Bobby Orr, My Hero; Why I Play the Clarinet; and Lippizaner Stallions: The World's Smartest Horses.

As always, Eric didn't bother much with the response. He was pleased that his teacher selected him as one of the two students in the class to move on to the next level of competition, but only because that gave him an opportunity to improve the speech.

And this was where I came in, and where all the trouble started. My own speech had been about comic collecting. But since I was a nervous speaker and had to read almost entirely from little note cards (whereas Eric had practically memorized everything), I was not chosen, much to my relief, as one of the two class finalists. This "loss" freed me up to help Eric, something I always did with pleasure, feeling privileged to be included in his intellectual pursuits. No topic was dull if Eric was excited by it, and certainly the life of Hitler was dramatic enough. Besides, I had more than my share of free time because of Eric's Indonesia project.

In the end, my help didn't amount to much, but it was enough to implicate me in Mr. Southern's eyes. Eric was supposed to repeat his speech to a larger assembly of all the senior grades, held in the multi-purpose room, a square, wall-to-wall carpeted space about half the size of the gym. Here, all the events not quite large or important enough for the gym were held. The same variety of flags, the same wooden podium, the same arrangement of students sitting cross-legged on the floor and teachers ranged along the walls, the same palpable excitement and buzzing murmur before the speeches began.

The first speaker in Eric's grade, Bernice Cavett, delivered a speech about the black panther. She also began dramatically, calling out a warning to prim Mrs. Smithers: "Mrs. Smithers! Don't move! Right behind you, it's ready to pounce!" And then we heard about the animal's various habits, where it lived, etc. The teachers loved all this—Bernice had a reputation as a teacher's pet, but those of us who knew about Eric's speech scorned her syrupy, adult-flattering delivery, born out of piano recitals and other public displays of cleverness. The next two speeches were fine, but in no way unusual, and by the time Eric's turn came around we were all beginning to get restless.

Looking back a few days later, I couldn't imagine how we managed to get the projector into the room. No doubt the teachers all thought that someone else's student needed it. In any case, no one questioned its presence, just as no one questioned chubby Avery Perich for putting it there at our request. Avery, the audio-visual monitor, was easily manipulated by the promise of mint wagon wheels. By the time I rose and took my place at the projector, and Eric had stood, back to the audience, preparing himself, both his teacher and mine must have been too surprised to stop us. Either that or they each assumed that the other had okayed this arrangement. Meanwhile, I felt the whole crowd surging with barely repressed excitement. Their eagerness almost carried me off with it, so that I would have missed my cue.

But it all went off just as we had planned, except for the initial titters that greeted Eric when he finally turned around. He had gelled the curls over his forehead into straight bangs and slicked them over to one side. A short, black moustache made of bristles from an old shoe brush was taped to his upper lip. Though the effect was comical, once Eric started his speech the titters faded away.

The early part of the speech was essentially the same, though we had added more and better props. The hand-pistol was now a realistic toy replica. When Eric discussed the Night of the Long Knives, he pulled a large carving knife from the Adidas bag at his feet and waved it threateningly at the crowd while kicking out as if he were smashing windows. With delight, I noted that Mrs. Smithers appeared decidedly more anxious than she had at the mention of Bernice Cavett's black panther. But her anxiety might have been mounting distaste. It didn't really matter. Eric had the crowd's full attention and he was building steam. I didn't notice exactly when the principal entered the room. I didn't see him before the lights went down, but he was definitely there when Eric delivered his conclusion.

Before that, however, came the moment that really got us into hot water. "The Jews," Eric had explained to me late one afternoon at his house after I had delivered his parents' copy of the *Sun*, "Hitler hated them. He wanted to wipe them off the face of the

earth!" Eric spoke with a sort of gleeful incredulity, as though
something he had long suspected had been confirmed by what he
had read about Hitler and the Nazis.

"The final solution," Eric continued, rustling through a sheaf of
papers, his words coming faster and faster. "That's what they called
it. And not just Jews either. Gypsies, retards, cripples, professors—
everybody they didn't like." He glanced up at me from the page he
had found, his eyes wide, his lips wet as he kept licking them. "And
they killed ten million! Can you believe it! Ten million people.
That's everybody in Vancouver ten times over." Breathlessly, he
related the stories of the concentration camps, and the gassing, and
the Warsaw Ghetto. I listened, awestruck, but as much by Eric's
excitement as by what he said. It was impossible to take in the
enormity of the facts. Or rather, I couldn't rise to Eric's level of
passionate incredulity. He left me behind, as he so often did, but,
as always, I learned something in his wake, if only the sheer joy
to be gleaned from increased knowledge.

Finally, after he had discussed Auschwitz and Dachau and the
other camps, after he had related some of the brutalities—babies
ripped from their mothers' arms and smashed against brick walls,
old people made to dig ditches—Eric slowed down and we
discussed how much of this material he should add to his speech.

"It's the most important thing," he argued. "If Hitler hadn't
hated the Jews so much he probably would have won the war."

I nodded, still lost.

"Einstein was a Jew," Eric added. "And he left Germany. And so
did lots of other scientists. If they had stayed, Germany probably
would have had the bomb before us!"

I was with it enough to realize how disastrous that would have
been. But I still couldn't keep up with Eric, and so I didn't even try.
What did I know about Jews? I didn't think I knew any, but I

wasn't brave enough to ask Eric. Later, I casually asked my mother. She just answered that they were a kind of people, like Negroes or Indians, and that they were very smart. Mr. Weintraub was Jewish, she said, adding that it was impolite to use the word "Jew." I liked Mr. Weintraub. He owned the drugstore where my mother worked part-time, and when I stopped in he sometimes gave me a comic book. I couldn't understand why anybody would want to kill Mr. Weintraub because of something he couldn't even help.

In the end, we added only a five-minute section on the Holocaust to the speech, and Eric hit on the brilliant idea of showing a brief clip of the concentration camps. He had been to the National Film Board office in Vancouver and had rented a documentary. I hadn't seen it yet, but Eric had described it to me. It sounded a bit gross, but as far as Eric and I were concerned, that would go over well with our peers.

Now, sitting behind the projector, waiting for Eric to say "And here is what the Allied armies found when they liberated the camps," I leaned forward with anticipation, almost forgetting about the crowd.

The eerily silent footage lasted only about a minute, but that was more than enough time to reveal the horror of the Holocaust. Graphically, unapologetically, the film showed a bulldozer pushing a tangled heap of corpses into a great pit—arms and legs were sticking out everywhere, and there was a palpable sense of softness, almost of ooze, as the mud-soaked bodies rolled over each other and toppled in sickening lumps into the opened earth. I stared with my mouth open. I had never seen anything like it before, though I had watched war movies on TV, and sometimes, with my father, episodes of the TV series *World at War*—I thought I must have missed the episode on the Holocaust, or else it had not been so graphic. Yet the image of the corpses did not make me sick or angry or particularly upset. I was simply amazed, and felt a strange attraction to the gruesome. After all, this was just a film, and it was historical: I could treat it with the same degree of detachment and unreality that I treated a gory comic.

But when I stopped the projector and Avery Perich flipped the lights back on, I could see that not everyone in the room shared my response. As Eric went on with his speech in the same commanding, dramatic voice, bringing Hitler's violent story to its violent end, I noticed Miss Prentiss and Miss Hanlon, two of the younger teachers, holding handkerchiefs to their mouths. A few of my fellow grade four students had started to cry and some of the older girls looked ill, though they were desperately trying to appear otherwise.

Most dramatic of all, though, was Mr. Southern's reaction. He stood against the near wall, just inside the door, his body stiff, his arms crossed over his chest. He had turned a violent shade of red and his nostrils were flared. He glared intently at Eric, and then, to my horror, at me. I swallowed hard and looked away immediately. Was he upset because we had changed Eric's speech, because it was now too long? No, he couldn't have known that we had changed it. Why, then, was he so angry?

The moment the assembly ended (after Johnny Van Dusen's speech about his trip to Disneyland, a big hit with the crowd, in no small part because of Johnny's use of gimmicks—he even had Jeff Bingam wear a Goofy mask and toss super goobers to the front row) the principal called our teachers over to him. After a brief conference, during which Miss Coronet and Mrs. Wilkins shrugged a lot, gesticulated wildly, and shook their heads, Mr. Southern stormed out of the room. I sighed with relief, believing that that was the end of it.

Unfortunately, Eric and I were told by our teachers to report to the office immediately. We were so puzzled and preoccupied as we walked down the hall that Eric didn't even think to remove his fake moustache.

"What's bugging him now?" he said with irritation, though I could also detect some nervousness in his voice. I knew he was rightly proud of his speech and the effect it had had, but Eric wasn't always sure of himself. Now, judging by the way he was whistling and carelessly smacking his left hand against his hip, I knew he was dreading the meeting with Mr. Southern.

I didn't respond to Eric's question. The last thing I needed was the close scrutiny of the principal, now that I had just handed in my report on Indonesia.

The pretty Miss Templeton smiled as she ushered us into the office along with a great wave of flowery perfume.

"What have you two done this time?" she said cheerfully, making me optimistic that things might not be as bad as we were anticipating. Then she dashed my hopes by shaking her head and lowering her voice to say, "Whatever it is, you sure have made him mad."

Then she was gone, a fresh torrent of her perfume wrapping us in an unpleasant embrace. We were alone in the western-themed room again, with Lester Pearson grinning down at us and the harsh rhythms of Deuteronomy reverberating off the walls.

Ten minutes later, when the suspense had almost become too much, Miss Templeton reappeared and said that we could go. She seemed every bit as surprised as we were.

"Go on," she urged us, "before he changes his mind."

We literally ran from the office, and only stopped to consider our good fortune once we had reached the hallway outside the boys' washroom.

Breathing hard, Eric suggested that Mr. Southern must have learned from Mrs. Wilkins that Eric had changed his speech.

"That's against the rules," Eric frowned. "But we didn't change it that much."

"But he was mad before he knew that," I argued. "He was mad when the lights came on."

Eric chewed his top lip, then peeled the moustache off. His bangs remained gelled and brushed over to one side. "Maybe it was the film," he considered. "Maybe he found out that we didn't get permission to use the projector."

Maybe, I thought. But still, the timing of his anger seemed all wrong. Anyway, what difference did it make? He had let us go, hadn't he?

"Ah, who cares?" Eric blurted out. "He's always mad about something."

Just then George strolled past us, pushing a wide broom. Grumpy as always, he muttered something incomprehensible as we moved out of his path. His appearance seemed to confirm Eric's last point and gave us the opportunity to stop talking and return to our classrooms.

"I wonder if you made the finals," I said before we parted.

Eric grinned. "I don't know. I would have for sure if I had tossed peanuts around."

All of this happened before lunch. I had begun to think of other things by the time school was almost over and the PA system crackled ominously to life. With a sinking stomach, I heard Miss Templeton call Eric and me to the office. Her tone was not cheerful, but businesslike. I hardly had the strength to rise from my desk. Oh god, I thought, it couldn't be Indonesia already, could it?

The hallways never seemed quieter or narrower. Somehow I reached the office, convinced that every step I took was bringing me closer to a monumental disgrace. All the way there I cursed Eric for coming up with the idea to copy his project. I could have found the time to do a report on England, even if the flag was more involved and it was hard to keep all the kings and queens straight. It was the first time I had ever seriously questioned Eric's judgment, and that added to my disoriented state as I stepped into the outer office to find Eric standing sullenly beside Mr. Southern.

The principal looked much calmer than the last time I had seen him. His face had reverted to its chubby, elfin quality, the violent red drained out of it leaving two ruddy dabs near his cheekbones. His hair, as usual, was freshly gelled and stiffly constrained in dark furrows. I could smell the cloying scent on it before I had approached to within a few feet. When I stopped in front of him, Mr. Southern unpursed his thin lips to say, without any inflection that I could interpret, "Now we're all gathered." It seemed a strange comment, the "we" hanging ominously over us, a word that must have slipped out mistakenly from one of the principal's assembly speeches.

I looked at Eric to see if he had noticed. He just stood beside Mr. Southern as if tethered there, and looked at me with no change in his glum expression. Eric's glumness chilled me to the bone. I found it more unsettling than Donald Bints's spiralling misery at the paper shack. What did Eric know that I didn't? I was about to look away from him, despairing of any explanation, when he scowled further and nodded toward the inner office.

Just as I mouthed a "What?" at Eric, Mr. Southern flicked out the bottom of his ever-present bolo tie, cleared his throat, and said sternly, "This way, gentlemen."

I began to tremble at the sight that greeted us behind that closed door. Right there, under the beaming, cherubic face of Lester B. Pearson, a foot or two away from a giant prickly cactus, sat my father, his head bare (almost unheard of outside the house), his large hands clasped to his knees, the pale blue dress shirt and navy tie he only ever wore to bowling banquets and weddings looking crisp as autumn leaves.

As we came in, my father lifted his head slowly and looked at me. The expression on his wind-weathered face could only be described as helpless. I saw no anger there, no fatigue, just a kind of nervous confusion. It was as if someone had taken the river right out from under his boat and had marooned him here amongst all these strange artifacts, the cactus and the ex–prime minister and the cast-iron horse, not to mention the desk and filing cabinets.

I should have smiled at him reassuringly, but I was too shocked to do anything but blush and look away, too ashamed to hold his gaze.

My mother's expression was equally unhappy, but not quite so lost. She too was dressed for the occasion, wearing a neat blouse and slacks, her hair in a kerchief, her face freshly made up. If I hadn't known any better, I would have sworn that they had just returned from the community centre, bearing trophies for High Average and High Single Game. Instead, my mother clutched the black purse she held on her lap, while my father's knucklebones turned whiter as he gripped his knees. Over the silence between us, I could almost hear my mother say, "Callum, what on earth have you done? Look, your *father* is here!"

But I couldn't look at him again. Instead, I turned my attention to Eric's parents seated nearby. Mr. Turnbull, tall and lanky, had one long leg casually crossed over one knee and was calmly smoking a cigarette, holding it between a V in his fingers, his hand propped under his chin dark with five o'clock shadow. His eyes seemed to shine behind his glasses and he wore a smirk on his narrow, wolfish face. But what distracted me was the sock on his left foot, exposed because he had lifted his leg onto his knee. It was an argyle sock. For some reason it hypnotized me, as though it were the skin of some exotic snake that had crawled there out of one of the principal's cactus pots. All through the conversation that followed I kept expecting that sock to strike. But it remained coiled just under the tan pantleg.

Mrs. Turnbull, of all the adults in the room, appeared most relaxed. Where her husband seemed poised to leap out of his chair at any second, she sat as comfortably as she did at her kitchen table. With her short, auburn hair and delicate features, her simple pantsuit and lightly made-up face, she looked as if she were about to speak lovingly to the cast-iron horse hovering at her shoulder. Yet there was no frivolity about her either, and I found this as disturbing as her husband's aggressive ease and my parents' stiff postures.

What had they all been talking about? I wondered as I sat in one of the three chairs facing them and waited for my awful fate to unfold. Ridiculously, the word "Djakarta" kept popping into my head.

In his most officious and dramatic manner, Mr. Southern thanked our parents for responding so promptly to his "invitation," a word that widened the smirk on Mr. Turnbull's face and caused him to glance at his wife.

"I do not normally hold unscheduled conferences with parents," the principal continued, ignoring the puffs of smoke uncoiling toward him, "only under exceptional circumstances."

My mother stared at me, her eyes widening. My father dropped his own face back to his clasped knees, his hands as permanently fixed as the iron horse's mane.

Mr. Southern took a long while getting to the point, a delay that made Mr. Turnbull shift position and butt out one cigarette while noisily lighting another, much to his wife's scowling disapproval. At one point, Mr. Turnbull suddenly shook the lit match out and muttered what sounded like "Goddamn."

Mr. Southern paid no attention. He was too busy explaining the spirit of United Nations Month, why he thought it was so important for today's generation of youth to take an interest in the affairs of the world.

"Ours is an international community," he intoned, warming to the subject as he always did. Across the room, beaming straight at him, Lester Pearson seemed to egg on each word. "And I feel it is imperative that, if your children are to thrive in the world of tomorrow, they understand and take up the responsibilities of this wider citizenship. This involves, as I'm sure you realize, developing a certain sensibility to different cultures, different ways of life, even if they seem strange to us."

Again, Eric's father grinned knowingly at his wife, nodding his head in a manner that suggested she should look around the office. But Mrs. Turnbull paid no attention. She sat forward on the very edge of her chair, listening intently to Mr. Southern, her tiny jaw lifted slightly.

I had avoided meeting my parents' eyes, but I could hold out no longer. My father still sat with his hands on his knees, his head hung out over the floor. He slowly raised his head every ten seconds or so, as if it were made of stone. I suddenly realized that he wasn't smoking. The absence of a cigarette in his hand or mouth was even more unusual than his bare-headedness. Maybe he thought it wasn't proper to smoke at school. But why hadn't he lit up when he saw Mr. Turnbull doing so? Maybe he had left his cigarettes at home? My mother, meanwhile, reassured me by fiddling nervously with the brass clasp on her purse, something I had seen her do at the doctor's office or wherever else she had to wait for an appointment.

"And this lack of sensitivity," the principal went on, his fleshy jowls particularly gruesome in profile, "is what has caused me to ask you here this afternoon on such short notice." Then, abruptly, he turned to Eric and me. "But perhaps your sons should explain what it is I'm referring to."

Oh no, I thought, does he mean something about the speech or about Indonesia? I mutely appealed to Eric, but he returned my confusion, then shrugged innocently at his parents.

The silence grew heavy. I could hear Miss Templeton's typing outpacing my heartbeat and my blinking eyes. Tap tap tap tap tap. It was the same lonely rhythm I had heard so often in the apartments of my elderly subscribers, only this sound was more intense, like a mantelpiece clock gone mad.

"Oh for God's sake," Mr. Turnbull said impatiently, dropping his raised leg, and the argyle sock with it, dramatically to the carpet. "What's all the mystery about?"

Very patiently, as if he had been expecting this interruption, Mr. Southern said, turning slightly away from us, "I thought it best to give these young men a chance to admit their own misjudgments."

"Eric?" Mrs. Turnbull appealed softly. My parents seemed content to let the Turnbulls take the lead.

"I don't know," Eric mumbled. "I guess it's because my speech was too long."

Mr. Southern's chin began to quiver and his sigh could probably be heard out in the hallway. "Come along, now," he said with mounting annoyance, "let's have the whole story."

"I don't know it!" Eric insisted, looking wildly at each of us in turn.

"Very well, then," the principal said dismissively. "Callum?"

I knew it was Indonesia; it had to be. But I just couldn't bring myself to admit the cheating in front of my parents, both of whom were looking at me, my mother all eyes and my father with a weary appeal. I wanted to release him from his stiff posture, just as I wanted my mother's eyes returned to their normal shape, but it was impossible. I could not hear myself say "I copied Eric's project," because then I might blurt out "And I stole some cloves from Lums' store because cloves are one of Indonesia's major exports." I wasn't sure which crime was greater, but I certainly didn't want to find out.

The typing in the outer office pounded away at my eardrums, so loud that I almost didn't hear my mother when she said, "Callum, you answer Mr. Southern."

Eric came to my rescue. "We bribed Avery Perich with wagon wheels to let us use the projector."

Oh good! Thank you, Eric, I cheered silently.

"You're not helping yourself, young man," Mr. Southern said severely. "All this stalling will only make things worse."

"Oh, this is ridiculous!" Mr. Turnbull sat tall and straight in his chair, his billowing cigarette orchestrating the air in front of his scowling face. "What is it the boys are supposed to have done, Southern? I'm a busy man. I haven't got time for fun and games."

Mrs. Turnbull reached out and touched his elbow.

"Yes, yes, all right," he spoke sideways to her.

The principal met the challenge head-on. He even seemed to be enjoying himself. After a dramatic pause during which he lowered his head and straightened his bolo tie, he said with much gravity, as though addressing a large assembly, "Your sons, I'm sorry to say, upset a great many people this morning with a degree of coldness and insensitivity that, quite frankly, I was astonished to witness in boys of their age."

Upset? I suddenly remembered the young teachers holding up their handkerchiefs. But that wasn't our fault, it was the Nazis'.

"In fact," Mr. Southern went on, "I have never seen the like before, in nearly twenty-five years as an educator." Some of the restrained gravity left his voice, replaced by genuine outrage. "It's one thing to desecrate the Nativity, which is insensitive enough, and which I found personally insulting and upsetting. But it's quite another, at a time scheduled specifically for celebrating the brotherhood of man, the link between all nations and peoples, to show such horrible images to a roomful of people who have come together for the purpose of goodwill, who are expecting to be informed and entertained, not brought to tears and even illness."

I knew that my mother's face had almost vanished now, swallowed by her eyes. But I didn't have the nerve to look at her.

"Out with it, man!" Mr. Turnbull snapped. "Enough of the song and dance!"

Mr. Southern did not even flinch. He cast Mr. Turnbull a dismissive look, then continued in the same angry tone. "Whether it's United Nations Month or any other time, to show a film of the Nazi concentration camps, a film that shows human bodies being bulldozed into a pit, is beyond poor taste and judgment. It reveals a callousness very disturbing to see in such young children." He calmed down slightly, and took a deep breath. "Admittedly, the teacher in question should not have allowed a speech on Adolph Hitler to reach the multi-purpose room in the first place, but she assures me that the original speech only referred to the camps in passing, and certainly did not include a film."

"You're kidding, aren't you?" Mr. Turnbull exclaimed, pointing at the principal with his cigarette, then turning to his wife and my parents. "He's kidding, isn't he?"

"I assure you, sir," Mr. Southern flared up, "I take this matter very seriously."

Now the conversation began to outrun my understanding. I realized that the film clip had upset some people, but I didn't think that Eric or I would be held responsible for something that the National Film Board had made.

·"Seriously?" Mr. Turnbull scoffed. "I hardly think so. If you took this matter seriously, you'd realize what a horse's ass you're making of yourself."

"Philip!" Mrs. Turnbull exclaimed.

"No," he said, his face more flushed than it had been. "I've had enough of this. The man can sit there and tell us that he's an educator—such a fine word—and then say with a straight face that one of the most significant historical events of this century is not a fit subject for study. It's ridiculous. No, it's worse than that, it's disgusting. Are we supposed to sit here and listen—"

"With all due respect," Mr. Southern interrupted, his chin raised slightly. "I would ask you to consider your tone of voice. There's no call for getting heated."

Mr. Turnbull lurched forward, his eyes widening. He seemed to be appealing to my parents. "No call?" he spluttered. "No call?" His wife touched his elbow again, which calmed him. He laughed briefly, more of a snort than a laugh, and stubbed out his cigarette. The act seemed to calm him even further. He fumbled for another cigarette, and then directly addressed my parents. "Am I wrong?" he said, striking a match. "You tell me if I'm wrong."

My mother looked directly at Mr. Southern. She stopped fiddling with her purse clasp and said in a strong but unexcited voice, "I'm not sure I understand. You say that the boys gave a speech about Hitler and that they showed a film of the concentration camps?"

The principal nodded.

"Callum," my mother said softly, leaning forward. "I thought you were giving a speech about comic books."

"It was not his speech," Mr. Southern interrupted. "I understand that he was an assistant, so to speak."

"Ah, Eric the ringleader." Mr. Turnbull grinned.

Mr. Southern shrugged. "If you like. He is older and so he does have the greater responsibility. Which is why, if I recall correctly, I did not call you . . ." He paused, looking at my parents. "About the desecration of the Nativity."

My parents seemed completely lost now.

"I beg your pardon," my mother said. "The desecration of what?"

I thought my father's neck would snap from the strain of holding it up so long. To my relief, he finally lifted his hands off his knees and leaned back.

Mrs. Turnbull spoke quietly to my mother, and very succinctly explained about the taping of Eric's picture onto the baby Jesus. "But I didn't realize that Callum was also involved," she concluded.

My father, much to my delight, smiled despite himself. He looked at us the way he looked at someone on the wharf who had done something out of the ordinary. He was not an intellectual by the strict definition of the word, but he greatly admired displays of wit.

"Well, Eric," Mr. Turnbull said in mock sternness, "what have you to say for yourself?"

"Philip, please," Mrs. Turnbull said wearily. "You're not helping." She turned to Mr. Southern. "I'm afraid I can't agree with you," she said calmly and respectfully. "I do understand that the Holocaust is upsetting, but it's an important part of history. I cannot see it as anything but dangerous to hide such things away from our children." Diplomatically, she added, "But perhaps there is an appropriate age that some reach sooner than others."

Mr. Southern smiled pleasantly, clearly appreciating her tone of voice. But he would not concede her point. "It is not a matter of hiding, but a matter of forgiving and moving on. It is of no use to dwell on the mistakes of the past. What I want for your sons, as for all students, is something more positive, something they can build on to help make the world a better place."

"Good god," Mr. Turnbull sighed heavily, waving his cigarette again. "It's not all *Paddle-to-the-Sea,* you know. The world's a hard place. You're old enough to have figured that out by now."

The principal's voice was becoming strained. He gripped the arms of his chair a little tighter. "The world's as hard as we choose to make it," he said, reaching out to adjust a small photo on his desk.

My mother suddenly spoke up, breaking the tension between the two men. "I'm sorry, I'm afraid I'm still not clear what has happened. You say that the boys taped something onto a little wooden Jesus and showed a film about bodies being pushed into a pit?"

There was a prolonged silence over which my mother's puzzled face hovered like a moon.

Mr. Southern spoke with less patience now. "I have put the matter of the Christ-child in the past. But this matter of the film, I felt it was serious enough to discuss with you in person."

Mrs. Turnbull nodded understandingly. "Yes, we do appreciate your concern. But I'm sure that the boys meant no harm in showing the film. In fact, I can guarantee that they didn't even realize they were doing wrong."

"Well, of course not," Mr. Turnbull joined in, the argyle sock back up on his knee. "Because they weren't doing wrong. What are they supposed to do? Pretend that the Nazis were good-time Charlies just out for a few laughs?"

Mr. Southern stiffened noticeably. "Your sarcasm, sir, is not appreciated." He raised his voice to drown out a response from

Mr. Turnbull. "But the wrong exists. It's a matter of sensitivity toward others. Two of our young teachers, one of whom is of German extraction, were particularly upset by the film, and several students were crying along with them. And . . ." He outspoke Mr. Turnbull again, the latter waving his hand dismissively and taking a long drag on his cigarette as the principal continued. "It wasn't just the film. Your son also went to the extreme of dressing up like Hitler."

Everyone looked alarmingly at Eric, who blushed and lowered his head.

"Eric, is that true?" his mother asked.

"Well, yeah," he mumbled. "But just the moustache and hair. I didn't wear a uniform or anything like that."

"Oh, Eric," his mother sighed. Even his father seemed momentarily at a loss. Eric, feeling the need to defend himself, blurted out, "But Johnny Van Dusen had someone wearing a whole Goofy mask!"

Mr. Turnbull guffawed.

"I fail to see the humour in this, sir," the principal remarked sourly.

"Quite right," Mr. Turnbull agreed, rapidly licking his lips and glancing around the office. "It is clearly wrong to dress up like someone else when you are giving a speech." His grin widened unpleasantly.

Mr. Southern, reddening slightly, glanced at the large portrait over my parents' heads. I followed his glance, and saw that my parents were struggling to follow the conversation; they both had their mouths slightly parted. My father intermittently looked with longing at Mr. Turnbull's dancing cigarette.

"Surely," the principal said, straightening his shoulders, "you would not be suggesting that dressing up as a Nazi and paying homage to a much-loved former prime minister, a man of courage and vision who worked all his life for peace, are at all the same?"

"Six of one, half dozen of the . . ."

"Of course he isn't suggesting that," Mrs. Turnbull said, casting a sharp look at her husband, who had returned to smoking casually. "Eric," she abruptly changed the subject, "is often too enthusiastic, I admit. And I have spoken with him about this. I agree with you, he does need to think a little more about the feelings of others. However, I think you're wrong if you believe the boys deliberately set out to hurt anyone. I know they would never do such a thing."

Mr. Southern seemed unconvinced, but more or less satisfied. "Perhaps that's so. They are certainly both very bright. Of course, that is not everything in life. One must be able to get along with others." He looked challengingly at Mr. Turnbull, who smiled sardonically.

The meeting seemed about finished when Mr. Turnbull suddenly addressed my father. "And what do you think?" he said loudly, pointing his cigarette. "Is your son a threat to society?"

My father looked hard at me for a few seconds. I noted the deep lines around his mouth and a small dab of blood on his lower jaw where he must have cut himself shaving. When he finally smiled and winked at me, I felt a rush of pure affection, followed by sickening guilt as he said, "Callum's a good boy. I don't suppose I have to worry about him."

My mother's broadening smile only made things worse. Right then, I made a vow: no more cheating, no more shoplifting, and no more helping Eric at school!

Meanwhile, Mr. Southern had cleared his throat nervously at my father's reply, and even Mr. Turnbull looked cowed by it.

The awkward silence was finally filled by the principal.

"Very well. I'll assume that there won't be any further incidents of this sort. I am satisfied that the boys have learned a valuable lesson and that you'll take whatever punitive steps you feel are appropriate." He stood and extended his pale right hand, on the index finger of which was a large pewter ring. My father shook the hand firmly and smiled without much warmth. Mr. Turnbull ignored the hand and busied himself by butting his cigarette into a cactus pot. The principal said pointedly to Mrs. Turnbull, "Thank you for coming." Then he ushered us out into the hallway, sending us off with the hope that he would see us again at the public-speaking finale.

A few minutes later, the six of us stood outside in the wan, rare sunlight rapidly dissolving into dusk. My parents and Eric's had never met before, and so there was some awkwardness in the over-hanging silence. Mr. Turnbull finally coughed and said heartily, "Well, there's nothing like a little cabaret to make the afternoon slide by."

My mother lowered her voice even though there was no one around. For a moment, she seemed to forget that Eric and I were listening. "That was very odd. To be honest with you, I don't know what he expects us to do now."

"Nothing. The man's certifiable," Mr. Turnbull said. The broken veins on his long nose and cheeks pulsed vivid red in the sunlight. He took his cigarette pack out of his shirt pocket and fumbled it onto the pavement. Scowling, he left it there as he continued to speak. "He should be in an asylum. Lester Pearson, for chrissakes! Waffling, Ontario Presbyterian rich boy. And all that cowboy business. It's no wonder the boys upset him. They're more with it than he is."

With great pleasure, my father pulled out his own cigarettes, lit one, and offered another to Mr. Turnbull, who took it and fell into a dark silence.

My mother and Mrs. Turnbull neatly turned away from the matter at hand to exchange pleasantries. Then they complimented each other on their respective sons, how nice it was that we both enjoyed reading and writing so much. The subject of the concentration camps and the Nativity never came up, and our two families soon parted.

This whole time, Eric and I stood almost motionless, just eager to get home. Tacitly, we understood that we'd talk things over later.

So the afternoon deepened to darkness. My father lifted my bike into the back of Mr. Ely's truck, which he had borrowed, and drove me to the paper shack. During the short drive, all either of my parents said about the meeting was, "You'd do better to concentrate on your own homework and let your friends do theirs," advice I was more than ready to follow.

But now I had Clive Withers's biting comments about my lateness to contend with, not to mention about thirty papers to deliver. "No rest for the wicked," I could imagine my mother saying, the words dropping heavily at my back as I pushed my bike over the gravel toward the skinny, amber-lit doorway of the shack.

fifteen

I SUFFERED TERRIBLY in the days following, convinced that my Indonesia project would cost me my freedom and what was left of my self-respect. Once, I even woke in the middle of the night from a nightmare in which I had been searching hopelessly for cloves in the capital city of Djakarta. During the day, whenever I imagined my teacher sternly calling me up to her desk, the copied map and flag in front of her, I shuddered and closed my eyes, hoping the awful vision would vanish.

Yet the anxiety did not prevent me from enjoying the small fame that Eric and I had won in the playground. We had also looked forward to regaling Mr. Bradlee and Jamie with the full story down at the bookshop. Eric had brought along a copy of the speech for Mr. Bradlee to read, which he did with rare solemnity, his submarine sandwich slowly dripping mustard onto the counter beside the pages as he pulled at one end of his moustache with his free hand.

"It's very good, Eric," he finally said, looking up without a smile. "Yes, very, very good." He wiped the mustard splats away with the sleeve of his sweater, then slid the speech to Jamie without further comment. I glanced at Eric to see if he was surprised or disappointed, but he had launched into his *Hogan's Heroes* German accent to explain how his father had argued with Mr. Southern. Surprisingly, Mr. Bradlee scowled and shushed him (a surprise because there was no one else in the shop).

"Not so loud, not so loud," he said, then turned up the volume a notch on the radio.

Eric hesitated, unsure of whether to finish his story. But Mr. Bradlee solved the problem by encouraging him to "go ahead, just not so loud." He then busied himself around the cash register in a way that suggested he was only half-listening.

Jamie was a more satisfactory audience. He was particularly interested in what Eric's father had said to Mr. Southern.

"No kidding? Really?" he responded when Eric told how his father had said it was ridiculous to dress up to give a speech. "He really said that? What did Southern do?"

When Eric answered, Jamie whistled quietly and looked at Mr. Bradlee. The latter had paused to listen, but he only shook his head slightly.

"Your dad is something," Jamie remarked. "My dad would never have said anything like that."

I suddenly felt annoyed. My father's few words, I had somehow sensed, were more impressive and effective than Mr. Turnbull's outbursts. But Eric, for all his brains, clearly hadn't recognized this fact, because he only mentioned my father in passing to get to his father's comment that the principal belonged in an insane asylum. Again I was annoyed, but it was really Eric's story, after all, his speech, his film. And I couldn't deny that his parents had spoken up more than mine. Besides, I was equally seized by Eric's storytelling powers. With his amazing memory, he re-created the meeting in the office almost word for word.

Ultimately, though, even this drama had a short shelf life for us. Once we had learned that Eric didn't make the finals of the public-speaking competition, we put the whole business behind us and moved on to other things.

I received my Indonesia project back. With little pleasure, I read my teacher's glowing comments under the large A+, her particular admiration for the taped spices page (Very inventive, Callum!), as well as the flag and map (Beautifully done!). I had gotten away with it and should have been proud. Instead, I felt lousy. I felt even worse when Eric delightedly told Mr. Bradlee about it. I should have revelled in this proof of my daring, but my cheeks burned and I changed the subject to the new issue of *The Amazing Spiderman* that had just come in. Fortunately, Mr. Bradlee, as if sensing how I felt, obligingly plopped the comic on the counter for us to flip through.

And that was it for United Nations Month. It ended as it always did, with a large assembly in the gym, topped off with a patriotic speech by Mr. Southern, once again in bow tie, which included several minutes of praise for Lester Pearson. Eric and I both had our excellent marks, but the excitement over how we had earned them soon dissipated. The school year trudged on through February, with fractions and book reports and phonics and National Fitness Testing (including the dreaded flexed arm hang). The prime ministers scowled down at us as we tramped the muck of the wintry weather into the hallways, where George plowed along as if at the dead leaders' bidding to mop up the grey pools we left behind, his unintelligible muttering almost motherly compared with the sound of the sleet and drizzle that never stopped tapping at the classroom windows.

For much of that drab month I relied on Ezra for excitement. No matter how dull school or the weather became, or how much of a cold slog delivering papers proved to be, I had only to call up the image of Ezra's dark face through the grocery curtain, or of his fleet form stealing from streetlight to streetlight along the banks of the river, to believe in the imminent possibility of drama. And the possibility was enough. As long as Jerris and I could trail him, as long as he appeared suddenly around a corner or at the crest of the dyke, my days retained an undercurrent of delicious tension; they even turned over like pages bound for some thrilling conclusion that, happily, never arrived. It didn't matter what the truth of his involvement with the Lums was; I was content to speculate on it and to pursue its shadows, feeling myself at once the spinner of the web and the fly trapped in it. Jerris, in his eagerness to follow me, provided a wonderful, receptive audience, and though at times I grew impatient with his own ideas (which I thought lacked sophistication, were more like *The Rawhide Kid* than *The Amazing Spiderman*), I was happy for his company. After all, I could not pretend a greater courage than I possessed; Ezra's blank stare continued to disturb me.

One night, I even woke in a cold sweat, terrified by the image of Ezra at the controls of a bulldozer pushing a thousand of his own bloodied, wide-eyed selves over the dyke and into the river. And laughter came from the lips of the driver and the lips of the dead. I had to switch on my light and read comics for a while before I calmed down enough to fall back asleep. But even then I kept seeing Ezra push in from the edges of the pages, as if he longed to be part of every kind of action at the same time that he remained separate from it. I often had to remind myself that he really existed, was a part of the town, that my parents knew him and that others saw him in the streets or at the wharf. And always,

always, in part because Ezra continued to see the Lum girls and often laughed openly at their brothers, I felt some vague climax approaching.

But when it came, I was not at all prepared for it, nor for the manner in which it happened.

sixteen

A FEW NIGHTS AFTER the end of United Nations Month, I was at the wharf with my father, checking the boat, when Mr. Graveridge strode heavily toward us over the planks, his bootsteps like clapping hands, his long shadow in the wharf lights reaching us before we could read the expression on his face.

"Evening, Mack, young Callum," he began soberly. I looked up at him. He was solid and black as a piling. His long, silvered hair hung brittle as dried moss from his black sou'wester and swung as he stepped aboard the *Nautilus*. She rolled with his weight and the calm harbour water sloshed a little as she righted herself. Mr. Graveridge didn't follow up his greeting immediately, so my father offered him a cigarette.

"Mack," he said, refusing the smoke with a wave and clearing his throat with a low rumble, "I wonder if you'd lend me a hand for a bit." He paused, spat in the water, then solemnly added, "It's Ezra."

The name echoed like his bootsteps and finally died away in the marsh. My father stood up from where he'd been bending into the main hatch. "Sure, Rod, whatever you need."

"The silly beggar won't listen to me," Mr. Graveridge explained as we headed up to the dyke. "I figure maybe someone else could get through that thick skull of his before he does himself an injury. Peggy told me you were down here."

"Where is he?" my father asked, our bootsteps crunching the gravel of the dyke as we hurried westward out of town (in the general direction of Lums' Grocery, I realized with excitement). The muddy riversmell swirled up from the tide, cloaking us. I could hear the current rushing along at our side, bringing everything with it—sticks, fish, oil, garbage—from the Mission Bridge down.

Mr. Graveridge laughed mirthlessly. "At my place. Drunk as a skunk. I locked him in. Christ knows if there'll be anything left of the place."

Even I knew of Ezra's reputation as a drinker. He often consumed prodigious amounts, after and during which he was capable of much violence if provoked. Once he even stole the seiner of a man he didn't like and ran it aground in the marsh. Similar incidents must have been on my father's mind because, as we approached the broken Home Oil sign, its neon glinting like light off bits of a smashed bottle, he said, "You get on home, Callum."

I was about to plead my case for coming along when a shotgun blast tore the silence and rippled the gravel twenty or so feet ahead of us.

"Jesus Christ!" my father gasped. "Where did that come from!"

We all spun wildly, as if we could trace the path of the shell in the darkness. Nothing moved on the street below or on the river.

"Goddamnit, Ezra!" Mr. Graveridge bellowed. "You could have killed somebody!"

We stood motionless. There was nowhere to take cover.

"I thought you locked him in," my father said in a hushed voice, pulling me to him. The rough wool of his jacket scratched my cheek, and I almost choked on the thick smell of cigarette smoke wound through it.

Mr. Graveridge scowled. "I did. The beggar must have smashed his way out." He lowered his voice. "It's different this time, Mack. I can't explain it, but something's happened. Something must . . ."

Suddenly, Ezra's cackle, eerie as a loon cry, broke out from the direction of the Home Oil site.

My father positioned me behind him and held me there by my wrists. "Where is he?" he asked anxiously.

But Mr. Graveridge had already moved toward the dim neon light falling on the gravel. He muttered deep in his throat as he went, then thundered out, "Ezra! Where in blue blazes are you!"

A rapid burst of words scattered around us. "Fuckin-kill-them-goddamnit-kill-them-both-first-chance-goddamnit!" Another shot followed, but the shell hit the river some distance from us. My father flinched anyway and tightened his grip so firmly on my wrists that they hurt.

Mr. Graveridge reached the base of the neon sign. A faint blur of blue haloed his head. He was facing away from the river toward the oil tanks. "Ezra! Mack's here! And his boy! Do you hear me! You don't want to shoot them, do you!" He quickly told my father to say something.

My father hesitated. I suspected he was deciding what to do about me, whether to send me off at a run for home or to keep me with him. He finally edged forward, releasing my wrists, his body between the source of Ezra's voice and me. After ten feet he stopped and shouted, "Ezra! It's me, Mack!"

There was a brief silence before his response. "Mackie-you-old-bugger-better-get-down-there-pump-her-out-lots-of-rain-goddamnya."

The relative sanity of this outburst decided my father. He knelt and with great urgency told me to run as fast as I could home, using the back way. "As fast as you can," he repeated.

I sprinted up the dyke until I got winded. But I was too excited not to circle around via the river road until I could see the oil tanks. I realized that this was the big moment I'd been waiting for, but I could hardly believe that it had come. Everything was happening too fast for me to do much else besides take up a good position from which to watch the drama unfold.

Under cover of one of the larger plum trees, I was close enough to see the lead-pencil smudges of my father and Mr. Graveridge on the dyke. I could also hear the shouted words between them and Ezra. Gradually, following the back-and-forth exchanges, I focused on the top of one of the tanks, which loomed up, slightly to the west, between the dyke and my position.

The full moon, the size of a seal's head, appeared to drift slowly over the scene, clouds trailing from it like seaweed. It cast a shuttered light that occasionally shone bright enough to heighten the dark outlines of the tanks and the two figures on the dyke. But I did not look away from the moon. Another figure jerked against it, sticking up vividly from the nearest tank. As I watched, I finally discerned the extra length of dark against one of Ezra's arms. He held it tightly, as if it were strapped to him, but the barrel extended a foot beyond his hand until it looked as though he were deformed.

"Throw it down, Ezra!" Mr. Graveridge shouted.

I looked to the dyke. The two figures had not moved. I looked back up at the moon. A large, scudding cloud suddenly smothered it, and Ezra vanished briefly. As the light gradually swept back over the tank, I held my breath, uncertain that Ezra would still be there. It was impossible to predict what he would do. Even if he jumped I wouldn't be surprised. He had never shown much concern for his physical well-being. And now, as Mr. Graveridge had said, he was drunk and capable of anything. Or was he drunk? Could all this be just another act designed to confuse the Lums, keep them from guessing that he was, in fact, preparing to outwit them?

I tried to believe so, even though I half-accepted the shattered quality in Ezra's laugh as genuine and dangerously unpredictable. Suddenly, I felt afraid for my father. Was Ezra cracked enough to shoot him? I remembered how he had thrown my father away from the pump. He hadn't been drunk then. And what did Mr. Graveridge mean by "something's happened"?

Moonlight spilled over the top of the tank and down to the gravel below, then spread rapidly over the thirty yards of dew-bowed grass to the cracked pavement of the river road. By the time it lapped at the trunk I crouched against, I was staring up at the source of it again. The black figure remained, motionless now, the longer arm raised to shoulder height and pointed upriver.

"Ezra! For Christ's sake!" Mr. Graveridge sounded more exasperated than concerned. His words bounced hollowly off the tanks.

"Ezra, it's Mack here. Come on down and let's have a drink." My father sounded calmer than before, but I noticed he still hadn't moved closer. I figured he also believed Ezra capable of shooting him, if only by accident. Mr. Graveridge must have realized this too, for he had not moved away from the neon sign.

It became very still. A bullfrog gulped in a nearby ditch and the wind rattled some smaller branches above me. Ezra did not move, though wisps of cloud burned like smoke off his shoulders. I waited for the gunshot. Instead, Ezra's rapid-fire words kicked into the silence, less manic and angry. I had to strain to hear them.

"Sons-of-bitches-sons-of-bitches."

There was a brief pause. Suddenly, his figure jerked back against the light, and, a split second later, the shell burst.

The two figures on the dyke whirled with the sound. One collapsed. Rising, I saw the dark figure against the moon, poised at the edge of the tank. The gun dangled loosely.

Ezra broke off the sky like a branch, but soundlessly. I thought I could see his body falling for a long time, but it must have been my imagination. The silence remained. I ran into it, trying to find two figures on the dyke. I ran without pause, as though I could keep the bodies from hitting the ground, as though there was nothing solid beneath any of us, just riverspill and the gathered rain and the letters of a broken word being spelled out relentlessly to the moonless sky.

seventeen

WHEN I REACHED THE BULK of the oil tanks I saw a shape sprawled on the gravel, the dried residue of spilled oil forming a loose pattern around it. My blood pounded and pounded in my ears. I tried to listen beyond it for some sound off the dyke, but heard only the wind.

The body lay motionless and silent. The same smell rose from it as rose from the surrounding splotches of oil. I looked to the dyke again. Only one figure stood outlined against the sky. I was about to cry out to my father, praying the figure would turn, when everything changed.

The black clouds slid like grease off the moon and a thin, viscous light washed over the dyke. The oily smell thickened. I watched the light spread over Ezra's ungrinning face, blackened by his beard and, higher up, what looked like blood. His skullcap lay a few feet from his head like another splotch of oil, and the gun rested slightly farther off, pointing back toward him and the dyke. The angle of its barrel turned me around again.

The figure at the top of the slope, fifty feet away and thirty feet up, hadn't moved. Then suddenly it disappeared, as if another, silent shot had hit its target.

"Dad!" I cried out and ran to the base of the dyke.

The figure rose and scrambled a few feet down the packed-gravel slope toward me.

"Callum? Are you all right?" It was my father's voice, anxious but steady.

I hurried up the slope. "I'm okay," I gasped, halfway to the top.

My father's face was grim when I arrived.

"Is Mr. Graveridge shot?" I asked, peering around him.

But the answer came from the top of the dyke where no one stood. "Never mind about me. Go on, Mack, get yourself down there and see to the lad."

My father looked at me and said quickly, "Hurt his ankle. Turning too fast."

I assumed Mr. Graveridge was referring to me when he said "lad," and I almost shouted that I was all right. But as my father started down at a run, I realized he had meant Ezra.

I followed, wanting to explain what I had seen at the base of the oil tank but not really sure what it was. Ezra's stillness couldn't mean death. How many times had Spiderman or Batman feigned it, just to spring up in the next frame, energized, better than ever, the darkness of the world cast back like so much dust? Besides, hadn't Ezra already risen from the dead? I had stood with Jerris in the marsh and seen the bloodstains, and I had been there when Ezra reappeared as if nothing had happened. No, there had to be more to his stillness than even my father or Mr. Graveridge understood. I almost expected Ezra to wink at me the first chance he got. And the expectation thrilled me. I hurried down the slope.

When I had caught up to my father he was already bent over the body, putting his ear to Ezra's lips. Then he grabbed one of his wrists and held it gingerly between his fingers, as though weighing it. I stared at the blank face, waiting for one eye to open, to flash out at me like the exposed moon. But Ezra must have had a better reason to keep both eyes shut. How much could I really know of his secret plans? I was scared, too; he looked badly hurt. Maybe he wouldn't get up.

A car passed on the road below us, the sound of its engine harsh and invasive. Once it had faded away, my father told me to run home and tell my mother to call for an ambulance.

"Be sure you tell her I'm all right," he added.

I ran so quickly through the clutching overhang of the orchard that I was speaking to my mother in our warm kitchen even before my eyes had closed on the dull neon and the broken body and the faintly gleaming oil tanks.

eighteen

TWO DAYS LATER, on a drizzly, still afternoon, I arrived home from my paper route just as my father was heading out the door. Something in his movements, an unusual haste, suggested that he was going somewhere other than the wharf. Ever since the shooting I had become especially sensitive to subtleties in the behaviours of others, on the alert for anything that might give me important information about Ezra.

There hadn't been much. According to my parents, he was unconscious in the hospital in Steveston, but they wouldn't say how badly he was hurt, or even if he was likely to survive. Unable to find out more, Jerris and I had become desperate; we hung around the Lums' store and the tree lot every chance we could get, hoping the pig-faced man would make an appearance. But everything was ordinary, except that Ezra had disappeared again. This time, though, I had seen him strapped onto a stretcher and lifted into an ambulance. That couldn't possibly be part of some ingenious plan. Yet, despite the evidence of my own senses, my own instincts even, the idea of Ezra as indestructible would not die completely. For if he had been drunk, had tried to shoot my father or Mr. Graveridge, and now did lie close to death in hospital, then what could be extraordinary about Chilukthan, or anywhere?

My father's urgency, at least, was unusual enough to be marked. More than that, it was downright strange that he'd be leaving the house so close to suppertime.

"Hey Dad, where are you going?" I asked excitedly.

Frowning, he glanced over his shoulder at the house, then looked back to me with an apologetic smile. "Just for a little boat ride. I'll be back in an hour or so."

"Can I come?" It didn't matter to me where he was planning to go. Just being around the waterfront or on the river seemed to increase my chances of finding out more about Ezra.

He paused, opened his mouth to speak. But a shaft of light from the porch doorway washed onto the wet gravel and my mother appeared.

"Make sure he wears a life jacket," she said in a tired and accepting way. "And here's a sandwich for you." She handed it to me, shaking her head. "I knew you'd be back before your father left. There's just no keeping you away from that waterfront these days." She sighed and pulled the collar of her jacket tight around her neck. "Callum, you listen to your father. And stay away from the sides of the boat!"

I nodded and hurried after my father through the plum trees onto the dyke. To my surprise we started to walk east, instead of west toward the town. In a moment, we had passed under the blinking neon of the Home Oil sign, and I looked back nervously. Though I had stared at the tanks many times since the shooting, this was the first time I had done so in the company of my father. His presence brought the incident back with a greater clarity—I almost saw Ezra's outline dark against the grey shivering of the rain. But there was nothing there; the only sound was of the river lapping at the wharf below our feet as we walked quickly toward the gas barge at the far end. Halfway down the wharf I saw that the *Nautilus* was moored at the barge. With mounting excitement, I also saw the tall, bulky figure of Mr. Graveridge standing on the deck. He held the outside steering wheel with one hand, spinning it casually as if it were no larger than a cookie.

"Afternoon Mack, young Callum," he said soberly. "Sorry about the hour, Mack. But I don't much care to be out late. The cold sets into me bones."

"That's all right, Rod. I'd have taken you over earlier except I had a few things to do to make sure the old girl would get us there and back without any trouble."

"Where are we going?" I cut in now, almost breathlessly. For a few seconds I wasn't even sure the words had come out.

"Steveston," my father said tersely, and dipped into the cabin to start the boat.

Mr. Graveridge laid his huge hand gently on my shoulder. "To the hospital, lad. To check up on poor old Ezra." He grimaced as he turned to face the channel, his sore ankle obviously still paining him. "He's not likely to have any other visitors, the poor sod."

A few moments later we had untied the *Nautilus* and were idling downriver, the grey waters parting and falling away evenly behind us. The rain fell lazily, in shivers, as if the whole sky were a branch shaking off droplets. Mr. Graveridge folded himself through the cabin doorway with a groan, eager, I supposed, for the faint warmth beyond and maybe a "spot of tea," as he called it. I stood on the main fish hatch, holding the bright red life jacket in one hand and the damp sandwich bag in the other. There wasn't anything to do but look at the scenery.

On the mainland bank sat a number of derelict boatworks and sheds, many with their windows smashed, their weighs empty, and their planks moss-covered. Wooden skiffs half-filled with rainwater slopped up and down beside oily, chipped pilings, while others, turned bottom-up on cluttered wharves, were black as mounds of earth. No one was around. The newer gillnetters had been drydocked, and the older ones, like my father's and Mr. Graveridge's, seemed so much a part of the weather that there was no point in separating them from it. I looked to the other side of the channel, to the silt islands. These were uninhabited, lonely places, though a way up in the rushes, tucked into the shelter of a marsh willow or cottonwood, a loner of a fisherman sometimes banged together several pieces of driftwood and old planks and lived there under the grey smoke-scraggle of a wet fire.

Our boat cruised slowly past, its familiar chug-chug-chug offering some warmth amongst the damp isolation. Soon we reached the bottom of the channel, before the Pheasant Island Bridge, where the river separated in two directions: south and west to the gulf and north toward Steveston. We took the northern channel up the east side of Pheasant Island, passing empty potato and corn fields and massive old barns so rickety that it was easy to believe the next wash of moonlight would collapse them. A few pieces of machinery loomed up out of the dusk, a combine and a tractor so rusted that they looked more like salvage that a dredging crew had brought up from the silty river bottom. Here, too, blackened wharves with sinking skiffs hung out from the tide-gnawed edges of the land. Spidery strands of web hung off swaybacked net racks. Several dozen loose corks, fast losing their colour, dotted the flaking wood. And a half-mile back over the sodden fields, a single yellow light in a window proved that the Lab that ran down to bark at us as we drifted by actually belonged to someone.

We ran north with the current until we left the tangle of sloughs and islands behind and briefly headed west toward the gulf. Up ahead I could see the lightship, the blinking beacon along the Steveston breakers that marked the end of the river and the beginning of the ocean. But we weren't going so far. We skirted another small island then cut back to the east, along a sprawl of wharves, gas barges, sheds, and abandoned canneries that made up the Steveston harbour. The government wharf was larger here, but as flaking and oil-smeared as the one in Chilukthan. Many different kinds of fishboats—gillnetters, trollers, seiners, and trawlers—rocked gently together, giving off an intermittent, fading sound, as of guitar strings plucked a few seconds before. Up on the dyke a big pyramid of crab traps rose like a barbed shadow out of the rapidly descending dusk. Two hatless Japanese men stood gazing out at the rain from the upper wharf, their cigarette smoke just visible, their voices unheard, though I could see their mouths moving. A half-dozen gulls screamed and wheeled over us. The blended stink of rotting fish and creosote drenched the air.

We tied up at the Canadian Fish Company docks (the company my father delivered his fish to) and walked up the gangway in the fine, slanting rain. My father and Mr. Graveridge moved in an aura of cigarette smoke that gave them a ghostly appearance. But their bootsteps fell heavily on the wet planks, drowning out my own, as we climbed from the tide line, finally reaching the all-but-empty parking lot of the cannery. A lone freezer truck sat off to one side, its CanFish logo almost faded away, its tires soft. We hurried through the shallow puddles on the asphalt, cracked here and there where weeds had broken through. Steveston was quiet in the falling dusk. Winter emptied the streets and wharves here just as much as it did at home, since Steveston was even more of a fishing town than Chilukthan. The businesses—small marine-supply shops, diners displaying handwritten "Halibut and Chips" signs in their windows, a barbershop with a striped pole, bait and tackle shops, the offices of the local newspaper and of a marine insurance agent—were already darkened. But none was so dark as the Gulf of Georgia cannery, a hulking, ramshackle building boarded up behind a ragged chainlink fence. I was certain I heard a low moaning come from those shadows as we hurried by, but the wind had picked up out of the west and I knew I was in a state ready to imagine anything.

The hospital, a large, dirty-brick building caked with moss, loomed out of the surrounding drabness like a fish aquarium. A few cars slid in and out of the glowing parking lot, their tires sloshing. Just before the entrance, I was surprised to find a large statue of a fisherman in a sou'wester holding a gaff hook. It stood in the middle of a pool of brackish water that contained a fountain that wasn't spouting. The statue was a dull, green-tinged copper, and the fisherman's smile looked as if it would crack at any second. Walking by, I saw that the brackish water was scaled with pennies, nickels, and dimes. I didn't have any change in my pockets, which upset me, since I knew exactly what I would have wished for. But the money didn't matter; I made the wish anyway, and kept right on making it.

We hadn't spoken since leaving the wharf. But now, in the bright lobby, facing the white-clad nurses and the sober faces of other visitors and the strange, far-off dinging noises that never ceased, my father and Mr. Graveridge turned to each other.

"Better get the room number," my father said quietly.

Mr. Graveridge nodded and removed his skullcap. He crushed it in his hand and the water dripped onto the shiny floor. "Aye, let's be done with it. I'm not a one for hospitals."

Now he and my father held their skullcaps to their bodies; in all that brightness, it looked like they had holes in their chests.

Before long, we found our way to an elevator, ascended a dozen floors, and walked down a hallway lined with watercolours of fish-boats and harbours. Mrs. Ely's are better, I thought with sudden pride. And the thought brought Jerris's grinning face to mind, which made me determined to concentrate on every detail of this unexpected visit.

Hesitantly, we walked into a large room holding eight beds, most of which were enclosed by curtains on wheels. The room was dimly lit and quiet except for a dull humming that seemed to come from the walls. Occasionally a nurse appeared, looked around briskly, and left again. I suddenly became aware of someone snoring behind one of the curtains, a sound like the half-hearted tearing of paper.

Ezra can't possibly be here, I thought, still hopeful. But then, in a flash, my hopes were destroyed. The sight of Ezra in the bed closest to the window shocked me. Against the stiff, starched bedsheets, he was even blacker than usual. A thin tube ran out of his bared sinewy arm to a metal stand holding a plastic bag of clear liquid. The liquid dripped soundlessly into the tube.

"Agh, good Christ," Mr. Graveridge groaned, bending over Ezra's still face. It was puffed on one side, scraped almost raw. His usually vivid red lips were pale. And, most disturbing of all to me, no smell of oil or smoke or fish came off him. In fact, all I could smell was the lingering, unpleasant odour of some sort of cooked meat. In all this, Ezra seemed more dead than he had lying on the gravel by the oil tank.

Mr. Graveridge suspended his hand over Ezra's brow, as if trying to read his thoughts.

"Poor begger," he said. "And what in Heaven's name have you got to come back to?" He paused before adding in an undertone, "If you come."

I stood with my father at the foot of the bed, feeling numb. It really was Ezra, there could be no doubt. All my wishing had made no difference; there he lay. I felt an overwhelming urge to turn around for home before this awful image was permanently imprinted on my brain. "Get up," I whispered desperately under my breath. "Come on, get up." But he didn't even open one eye.

Mr. Graveridge lowered his hand and gently stroked Ezra's forehead.

"Stone cold," he announced, and turned back with such a collapsed look that I shuddered. My father cleared his throat uncomfortably, then moved around the bed and awkwardly, lightly patted Ezra on the shoulder.

"He'll be all right," he said. "Comes of tough stock."

I knew my father meant well, but the words sounded hollow even to me. Tough stock? What was so tough about falling off an oil tank without anyone around to push you? What was so tough about letting the Lums win so easily? A strange combination of rage and loss threatened to overwhelm me, but I concentrated on the distant humming until I calmed down.

The three of us stood there a few more minutes, as if waiting for someone to arrive and tell us whether Ezra would pull through or not. Finally, we left the way we had come. Mr. Graveridge stopped at the nurses' desk to make inquiries, but found out only that Ezra had a severe concussion and was unconscious. "Time will tell," he repeated to us with a weary shrug, as if Time was some sort of official who looked down on people if they were only poor salmon fishermen.

It was dark when the *Nautilus* chugged back out of Steveston harbour and turned south for Chilukthan. The rain had stopped, but it was colder. A slick glaze on the water reflected the wharf lights, and the river looked like a huge stretch of black ice. My

father and Mr. Graveridge stayed in the cabin, wrapped in cigarette smoke and long silences. I decided to go out on deck. The
yellow warmth of the cabin was too much like Ezra's hospital
room, which, I suddenly realized, had made me uncomfortable in
much the same way that Mrs. Edmundson's living room had,
with its humming radio and odd smell and the weight of the air.
Though bitingly cold, the darkness was at least clean and fresh.

I stood on the main hatch, munching the sandwich I'd taken
from my coat pocket. The stars glistened over the gulf. All of a
sudden I could taste the salt at the back of my mouth, almost
down into my lungs, as though great gulps of the night were filling
my insides. Everything I had seen on the trip to Steveston had
disappeared. Even the barking dog on Pheasant Island was quiet,
and the light in the farmhouse window was out. Most of the way
home we travelled from dark to dark, and I strained to pick out a
tree or moored boat along the banks.

Finally, on the approach to Chilukthan harbour, the small, full
moon slid out from a cloud and a dim whiteness lay on the water.
The moon itself was brighter than its light. It was as white against
the sky as Ezra's face had been black against his bedsheets.
Somehow, staring at the moon, I kept seeing Ezra's face sinking
and then, magically, disappearing. The image seemed vaguely
familiar, something I had seen before, long ago, something
connected to Ezra and the river, but I could not recover it; it had
gone with the dog's bark and the farmhouse light and the rusted
weighs and broken skiffs. I stared at the moon, its one faint crater
a dark body falling again and again from a great height. For the last
time, I felt the strange, delicious closeness to Ezra; it seemed that
I had only to lean a little farther into the surrounding dark to
recapture his grin and his rapid speech, the vague image that was
trying to float to the surface. But I did not lean any farther. And I

did not even want to. There just wasn't any point. Dry-mouthed, I hurled the crust of my sandwich onto the black, flowing waters.

A few days later, Jerris and I were sitting on the stone staircase of the museum, under the broken face of the clock, going over for the hundredth time the possible explanations for Ezra's bizarre behaviour. We'd pretty much narrowed the reasons down to something connected with his brothers and the Lums (I'd overheard Mr. Graveridge bitterly mumble something about those "greedy bastard brothers of his" being behind it, something about "money like mother's milk to them," which I didn't understand), when Jerris suddenly shouted, "Hey! Look!"

And there was Ezra, head down, moving rapidly along the other side of the street. There could be no mistaking him, that blackness, that hurried pace. But he did seem slower, as if he were dragging something we couldn't see.

"Come on!" Jerris nudged me, and we followed Ezra as he headed up the dyke toward the harbour. In a few minutes he'd ducked into the cabin of his boat, and that was that. I couldn't believe it. What if he *is* dead, I thought suddenly. Maybe that was his ghost. But I didn't say that to Jerris. He hadn't stood on the deck with me the other night and stared at the moon, so I was doubtful he'd know what I meant. Besides, I was pretty sure that Ezra's ghost would do something a lot more interesting than just walk through town and climb onto his boat. He'd do something more dramatic, take revenge on his brothers or the Lums or whoever had driven him to the top of the oil tank.

Jerris and I waited on the dyke for fifteen minutes, until Jerris suggested that we sneak down to the boat and try to look inside. I thought about it, but decided I'd rather go and finish my papers.

"I don't think you'll see anything," I added. "He's probably just lying down. I mean, he just got out of the hospital."

"Okay, I'll go," Jerris replied quickly, not even turning his head. I figured he'd still be hanging around the wharf by the time I finished my route.

Over the next few days, at Jerris's insistence, we renewed our surveillance of Ezra and his favourite haunts, hoping for an encounter between him and the pig-faced man, or him and his brothers or the Lums, but nothing happened. Ezra seemed different. He moved a little slower, almost as if thinking about each step. And there was something else, something I couldn't quite pin down. As I watched him follow his usual routes, as I searched for some sign of his old burning, I sensed that his darkness had dimmed. It was a feeling I couldn't shake. It made me so uncomfortable that I didn't even say anything to Jerris about it. How could I explain? There was Ezra, head down, hurrying to the diner, back to his boat, rowing across the channel to feed the birds and the rabbits—what was different? When I asked my father about him, he just shrugged and said, "He seems all right. Isn't talking much, but that's not unusual. But I guess it'll take him awhile to get over that fall." There was something hesitant in my father's voice, as though he worried that Ezra might never recover from that night. But I knew it was futile to press for such speculation. As far as adults were concerned, if things appeared to be normal, that was good enough.

I began to share that view as the uneventful days turned into weeks, but Jerris's interest in Ezra remained at a fever pitch. He was always wanting to follow him around, convinced that Ezra was planning some kind of revenge on those who had hurt him. Eventually, I didn't join Jerris any more. His refusal to give up on

Ezra as a source of excitement seemed embarrassing, even childish. Besides, I had so many other things to keep me busy: school, sports, comics and books, my paper route. Jerris wasn't much interested in anything but the river and fishing, so it made sense that he'd stay caught up in the mystery surrounding Ezra. For a while, whenever I saw Jerris, I'd ask him if anything interesting had happened, but nothing ever had, and eventually I stopped asking and even Jerris didn't bother to talk about it. Finally, another event diverted my attention completely from Ezra and Jerris.

One afternoon, pedalling through February's grey doldrums with my papers, I arrived as usual at the duplex, only to find Mr. Edmundson loading his mother's belongings into a small U-Haul trailer.

I must have looked puzzled as I coasted toward him, for he immediately explained that his mother was waiting in the car.

I braked beside the rickety steps where he had paused to speak.

"It won't take long to gather up her things," he continued, his face vividly red and dripping sweat, his hands rapidly brushing at his thighs as though to remove some invisible lint from them. "Especially not if you lend me a hand."

I parked my bike under the willow and followed him into the half-empty room. He gestured to some boxes stuffed and over-flowing with newspaper. "Might as well start with those. But be careful, it's china."

Concerned, I asked him where his mother was going.

"A private home," he answered sharply. Then he grinned apologetically. "She'll be happier there. I know she will. More attention than I can give her." He chewed his bottom lip while blinking at some space beyond me. "Yes, it's better all around. It's the right thing. It had to be done."

I nodded to give him the reassurance he seemed to want. Then I helped him empty the oppressive room until only the radio and its cabinet and the framed photographs and collector's plates on the walls remained. The presence of Mrs. Edmundson's first husband, Arthur, swelled to fill the emptiness until I was convinced that if we had switched on the dark, silent radio its marine glow would have trembled with his long-dead voice.

When Mr. Edmundson said not to worry about the things on the walls, I was relieved. Somehow I could not imagine reaching up to that sadly knowing expression. What might come out of it at my touch? A scream, a laugh, or some sound I couldn't even imagine? As long as the walls remained covered, I could also tell myself that Mrs. Edmundson hadn't gone completely; the place was still hers, and I would continue to think of it that way once I had turned away from her past's few frozen images. Yet as I stepped back into the cool, deepening dusk, I could not deny that I felt a burden had been lifted.

As I shook Mr. Edmundson's massive, sweaty hand and pocketed the money he owed me (plus a two-dollar tip he was happy to give on account of all my help), I knew I wouldn't enjoy seeing his mother one last time as I pedalled past the car. But she had her head bowed when I went by, so I couldn't even see if she was sad or frightened or excited. In any case, I understood that her expressions no longer accurately reflected her feelings. I decided not to say goodbye.

Later, when I had finished my route, I found that I had an extra paper, the one I should have left at the duplex. It suddenly struck me as odd that I had continued to deliver the paper to Mrs. Edmundson all those months. I looked at the front page, full of politics and war and weather predictions. What would she care about any of that? No more than I cared, I concluded.

And that small bond between us made me even sorrier that she was leaving.

I rode home and told my mother what had happened.

"A home?" She raised her eyebrows. "Well, it's about time. What home?"

"I don't know. He didn't tell me."

"In Chilukthan?"

I blushed. Why hadn't I bothered to find out? Was I so happy to be free of the responsibility of checking on her that I didn't even care where she had gone?

"Never mind, Callum," my mother said, offering the more accurate explanation. "I'm sure it's a very nice place."

I nodded, wondering suddenly that if the home were in Chilukthan whether I'd stop in for a visit. My face flushed even warmer when I realized that I had little desire to do so.

A few days later, as I sat at the kitchen table eating a bologna sandwich, my mother suddenly announced, in a tone both impressed and surprised, that she knew where Mrs. Edmundson had gone. "It's in West Vancouver, apparently," she said. "Very exclusive. Private rooms, a doctor on staff. She'll be well looked after. A place like that must cost a pretty penny."

And that was all. Before long, I started looking toward the back end of the duplex with a mercenary intent. With my income greatly reduced, I needed every new subscriber that I could find.

The winter drizzled on. In science class, we glued together the bones of a chicken. At the bookshop, Eric, Jamie, and I entertained ourselves by searching for the world's worst comic, finally choosing one called *Night Nurse,* which detailed, in terrible blocky illustrations, the working life of a registered nurse. We also awarded runner-up status to *Life with Archie,* the Christian version of the familiar strip, with its heavy moralizing and hokey happy endings complete with quotes from the Bible (but nothing from Deuteronomy, though Eric and I were always on the lookout). Donald Bints quit his route and, according to the gossip at the paper shack, was dropping acid. I hoped it wasn't true, since even the idea of drugs frightened me—I had seen what they had done to Peter Parker's best friend, Harry Osborne, in the infamous drug issues of *The Amazing Spiderman*. Besides, I was fond of Bints, and even though I had kept his secret about Mr. Vreen and his mom, I still felt guilty about his downfall at the paper shack. In any case, Bints dropped out of sight, and I was too caught up with other things to worry about him.

On rare occasions, Jerris helped me with my paper route or I went out with him on his trapline. We still had fun, but it was muted somehow, as if the ending of our mutual interest in Ezra had put a damper on everything else we enjoyed together.

By March, we hardly spent any time together at all. Only in the summer, once school had ended and we were released to the fields and riverbanks and orchards again, would we briefly resume our more intimate friendship.

nineteen

ONE COOL, GREY MORNING in March, I stepped out of the house to find a small silver bucket teeming with oolichan on the front step. My father did not fish for these tiny, greasy creatures, so I suspected that Ezra had made us a gift of them.

I returned to the kitchen with the bucket, and was about to show it to my mother, who was seated at the table, when she suddenly sighed over the local paper. "Oh Callum," she said, "what a shame."

The weight of the fish pulled on my arm and the metal handle burned cold into my palm, but I didn't put the bucket down.

"Mrs. Edmundson has passed away."

"Oh."

"Eighty-two she was," my mother continued after realizing that I wasn't going to cry. She read from the paper. "'Predeceased by her first husband, Arthur Merkisvale, and her second husband, Reginald Edmundson. Mourned by her loving son, Leslie.'" My mother looked up heavily again. "That poor man. He's going to miss her terribly."

I put the bucket on the counter by the sink and sat down to my bowl of cereal on the table, trying as hard as I could not to see Mrs. Edmundson's body stretched out in the armchair, her eyes and mouth open. She was my first human death. I did not feel sad so much as surprised by the humdrum nature of the event. I watched my mother's eyes scanning the rest of the obituaries and thought, "It's just something else to read about, that's all." Even later in the afternoon, when I delivered the daily paper that also announced her death to the new tenants at the back of the duplex, I wasn't greatly moved. Like Ezra, Mrs. Edmundson already belonged to the winter, to the past.

The second death was a greater shock. Only three days later, Mr. Edmundson's secretary found him hanging by his necktie from a ceiling beam when she came in to work. According to Norma Hazlitt, one of my mother's gossips whose husband worked on the local force, Mr. Edmundson hadn't even left a note.

It was understood that the "reason" involved his depression over his mother's death. Eavesdropping in the darkened hallway outside the kitchen, I heard my mother say to my father, "He must have felt terribly guilty about not keeping her at home. But his wife, Norma tells me, didn't like having her around." At which point my father interrupted with, "Well, it doesn't much matter now."

Nothing further came of it, at any rate. The suicide became another rare Chilukthan mystery, like the disappearance of the town butcher some years before. Mr. Edmundson's widow sold the house and, as far as anyone knew (she was not a friendly sort of woman) moved back to Ontario.

The obituary was short and blunt: "Leslie Edmundson, 52, of Chilukthan. Suddenly. Predeceased by his parents, Reginald and Vera. Left to mourn, his devoted wife Doreen." No service was held.

Soon both deaths were swept under by the sheer progression of days. I was troubled by the second death for a while, since I had known and liked Mr. Edmundson, and was shocked that someone so quiet could do something as violent as hanging himself. But I was never really close to him; his absence did not affect me profoundly. Nevertheless, I took a strange sort of pride in the fact that I had known him; the tragedy even raised my standing at the paper shack for a short while. Everyone wanted to know if he had always been "nuts." Inevitably, though, my answers disappointed; it just didn't feel right to lie about someone who had been so sad and was now dead. Besides, he'd been good to me. Eventually, Mr. Edmundson's death, like Ezra's fall from the oil tank, lost its hold on my imagination. Along with everyone else, I became preoccupied by the change of season in the air, by the promise of renewal. In a matter of weeks, buds appeared in the orchards and the river rose to freshet levels. The days grew longer, and even the rain had lost some of its darkness. School, sports, my paper route, the bookshop—everything seemed new again, as if the unusual winter had been a skin over all my activities that had now been shed.

Summer came in turn, and with it a whole range of images and sensations: the sour, rotting smell of the compost pile in our backyard as Jerris and I shovelled it over in the early morning, the blade silvered with dew, the long, segmented earthworms like jewels in the black mulch; the feel of the simmering heat coming up through our bare soles as we stood by the gas pumps at Onnoways' station; the nautical ding-ding of the bell hose when a car coasted over it; the whiff of chlorine wafting out of blue-pooled yards; the bubbly, sweet gulp of cream soda; the gillnet fleet drifting into harbour trailing flocks of screeching gulls swirling like blossoms going down a drain; the floury puff of a resin bag as the pitcher dropped it on the mound and began his windmill motion; the stars clustering until the sky became another fattened blackberry bush, ripe, sweet, and bee-hung; and, always, the vast companion motion of the river, sending out its unseen waves of brine and muck and rot, reflecting the vanilla clouds and depthless blue or the pewter scud of storms as the moon gradually thinned to a scythe to cut the season off while the gulls screamed and the mud grasshoppers whirred madly and the last worms turned soft and moist as we raised our empty hooks.

"Nothin," Jerris said, and flipped back his thick red bangs. He pushed himself up off his bare chest, almost a mahogany colour, and little flecks of wood chips and moss from the wharf stuck to his skin. His gapped front teeth shone whiter below a butterfly spread of freckles over the bridge of his nose onto his cheeks. By his feet, which were scraped and scarred from prickles and gravel, the bloodied mess of a bullhead lay startlingly red, its ugly mouth twisted grotesquely because Jerris had had a hard time ripping the hook out. "What do you want to do now?" He squinted at me in the late morning sun.

The slumbrous smell of creosote hung heavy on the air, stronger even than the mud of the lowering tide. The harbour was quiet. On the near bank, in the heat haze, the bleached skeleton of an old gillnetter seemed to shift its ribs in the rushes. Across the narrow channel, the door of one net shed had been slid open. A fisherman profiled in the dark interior mended a net.

"I don't know," I answered, deliciously, sensuously bored. "I have to go soon anyway." I had a ball game in a few hours, but since Jerris didn't care for organized sports, I didn't mention that I hoped to improve my batting average.

The sun beat down. A sparrow flitted soundlessly over us. Jerris began to wind his fishing line around a spool, his head bent to the task, his hands working rapidly. His shadow wavered at my feet.

"What are you doing later?" He glanced up quickly, then his bangs flipped over his eyes and he looked down again.

I paused awkwardly. Danny, one of my baseball teammates, was going to help me deliver my papers and then come to my house for dinner. After that, we'd likely call up another friend to play hot-box at the park. "Oh, I've got some stuff I have to do," I said finally, and bent over to drop my lead sinker into my plastic tackle box.

The little sound reverberated.

Jerris nodded. Then he turned and looked downriver. Far off, a tiny whirring noise like a mosquito grew louder by the second. We just stood and waited, not speaking, as an outboard appeared in the harbour entrance, its V-wake white as bone on the leaf- and sky-reflecting water.

A lone figure sat in the stern, one hand on the rudder, the other hand and arm holding something tight to his body. Even from a distance, the figure was easily identified. No one else who wore a plain white T-shirt looked so black.

I blinked at the wild black beard and long, greasy black hair and the dingy, blood-stained T-shirt as the outboard coasted alongside the wharf thirty feet downriver of where we stood. Ezra didn't seem to notice us. He clutched a wriggling burlap sack in one hand as he shut off the outboard and stepped onto the wharf, his gumboots muddy and a duller black than his shadow.

Muttering and cursing to himself, he suddenly stared straight at us and said "Tie-er-up-tie-er-up-goddamnya." Jerris hurried forward and grabbed the bilge-sopping rope out of the skiff. A heavy smell of gasoline filled the air as a cloud of exhaust drifted over the wharf.

I followed Jerris, my eyes fixed on the burlap sack.

"What have you got?" Jerris asked, double-hitching the rope to the nearest piling.

Ezra didn't answer. He dropped to his knees and placed the sack in front of him. Something pushed hard against the burlap. Suddenly the silence was shattered by a loud, hoarse squawk, as easily identifiable as Ezra's voice.

"What's wrong with it?" I asked, moving up to within a few feet of Ezra's bent head. Jerris stood on the other side of him. We waited. Ezra slowly pulled the sack open. His strong, grease-smeared hands tightened on the blue-grey wings.

"Easy-now-you-little-bugger," he grinned as the heron opened its sharp bill wide and lunged at him. Its ruffled feathers were more grey than blue. Its tiny eyes burned like embers set deep into a rock. The bird squawked a second time, more feebly, but the sound still tore into the silence.

Ezra muttered again. "Some bugger shot it," he said, adjusting one hand to push the feathers up below one wing and reveal a small messy hole. "Pellet gun, looks like." Then the muttering resumed.

Jerris knelt beside the bird and reached out to stroke it. After he had pulled his hand away, the heron snapped its bill a few times in the air as it tried to stretch its wings, then rapidly struck Ezra's bared forearm.

Ezra laughed wildly. "Goddamnya-little-bugger-feisty-eh-goddamnya." He gripped the bird tighter. Then he held it close, only a few inches from his face, and looked straight into its eyes. A trickle of blood appeared like a worm on his arm, but he paid no attention to it. "You-want-to-get-me-eh? You-want-to-poke-my-eyes-out?" He grinned until his teeth showed between his ruddy lips.

The heron didn't move. I had stepped back, waiting anxiously for Ezra to move his head away. But Jerris edged closer.

Finally, with another cackling laugh, Ezra pulled back. He glanced sideways at Jerris. "Hang-on-to-him," he said, and Jerris's hands suddenly replaced Ezra's. "Tight-goddamnya!" Ezra cursed. "He's-a-strong-little-bugger." Then he looked around questioningly and said, "Got a knife?"

I didn't move or respond. Jerris finally said "In my tackle box," and nodded down at the wharf. Ezra bent over, pulled out a jack-knife, and snapped it open. The blade caught the sunlight and glinted briefly.

"Tighter!" Ezra commanded. He closed his empty hand around one of Jerris's and then dug the point of the knife into the pellet hole. Blood dripped slowly off his arm and made a little pool on the planks the size and colour of one of the heron's eyes.

The bird squawked violently and tried to beat its wings. But Ezra and Jerris pinned them tight and held their heads back from the snapping bill.

Ezra flicked the pellet onto the wharf. It bounced twice and landed at my feet.

"That's-got-er," Ezra said, and flipped the knife shut. Then he closed his other hand over Jerris's other hand. Together, they got up off their knees with the bird held between them.

"Off-you-go-you-little-bugger!" Ezra shouted as they opened their arms wide. A rapid flutter, another harsh squawk, and then a smaller shadow loosed itself from the wharf. The heron circled over us once in its lumbering grace, its shadow fishlike as it slipped over the surface of the river and disappeared behind the cottonwoods on the harbour island.

I looked down out of the sun. Ezra and Jerris were still gazing after the bird. Their jaws were slightly raised, and I could just see the sunburnt, slowly working Adam's apple beneath the tangled mass of Ezra's beard. I looked back to the sky. But I could see only the leafy tops of the cottonwoods sharply outlined against the cloudless blue.

Jerris moved first, meeting my look with an expression I could not read. It vanished almost immediately, flipped back under his bangs. Ezra, meanwhile, swallowed faster and harder until I thought he was going to choke. Instead, he absently smeared the blood over his forearm, then grumbled indistinguishably as he lowered his head. He did not speak to us or look at us before he turned and walked rapidly down the wharf to his gillnetter, moored like a chunk of darkness that the sun hadn't been able to burn off.

"I wonder who shot it," I said once Ezra was gone.

Jerris shrugged and walked back to his fish lines without looking at me.

"I better go," I said.

"See you," he responded, his head still down, the bangs shrouding his face.

I hesitated, staring at Jerris's kneeling form. Feeling sorry for him, and for all the time we used to spend together, I almost said, "Aw, come on, come and play ball." But I knew he wouldn't want to, and I knew I was glad about that.

A minute later I was on my bike, pedalling quickly, the sun even warmer on my back and shoulders, the harbour and everyone in it falling away as the limed field and the batter's box and the hazy margins of the future moved closer.

epilogue

THE BUS CREPT FORWARD in the jam of traffic on the Oak Street Bridge. Slightly nauseated by the stop-go motion and the stifling heat, I looked away from the sun blaze off the steel hoods to where the muddy North Arm of the Fraser flowed sluggishly westward. One or two native fishboats, little more than skiffs, had their short lengths of gillnet out, the corks pearling the murky water (the salmon fishery had been shut down for the season to non-natives in an attempt to protect the depleted stocks). I shifted in my seat and looked east.

Several giant pyramids of sawdust, like the dregs of old sunsets, glimmered on the north bank outside the sawmills, most of which operated only occasionally due to a downturn in the logging industry. I thought of Jerris Ely. No wonder he lived way up the coast, in the bush the last I'd heard, eking out a living by trapping and by fishing when the authorities allowed it (and maybe even when they didn't). Looking out the window, I couldn't imagine how he could exist here; the whole south coast seemed now like the sort of enclosed space he had resisted so strongly as a boy. Sighing, I turned back to Ezra.

He'd hardly changed position or expression the whole time the bus had been caught in traffic. It was as if he didn't realize he was supposed to be travelling somewhere. His silence and stillness, exaggerated by the restlessness and complaining of the other passengers, were exactly like that of a piling graven with decades of mud and brine.

As the traffic began to flow again and the bus exited Oak Street to Granville, I tried to imagine what Ezra's sudden appearance meant. Was I supposed to take his vacant presence as a warning, a sign that I should count my blessings and get on with the business of life? Or was his feeble shell sitting there just another extension of the enigma he'd always been, so that he meant nothing, and the past meant nothing, and memory was useless in a world of violent headlines and relentless, dizzying images?

Bus-sick, sick with thinking, sick with the sense that the same meaningless newsprint was being dropped on the proliferating doorsteps of the world, I had just determined to put Ezra out of my mind when, suddenly, he pulled the bellstring and stood up.

In a few seconds he was standing by the back doors, just opposite me. The smell of stale sweat rose off his body. There were sharp creases in his incongruously dark-blue jeans. And then it struck me: where was he going? What business could he possibly have in the city?

I decided that my trip to the used bookstores could wait. The bus stopped at the intersection of Davie and Seymour and I followed Ezra off. To my disappointment, he didn't jaywalk across Seymour, but waited for the light to change, even though there were gaps in traffic. I waited with him, several feet behind.

It was blazing hot. I sweated profusely, and thought that Ezra must be boiling in his flannel shirt. But he didn't appear bothered. When the light changed, he crossed the street, moving with purpose but not as quickly as in the past. More surprisingly, he didn't lower his head at all. He didn't even turn it. It seemed he was walking a familiar route.

A few minutes later he turned down a dirty, narrow street. A minute after that he pulled open the front door of the Drake and Hen Hotel, a combination flophouse and strip joint. Before going in, he paused, just briefly, to look back. The paleness of his face over his grizzled beard hung a few seconds in the blaze of sunlight. Then the door closed.

By the time I reached the lobby, Ezra was gone. I talked to the desk clerk, a clean-cut, pink-cheeked preppy, probably a university student doing a summer job. A strip show for the business lunch crowd was in progress through a doorless frame nearby, and I almost had to shout to be heard over the throbbing bass. Smoke drifted everywhere, hanging like cobwebs under the mildewed ceiling. The dark, dingy lobby reeked of cigarettes, beer, and a smell like leaves decaying in a full rain barrel.

I didn't learn much, but it was enough. Ezra had been a tenant at the Drake and Hen for a few years. Some sort of social worker paid his rent with government cheques, even though Ezra didn't stay in his room every night (I wondered if he still spent some nights in Chilukthan, and whether he still had his boat). The clerk said he was no trouble, that he never went into the bar, not even to watch the shows.

"What does he do when he's here?" I half-shouted.

The clerk shrugged. "Feeds the pigeons out back sometimes." He nodded toward the parking lot. "Sits around mostly. But he's not here all that much. I think he rides the bus a lot. Used to be a fisherman, I think. Maybe he goes down to the water."

The clean-scrubbed, high-coloured face suddenly darkened with suspicion. "What do you want to know for?"

I explained briefly that he was from my hometown, which satisfied the clerk. He added, by way of ending our conversation, that Ezra was all right, that the drugs kept him tame enough.

And then I was back outside, blinking into the sun, breathing diesel fumes, walking with only a vague purpose north toward the skyscrapers. My whole body trembled. I couldn't get it to stop. Where was my father? Where was his world? The realization poured over me in a dark swell: I wasn't going to find it again, on any trip home. It wasn't fading; it was gone. And I saw that it was meant to be gone, that it had to be, no matter what frayed, dumb remnants of it paid their money and kept boarding a bus to the next day and the next day and the next, until a flock of grubby pigeons finally pecked at a rapidly stiffening palm of seed. I felt my lips forming the old question, even though the world, which never had any time for it, now actively scorned it and kept moving faster and faster away from the implications. There, in the long shadows of the North Shore Mountains, those mountains pale blue as a heron's body, and once so alive with creeks that my father had been inspired to spend his entire boyhood in a laughing, roaming truancy, I whispered our old lyric to his ghost.

But the only sound the air gave back was a soft click, as of a door closing, and there hung Ezra's pale face again, briefly visible in the doorframe of the flophouse. And suddenly I saw, with astonishing clarity, the lost image that I would always keep with me, just as the names on a cenotaph or the faces on a totem pole retain something deep in the stone and wood of the glory and the sorrow that raised them.

It had started to rain, but I couldn't see it in the air. The surface of the harbour channel was suddenly pocked with bubbles as if a school of tiny fish had risen to feed, and drops fell slowly off the metallic wharf lamps and the steel peak of the winch. My father flicked his cigarette overboard. It fizzled out just shy of the neighbouring boat's stern. Then he looked away from the iron wharf ladder climbing straight above his head into the grey overcast, and nodded at me.

"Come on. You might never see anything like this again."

I crossed the deck and hesitated beside him.

"Up you go," he encouraged, grabbing me under the arms and boosting me up to the first rung.

The iron was cold and wet. I gripped it hard. Above me, I heard low voices and idling engines but saw only a dark, smouldering cloud and the winch looming heronlike over the water. Invisibly, the rain touched my face. I moved up the ladder, keeping my eyes on the winch.

"Stay put when you get there," my father's voice swirled around me. "It'll be slippery."

I reached the top of the wharf and looked over. A couple dozen fishermen stood around in separate clusters, smoking and talking quietly. Several pickup trucks filled with wooden fish boxes were parked at random angles between the clusters. One truck still idled, another just arrived over the gravel road that led to the wharf. The crunch of its tires sounded unusually loud and slow. I looked to the left, in the direction of the winch.

Only one man was on that third of the wharf. Hunched over, he moved rapidly back and forth between the far edge of the wharf and the thick chain swinging loosely from the peak of the winch. The chain swung because the man had reached up and grabbed it with one dark hand, which retracted as quickly as it had appeared as if the air had burned it. I couldn't see his face clearly, but I knew who had towed the sturgeon into the harbour. The heavy black beard and black skullcap only confirmed it. My father and I, and a few others who had tied up on the opposite side of the channel, had watched him come in.

"He's going to the winch," Mr. Toukalous had said with surprise. "He's going to winch it up."

"Jesus! What for?" somebody else had exclaimed farther along the wharf.

No one answered. My father lightly touched the top of my head. "Might as well take a look," he said.

Across the channel, dark figures had emerged from boats and net sheds and drifted ghostlike up the gangways to the gravel road, as if summoned by the same silent voice. I helped my father untie our boat ropes, but wasn't much help, since I kept looking across and down the channel to the elevated main wharf where the coal-black boat had come to a stop.

Now I peered over the top of the same wharf, breathing the powerful oily smell of creosote, the rain soft but cold on my cheeks. Ezra suddenly sprang to the base of the winch and spun the wheel, releasing more chain, which he then grabbed and yanked to the edge of the wharf. For the first time I noticed the fat, steel hook; it was dull silver and gleamed a little as it dragged across the planks.

From just below, my father told me to keep going. Soon we stood side by side in the grey dawn light, staring at Ezra as he leaned over the far edge of the wharf. My father asked a man nearby what was happening.

The man, with a face flat and grey as a stone, laughed pointedly. "Don't want any help," he explained. "Wants to do it all by his lonesome."

I felt my father stiffen. "Well," he responded coolly, "it's his business. Not every day you bring something like that in."

The man snorted and turned away. Mr. Toukalos and Mr. Mawson walked over to join us. Both had cigarettes hanging from their mouths. They took the cigarettes down as if they were heavy, the red tips blinking as they shifted their hands. Like my father, they had been awake for over thirty-six hours.

"It won't take him long," Mr. Mawson yawned. "No dawdling for the likes of Ezra."

Mr. Toukalos and my father grinned. Then the clatter of the winch turning drew everyone's attention. The scattered clusters of men flowed together and formed a black line across the wharf. I stood at the front, resting back against my father's thigh. It began to rain harder.

Ezra had vanished over the edge of the wharf, but his activity was audible from below. He seemed to be exerting himself, judging by the gasps and grunts and the occasional thump of something heavy against wood. The winch kept creaking in slowly, picking up the slack of the long, thick-linked chain. I blinked into the rain. It had formed its own darker chains, a whole sky of them; they tightened against the grey light and seemed to creak right along with the winch. Breath and cigarette smoke swirled over us, rising with each turn of the winch, that sound like a machine gun in extreme slow motion. Somebody tossed a butt onto the planks. It blazed for a few seconds, a tiny dot of red, then fizzled into black. Up above the peak of the winch the stars were still out, but faint as fish scales on dry wood.

I looked down just as Ezra popped over the edge of the wharf, his face blackly grinning, rain silvering his skullcap and beard, dripping off the end of his pointed, bony nose and trickling off his matted jaw. With one quick push of his arms he hoisted himself into a crouched position on the wharf. From there he regarded us with barely repressed glee, as though waiting for a seal bomb he had hidden amongst us to explode.

But only the winch creaked on under the patter of the rain. Ezra stood and turned back toward his boat. Somebody in the crowd behind me broke our silence by shouting "Fer chrissakes, hurry it up will you!" But the words dissolved strangely in the heavy air; they didn't even echo. The rain, even harder, darkened the horizon, turned the light a deeper grey. The winch creaked on.

When the head appeared, I pressed back against my father. Wide as a barn beam and anvil-hard, it looked more like its own skull, as if the flesh had already rotted off or been stripped clean. Though I had seen smaller versions of the head before, I shuddered at the sight. It seemed to be eating the chain, the great vacuum mouth pursed out where the steel hook had been fixed, the long whiskers trembling like angled streaks of rain from the plated, prehistoric head. Dingy white and grey, almost moss-green along the top, the head rose slowly into the air, its gills the size of doghouse doorways, the same unbeckoning, cold dark beyond them, but also a little red, as if a match had been struck inside.

The body hung ghostly below. A less dingy white, the flesh shook grotesquely as it rose through the rain. Down both sides of the gut, thirty feet to the sharklike tail, a jagged raised white stitch seemed to hold the fish together. The fins were huge. What light the day possessed concentrated in them until they seemed flushed with blood.

I wiped the rain from my eyes, smearing my vision. When I had blinked it clear again, I noticed the spine. It appeared to consist of a row of tiny glass doorknobs, but the glass was murky from lying on the bottom of the river so long. After the winch finally stopped creaking I kept staring at the spine, wondering if I had the courage to touch it. I couldn't shake the feeling that Ezra had actually caught the skeleton of a giant sturgeon. Everything about it seemed like it had been dead a long time; even the flesh looked too cold to have ever belonged to a living thing.

But by now the thick musk of it had filled the air. Muddy, briny, the huge fish might have been a half-dozen fathoms of river bottom lifted to the sky. I liked the smell. The rain deepened it, washed it across the planks and our bodies until it hung from every chain the sky was dropping all around us.

A few men stepped over the black line we had formed on the wharf. They approached the sturgeon, craning their necks up to see the head. One patted the gut experimentally; his hand made a wet, hollow sound. Soon we had all edged forward to make a loose semicircle around the winch, everyone talking in hushed tones, guessing the weight. I heard nine hundred pounds, nine-fifty. Mr. Mawson figured a thousand was more like it. My father prodded me gently in the small of the back.

"Go on, Callum," he said. "Touch it."

I couldn't step forward with everyone watching. "I'm right behind you," my father encouraged.

The fish stretched away overhead like a church spire. I reached out. The skin was sandpapery and cold. I quickly drew my hand away and stepped back.

"It won't bite you," somebody laughed.

"I don't know. It might yet," somebody else joked.

Then everyone looked up at once, as if the sturgeon might actually be alive. I was dizzy from trying to see so far up and lowered my eyes.

Ezra stood only a few feet away from me. He wasn't looking up or down. The grin had left his level gaze, replaced by an expression I had never seen before. He appeared excited yet calm. His eyes

were glassy, but it was hard to be sure in the rain. So much moisture was spiderwebbed in his beard and on his skullcap that he
seemed more under the river than above it.

My pulse quickened when I saw the knife in his hand. The
blade was long and only dimly silver, but shone against the black
of his body. I looked back to his face. The familiar grin had
returned. Very rapidly, his eyes took me in, then forgot me. I shuddered and wiped some more rain off my face.

Along with the knife, Ezra had brought a wooden stool and two
metal buckets onto the wharf. He walked over to the soft belly of
the hanging fish and put the stool down. He stepped onto it, still
holding the knife.

"Ah Christ, you're not going to gut it?" someone complained.

Ezra raised his arm.

"Come on, you got to weigh it first. What's it weigh?"

"Weighs-enough-goddamnya-goddamnya," Ezra snarled and
plunged the blade into the white gut.

"You won't get nothing for it," the disappointed voice continued feebly, then was swept under the excitement caused by the
downward sweep of Ezra's arm.

A few guts spilled out in a whoosh of thick, black-red blood,
landing wetly and heavily on the planks. Ezra dropped the knife. It
fell almost without a sound on the bloody spot below. He put both
hands into the long, horizontal opening and began to pull, like
someone ransacking a closet. Slippery organs and long spools of
intestine joined the viscous mess on the wharf. The fish smell grew
heavier, saturated with blood. I didn't think Ezra would ever stop
tossing down the viscera. Even the grey dawn light became slippery
and red. The pelting rain seemed to pass through his hands.

Suddenly he jumped off the stool and grabbed one of the metal
buckets. Swinging it like a railroad lantern, he leapt back onto the

stool and stuck his arm past the elbow into the gaping fish. He made a peeling motion, a soft tearing sounded out of the rain, and then a black mass splattered into the bottom of the bucket. Ezra quickly jumped down again, placed the full bucket on the planks, grabbed the empty one, and returned to the stool. The same motion and sound were repeated. Soon, two full buckets sat to one side of the sturgeon's tail, a few feet from me, bright as headlights in the surrounding gloom.

"A small fortune there," Mr. Mawson said quietly.

Bitterly, another louder voice added, "You sell those to the Chinamen in the city, you're set for the year."

Ezra stood still, his grin even broader, the right sleeve of his black sweater dripping and slimy, his breath pouring out and rising in small clouds.

My father nudged me again. "Eggs," he whispered. "Take a look."

I stepped up to the buckets. They were filled to the brim with what looked like slimy black pearls floating in black blood. There must have been thousands of them. Stippled and crushed together, they reminded me of blackberries overflowing a pail. I leaned closer. The smell wasn't sweet, just heavy, bloody. I stepped back.

"A delicacy," my father explained close to my ear. "For fancy restaurants."

"No flies on you, you crafty bugger," Mr. Toukalos said.

Ezra's grin was so broad that his raised cheeks almost swallowed his eyes.

"Fuckin waste if you ask me," said the bitter voice. "Packer won't take it, gutted all to ratshit."

Ezra shrugged, then said rapidly, his words ending in a delighted cackle, "Give-em-to-Rodney. Pickle-em-goddamn-old-bugger. Chew-until-his-teeth-fall-out."

Some of the men stepped close to the hanging fish for a last look. I heard a few more slaps, some low whistles. Smoke circled the body like its own strange phosphor.

Just as it seemed the excitement was over, Ezra jumped back onto the stool. "Best part," he mumbled, reaching into the dark, flapping cut. He pulled out a large, sacklike mass, held it against his chest, and jumped down to the wharf. Then, placing the mass near the buckets, he grabbed the knife off the planks.

It was raining harder. Black bubbles burst over the sides of the buckets. Water streamed off the sturgeon's tail. The men pulled their skullcaps so far down that they became almost faceless, the lit cigarettes even more striking as a result. Two or three seagulls landed on the masts of Ezra's boat and began to screech, sticking their necks out toward the wharf. Others circled high over us, their cries weaker, like an echo.

Ezra sliced the sack open and began pulling out the contents. A crimson salmon, its head half-covered with white fungus; several large rocks; a sculpin; the skeleton of a small bird; handfuls of tiny fish like iron filings; a tin can; a long, rusted bolt; and then, most astonishing of all, a woman's leather boot with buttons, a small black book, and what looked like part of a wooden rudder.

A powerful stench worse than rotting garbage drifted up off the planks. I plugged my nose and stifled a gag. Several men cursed.

But Ezra's dark hands busily searched the rest of the sack. When he was satisfied that it held nothing else of interest, he turned and held up the boot. "For-your-old-lady-eh-Mackie," he grinned at my father.

"How about that?" he responded wonderingly, taking the boot and holding it out for me to see. "Belongs in the museum, this here."

The stench had driven some of the crowd away. An engine revved, then another. In five minutes, only about ten of us remained. I was expecting my father to say that we had to go when Ezra made one last trip to the stool.

"What's he doing now?" I whispered, gazing into my father's tired, stubbled face, wreathed with cigarette smoke.

He shook his head without looking at me. All his attention was focused on the great fish.

Ezra's upper body plunged into the gap. Once again, he tossed guts out behind him.

"There's nothing else," someone said. "What's he after?"

No one answered. The gulls went mad, their beaks wide open, their wings flapping. Rain blurred my sight but I was afraid to wipe it away in case I missed anything. I blinked and blinked until I saw Ezra pull himself out of the sturgeon. The rain slammed around him in dark shafts. But his grin remained, broad as ever.

I wiped my eyes quickly. He still stood there, his muscles tensed. The fish hung open behind him. And then, without a word, he turned and stepped off into the air.

I whirled around, but my father and the others were staring with the same shocked look. I whirled back. Ezra stood inside the fish as if it were a doorway. His black face broke into a peal of laughter. His hands held the flaps of the great belly open for a few seconds, their dark fingers striking against the dingy white of the flesh.

I stared and stared. I did not hear the gulls screeching or feel the rain streaming down my face.

Still laughing, Ezra slowly pulled the sides of the fish together. Only his face and hands remained in sight. I held my breath. Everything turned white and black, became sharper, clearer. I

watched as hard as I could. The open mouth, the hands black with blood.

Then the laughter stopped, and the face and hands were gone. The sturgeon hung motionless, whole again. Seconds passed. Nobody moved or spoke. Then the screeching of the gulls tore the silence apart.